OVERTIME

MAGGIE RAWDON

ONE

Joss

I'VE JUST SURVIVED BEING 30,000 feet up in a tin can hurtling through the air with nothing but a few inches of metal between me and instant death. A trip that involved one seatmate who kept trying to use me as a headrest and another who thought manspreading in the sardine can was appropriate all while the air temperature lingered maniacally between Sahara Desert and Arctic tundra. Don't ask me how it's possible, it's the airline's special brand of magic. The kind that comes with a side of ginger ale and cinnamon biscuits, which makes it marginally better somehow.

I'm currently being rewarded for my survival by having to navigate my way through a terminal full of people who also seem to be exploring that same oxymoronic liminal space because while half the crowd is crashing past me, dodging and weaving like they're running from zombies, the other half is stumbling around disoriented like they *are* the zombies.

I *hate* flying. Unfortunately, being a photographer frequently means shooting on-site, so I'm always on the run and airports are as much my home as anywhere else. I have so many frequent flyer miles I don't know how to spend them faster than I accumulate them. In the last few months, I've seen the inside of almost every major European city's airport lounge and sampled one too many overpriced airport sandwiches. It's gotten to the point that I've given up keeping any sort of real home in favor of living out of my suitcase ninety percent of the time. But right now, I'm headed somewhere close to home, or at least to some people who feel like home: Ben and Violet.

They'd been my roommates in grad school after Violet got rid of her first mistake of a boyfriend, fell in love—in large part thanks to my meddling, or at least I like to claim the credit for it —and then moved to Seattle when Ben was drafted by the Seattle Phantom. Violet has flown out to meet me a few times when I'm traveling but somehow, I haven't had the chance to visit her at home.

Truthfully it's on purpose; as much as I love the two of them, seeing or staying with them for any period of time makes me miss them more than I can stand. Staying with them also would make seeing the biggest fuck up of my life an inevitability, and that was something I *should* avoid. Something I'm already confronting as I pause in front of a newsstand to let a family trail across the walkway to the gate on the other side, as that fuck up smiles at me from the cover of a sports magazine. Because my biggest mistake is Colton St. George—the quarterback for the Seattle Phantom and one of Ben's closest friends. He's a media darling. The gorgeous, all-American Midwestern boy with the panty-dropping smile and the charm to match. He's also apparently, very fucking good at football. Or so I'm told because sports just really aren't my thing.

I feel the turn in my gut as I stare at his face, pausing and wondering if I don't need a $10 pack of gummy bears and an overpriced tabloid magazine for the road—because I'm not entirely sure if the grumbling is hunger or fear. It's anyone's guess at this point. But sugar and distractions might help either way.

"Phantom fan?" The guy next to me asks, noting I've been staring at this magazine cover for entirely too long.

"Oh, no. Just knew him in college."

"You knew St. George?" The stranger's eyes light up and then flick over me because I'm pierced, tattooed, with jet black hair and a dark streak of red on one side, wearing an all-black outfit that ends in a pair of Doc Martens that have seen better days. Basically the visual opposite of everything their beloved QB stands for.

Knew probably isn't exactly the right way to put it, but I'm not sure what is. Especially if I need to sum it up for a stranger. So *knew* is what I'm going with.

"Yes," I answer, and then hurry off again because even though my plane landed early if I know Violet, she's already downstairs waiting for me.

And sure enough, when I get to baggage claim she's there, standing up and bouncing when she sees me because the two of us revert to acting like teenage girls at a boyband concert whenever we're reunited, and I *love* it. I run the rest of the distance to her, wrapping her in a hug and jumping as we greet each other with a cacophony of giggling and general amusement. Is it a spectacle? Maybe. Do I care? Definitely not.

"How was your flight?"

"Awful. All I can say is thank the plane gods for noise-canceling headphones, snacks, and wearing layers."

"Did you eat something? Was the food terrible?"

"Passable. Honestly, not the worst I've had. Just glad I stashed snacks in my bag before I left. Oh, and I brought you some of the Swiss chocolate you love so much and some of the weird gummies that Ben likes."

"You're the best. I'm so lucky to have a bestie that gets to tour amazing places all the time."

"You could come with me more often."

"I might do that in the offseason. But for now Ben insists I'm his good luck charm at games."

"Will his obsession with you ever cease?" I pretend to roll my eyes but end up smiling because I love the two of them together almost as much as I love them each individually. They deserve each other, and they make me think that true love, *real* love—the kind that lasts forever and a day—is actually possible. Maybe not for me, but it exists and that's something worth admiring.

"I hope not." She grins and then we walk to the carousel to wait for the rest of my baggage. "Have you decided how long you're staying?"

"There's another shoot I have to do in six weeks, so it's just a matter of how long you want me really. But I don't have to stay with you the whole time. I can look for a hotel or a short-term rental. I don't want to crowd you. I know you said your other friend had to come stay unexpectedly."

"Yes, Harper. I can't wait for you to meet her. You'll like her. Her ex-husband is being an epic dick though. That's a long story. But we have plenty of rooms in the house. I don't mind at all, and I know Ben won't either."

"But what about stoic Midwestern farm boys who throw pigskin for a living?" I give her a look.

"*Right...* He's gonna be at the party tonight, I think. I hope that's okay. They're just so close still, you know, and I wasn't sure if you were gonna make it tonight or not."

"Don't worry. It's Ben's birthday. I'll be on my best behavior." I see my bag and grab it off the carousel as my thoughts drift back to him again. "He doesn't have a girlfriend now?"

"No. It's been a while."

"A date?"

Violet's eyebrow raises in suspicion at my curiosity.

"Just wondering." I shrug defensively.

"Mmmhmm. I'm sure you are." She eyes me.

"Don't give me that look."

"Oh, I will give you this look. And a few more looks. Probably a nudge or two. Then I might throw some meddling in for good measure."

"Don't," I say, flicking her a look and grabbing the second bag that's full of lights and prop equipment marked "FRAG-ILE" in bright blue ink.

"Do we need a cart?" She looks at the bags at my feet.

"Maybe..." I hedge. I mastered being able to wheel the two giant hard case bags and my backpack and carry-on, but I did look like a one-person circus doing it.

"Here, I'll get one." She nods to the wall where several are waiting to be checked out. I readjust my shoulder straps and take a deep breath.

I'm here to see my friends. Hang out with them like old times, laughing and taking a trip down memory lane and all the good things. I can just avoid the part where I stomped all over a guy's already broken heart for no good reason. After all, he's all grown up now, one of the most famous people in the country, and at this point, I'm probably nothing more than a blip on his radar. A smudge of a mistake that he learned from. No reason to think we can't get along now—all these years later.

"All right. Here we go." Violet rolls the luggage cart up and helps me load the bags onto it. "I need to get some luggage like this. Better than what I've got."

"Yeah, it's not cheap but it's worth it. No shooting equipment damaged so far—knock on wood."

"I'm so freaking excited you're here though, Joss. We have so much catching up to do. And I can't wait to show you the house and my studio."

"Well let's get going! Can we get a smoothie on the way though?"

"Obviously. I already know a place you'll like. Had it all planned out."

"And this is why I love you. Who needs men when I have a bestie like you?" I hug her from the side because in so many ways Violet really is my person.

"I mean, you do." She laughs.

"Fair enough." I laugh along with her because I don't have the heart to tell her I've had my own little dry spell when it's come to men lately.

She loves living vicariously through me. Hot Italian men taking me out for pasta and rides in their Ferraris. Climbing on a yacht on the Riviera with a guy who owns a vineyard. Hiking in the Alps with the Swiss mountain guide and eating fondue in an adorable hut at the top while he reads me dirty poems in German? That's what I'm famous for. Being melancholy because none of it hits the way it used to, and I'm bored of the fun I used to have? Not the sexy adventure anyone wants to hear about.

I'll have to tell her at some point. I need my best friend's wisdom and sage advice. But I'd rather pretend for a while longer. Especially since the last person on earth I want to know I'm not at the top of my game anymore is both on the front of a magazine and going to be sitting across from me at dinner tonight.

TWO

Colton

"THEY'RE IMPROVING," Ben notes as he steps up beside me at practice. He's my wide receiver and my closest friend. We've played together since college, and I'd be lost without him. We're watching the defense run their drills and the guys are currently practicing their man-to-man coverage and looking damn near flawless while they do it.

"A lot. This defense might be able to hold anything if they keep up like this." I nod before I take a long swig of water and we both watch for a couple of minutes.

"So are you still planning on stopping by tonight?"

"Of course. Wouldn't miss it."

"Then I've got something I need to warn you about." Ben's brow furrows and I raise mine in response.

"What's that?" I can't imagine what I need to be warned about. I'm at Ben and Violet's all the time as they've become the de facto team home and hosts. Not to mention Ben and I go running or go out on the kayaks semi-regularly.

"She's flying in today. I didn't know until yesterday. I think it was a last-minute thing, but she's had a break in her schedule, and Violet invited her to come stay with us for a while."

I don't need to ask who she is. I know. I take another drink of water, buying myself time because even though it's been years since I saw her last—since his wedding to her best friend —the mention of her still sends a shockwave down my spine. One that ricochets low and brings back memories that I try not to think about for too long. At least not in the bright light of day and not while I'm trying to focus on practice.

"I know she's not your favorite person," Ben hedges, his hand running over the back of his neck. "But she's staying with us for the time being so..."

"It's fine." I shrug. It has to be. It's been way too damn long for me to still feel anything about her, especially since she made it pretty damn clear how she felt about me. Or rather, didn't feel. I was a dumb kid with an already broken heart who didn't listen to her when she warned me that catching feelings was not in her wheelhouse.

"Sounds like there'll be quite a few people, so I don't think you'll have to talk."

I flash him a reassuring smile. "Hey, it's no big deal. It was years ago. We both moved on a long time ago. We were fuckin' kids. Or at least I was."

Years and a lifetime ago. I'd been a junior in college. The starting QB for the championship team, and she'd been working on an MFA in photography. If it hadn't been for Ben and Violet, I doubt our paths would have ever crossed. We are nothing alike.

I was raised in small-town Nebraska on a farm with a mom and dad who put emphasis on family dinners, Midwestern manners, and football as a part-time religion. She'd grown up in Chicago, an only child with a single mom who died young, and her only religion was art, with a side of sex and music. But despite all the reasons we didn't make sense, she'd been a soft place for me to land. When everything went to hell my junior year despite all outward appearances making it look like the best in my life, she was there.

At least she had been for a while. Until I said too much, and she ran like hell. Guess I'd be finding out tonight if time really does heal all wounds.

"Nothing still left there?" Ben asks quietly because if anyone understood pining after the older woman who doesn't care if you exist or not, he did.

"Nah. How could there be? I have no idea who she is anymore. And she definitely doesn't know me."

"You never know, maybe she developed an obsession with football stats in her free time." Ben can't even keep a straight face as he says it, and we both end up laughing harder than necessary.

"Something funny?" Waylon appears at my side, he's the center for our team and one of Ben's friends from Highland State. I came later after Waylon had already been drafted to the pros, but we'd grown close since we both played ball for the Phantom.

"Thinking about an alternate universe where Violet's friend, Joss, is a football statistician," Ben explains.

Waylon raises a brow as he pulls his long blond hair back into a low bun. "Do I want to ask?"

"She's coming to stay with us for a while. She and Colt have some history."

"With Joss?" Waylon looks perplexed at that idea because anyone who knows anything about her would. I'm not the kind of guy who ends up on her radar, let alone in her bed.

"Ancient fucking history," I mutter, shaking my head and eyeing Ben for opening his mouth. Not that I don't trust Waylon, but the less people know about it the better.

"I see." Waylon looks me over like he's trying to figure out how that puzzle fits.

"It was after I broke up with Kate." Another woman I could do without—my high school girlfriend who made me promise to wait for her when I transferred colleges, the one I'd been waiting for since we got together sophomore year, only to cheat on me with the quarterback on my former college team. The same quarterback who made it necessary for me to find a new team if I ever wanted a starting position.

The more I think about it, the more I realize it was a really fucking bad year for me when it came to luck with relationships or lack thereof. Unfortunately, while Joss was largely something of a legendary character who only really existed in Violet's stories about her adventures overseas, Kate still liked to make herself known in the present as a sports reporter who seemed to be getting assigned to my games with an increasing frequency. While I feel like that's a chapter happily put to rest, I've been getting the feeling that despite the fact she's married —she's been hoping the book could be opened again.

"Well that's a surprise." Waylon looks me over again. "I thought you were more the fifties housewife type."

"No one inviting me to the conference? Harsh." Tobias grips his chest dramatically. "Where's the fifties-housewife? I love a good game of dress her up, fuck her down. And those vintage dresses, fuck yes. Sign me up."

Tobias Westfield is my other wide receiver. He's a little older than Ben, from a football dynasty family, and the current crown-holding libertine of the team now that Alexander Xavier's stepped down in favor of monogamy.

"Is it necessary to hear about every single one of your fantasies?" I give Tobias a look.

"Just hoping one will inspire you out of your rut, Priest." He grins wide at me.

"There's no fifties-housewife. Just apparently Colton has a history with one of Violet's friends." Waylon grins, and now I know they're about to gang up on me.

"Oh yeah? You think he had a life before he decided on a strict diet of celibacy and reflection?" Tobias smirks.

"Sounds like it." Waylon needles.

"So what brought her up?" Tobias asks.

"She's coming to town to stay with Violet and Ben." I can hear the tone in Waylon's voice, and I shift my weight, pretending to be interested in the latest movement on the field. Watching Xander as he takes a guy down.

"Oh, that's gonna be fucking good. Can't wait. When does she get here?"

"Today," I answer before Ben can.

"She hot? Have a thing for older guys? Or tattooed wide receivers?"

"She's older. Closer to your and Violet's age," Ben explains.

"She prefers them tattooed but doesn't like athletes," I add helpfully.

"Well, clearly she made an exception once." I know Tobias well enough to know that he has zero intention of pursuing her. He's just trying to get a reaction out of me. But if she's anything like she used to be, she might pursue him, which gets under my skin.

"She won't again." I flick him a look that tells him to cut his shit and there's a low whistle from Waylon.

"Let's not piss off our fearless leader." Waylon laughs.

"Let's get back out there and throw, yeah?" I look to Ben,

and he nods, putting his gloves back on and jogging with me to the side of the field they're not currently running drills on.

I needed to focus on football. Zone out and just let my body take over. If I put in a hard enough workout I'll probably be too tired to think about her, and it's probably better that way.

THREE

Joss

WE GET BACK to Violet's house and after a shower and a quick tour of the place, which is even more stunning than she made it seem, we're finishing up prepping for the party.

"If I stay long enough, what do you say to an old-school Halloween party?" I wiggle my eyebrows at her.

"I think we can make that work. We'll have to get Ben and the guys convinced to dress up. Might be a few holdouts."

"I can convince them." I grin.

"Convince me of what?" Ben asks coming down the stairs from his own post-practice shower.

"Benny! Happy. Fucking. Birthday!" I yell, running for him, and he wraps me up in a hug.

"Jossifer," he taunts in a playful tone, using the nickname he gave me after everything blew up and he had to deal with most of the consequences. It had stuck long after since he liked teasing me.

"How dare you!" I laugh, hugging him tight.

"Missed you. You need to come to visit us sooner next time."

"I'll try. I got you candles for your cake, those weird marshmallow gummy things you like, and another present. I can't wait for you to open it." I scruff his head.

"You know I'm not a kid anymore, right? You told her I'm all grown up now, right, Vi?" Ben asks with mock concern.

"Yes, I told her all about how you and Colt are elder badasses now."

At the mention of his name, Ben's eyes snap to mine, a look there I can't quite read. I smile in return, but it doesn't seem to be enough to make him relax.

"She told you he's coming?"

"Yes, she mentioned it."

"No bloodshed, I hope." He gives me a meaningful look.

"I'll be on my best behavior." I grin.

"Oh good, we're gonna need it because Harper just texted me that Drew's coming with her."

"Jesus, Alex is going to murder him on sight if he touches her." Ben sighs.

"See, I'll be the least of your worries."

"Did you guys come up with any sort of plan to help Harper?" Ben looks to Violet.

"Joss has an idea about a calendar with mostly naked athletes in it. Or possibly a coffee table book. She's still deciding." Violet gives Ben an evil grin as he wraps his arms around her from the side.

"Why does that not surprise me?" He shakes his head at me.

"Because you know me well?" I offer.

The two of them kiss, and they look like the picture of wedded bliss even now, several years in. When they should be over it, yelling at each other about laundry piles and a lawn that needs to be mowed. But not them. They look like everything you might want if you believed in love.

"You two make me sick!" I yell but then can't help the smile that cracks across my face because I love them despite how disgustingly in love they are.

Just then the doorbell rings.

"Damn," Ben mutters kissing Violet one last time. "Already here I guess."

"Can you get it? I'm finishing up the stuff in the oven. Once Harper's here I'm sure she won't mind keeping an eye on the door."

"Yup got it." Ben disappears around the corner to answer the door, and I go to sit at the counter again, pulling up one of the barstools.

"Anything else I can do?"

"Nope. I'm going to let Ben and the guys handle the BBQ, so once this cornbread is done, we're good."

I hear the sound of male voices in the hallway, laughter, and then I can distinctly hear his voice as they get closer. One that's deep and sexy. One attached to—he walks into the room then and my mind blanks. Just a complete blank void and there's the sound of white noise in my ears as I stare at him. There's a reason he's on magazine covers. He's like the second coming of James Dean. If James Dean played football and was closer to Rock Hudson's height. Built like he could throw you up against a wall and fuck you hard.

I don't know why this man always has such a pull on me. He walks into a room and suddenly it's like everything stops but him. And he shouldn't, he really shouldn't. He's not remotely my type. Too pretty. Too clean cut. Too successful. Give me a lanky heavily tattooed and pierced starving artist with greasy-looking hair up in a bun. Bonus points for facial piercings. Maybe the occasional blue-collar guy with a filthy mouth and a secret love of alt girls when I need variety in my diet. Those are my kind of hot. Not Mr. Midwest Farm Boy Quarterback over here, walking in dressed like he just walked off a GQ casual photoshoot set with a perfectly styled and textured quiff. It's too fucking much. And yet, here I am gawking like Elvis has been resurrected.

"Hey Colt," Violet greets him.

"Hey Vi." He flashes her a bright smile, and I feel my stomach flip a little.

Remembering what it felt like to have that smile aimed at me. Anticipating I'm not going to get that reaction when he notices me any second now. I'm not prepared to meet him like this. With just the four of us in the room. I'd expected to come across him during the party, in a room full of people where we could exchange a slight half-nod smile thing that passed as acknowledgment and then move on. That would rip off the Band-Aid and then we could happily ignore each other. But not like this. No sooner I think it, his eyes turn to meet mine.

Fucking. Fuck. I can tell the second he looks at me that he knows what I'm thinking. That he still melts my brain and other parts of me. I want to run, but then I remember the lecture I'd been given about playing nice. So I panic, deciding I'll play it off with excessive cheerfulness.

I run and throw my arms around him, hugging him tight.

"Colt! I missed you so much! You look amazing!"

His hands wrap around my wrists, and he takes a step back, pulling away from me. His eyebrow raises, and he looks at me like I'm an over-exuberant fan.

"Uh, hi." Is all he manages to say, his eyes sweeping over me and finding me wanting.

The hot flush of embarrassment races through me. It's not visible on the outside because I'm well-practiced. But I feel sick. I glance at Violet, and she looks worried for me. I turn away from him, desperate to find something else to focus on, and I hear Ben clear his throat.

Kill. Me. Now.

"Oh shoot, I forgot to get the stuff outside set up. We've gotta pull the kayaks down and finish getting the balls and sports stuff out of the shed," Violet interrupts, looking flustered, and I can tell it's as much about the reunion as it is her genuine concern for setting up the party.

"I got it!" I practically shout. Any excuse to get away from him. "I know where the shed is, and I assume the kayaks are in the boathouse?"

Violet looks at me surprised. "I was just gonna have Ben and Colt—"

But before she can even finish the sentence the doorbell rings, and Ben flashes a look before heading off to answer it. And after that embarrassing debacle, I'm ready to get out of here anyway.

"I have it. Really."

"In those heels?" Violet nods down to the three-inch spike heels I have on, that I may or may not have worn for confidence.

"I have flats upstairs I can change into really quick."

"I've got it," Colton interjects, and Violet and I both turn to look at him. "It'll take me half the time, and I don't need to change to do it."

"I can do it," I argue. I don't know why I'm arguing, he's right. But I'd wanted out of this room. Fresh air. Time to myself to replay that stupid scene a few times until I'd been able to quell my anxiety by thinking of a time that was more awkward than that one, and by comparison make it seem less tragic.

"You can get a pair of flip-flops out of the closet." Violet nods to the door. "I just bought them."

"Thanks."

"I can get the kayaks if you want to get the stuff in the shed." Colton doesn't wait for an answer, opening the back door instead and taking off.

"Bastard," I mutter, hurrying to the closet and grabbing the flip-flops. I quickly change and then scurry toward the door.

"Be nice!" Violet calls after me.

"Oh, I'll be nice," I respond and hustle through the door after him. His stupid, giant ass gait already has him halfway down the hill. I have to run to catch up with him and then slow down my pace because I'm sure I look ridiculous running down the hill in flip-flops.

"You really didn't have to come. I've got it," I say, trying to sound calm and collected despite the fact I'm attempting to move at the speed of light because this man just made me feel an inch tall.

"The kayaks are high up. Ben usually gets them."

"I can figure it out."

"Or you could just get the things in the shed," he counters.

And I could. I could just get the things in the shed, but instead, I'm barreling down the gentle slope of the hill toward the boathouse trying to beat a man who could probably outrun me in two seconds flat if he bothered to put in any effort. I'm being stupid. Stubbornly stupid. But I can't let it go.

When we get to the boathouse though, I know he's right. There's no way I can get them easily, especially if I try to do it all by myself. But I'm determined to try.

I stand on my tiptoes and then use the tips of my fingers to press the edge of the kayak off the hook. I manage to knock it free, and one side comes down on me hard. I scoop my arms under it and catch it before it can crash to the ground. It hurts, but I'm used to hauling heavy camera equipment around, so it's nothing I can't handle.

The problem is what comes next—a giant fucking spider parading its way out from underneath the lip of the kayak onto my forearm and proceeding to make a quick march up my arm.

I scream. I jump. I yell fifty-something obscenities and then I lose my balance. The weight of the kayak only makes that precipitous situation even worse, and suddenly I'm tumbling over backward with the kayak falling hard on my legs.

FOUR

Colton

IT HAPPENS SO FAST I can't get to her in time, and she's on the ground with the kayak on top of her, viciously swiping at her arm and making tiny yiping noises like a small hurt animal.

"Fuck, Joss. Are you okay?" I rush over and lift the kayak off her legs but two red welts that look like they're ready to start bruising any moment are already on her shins.

"Get it off! It's in my hair! In my hair!" she screeches.

"What?" I ask.

"The spider. It's huge and gross, and I know it went in my hair."

I crouch down, leaning over her, and spot the offender as it crawls out onto her shoulder.

"It's just a wolf spider," I say, trying to reassure her that it's nothing venomous.

"I don't care what it is, Colton, just get it off!"

I swipe at it, knocking it to the floor and it scurries off, likely wondering what the hell it did to deserve this kind of afternoon surprise. She takes a deep breath and pulls her legs up to her chest, moving one from side to side to get a better look at the welt. I glance up at the kayak which looks like it has a bit of a dent on one side and frown. I can feel her eyes on me again.

"If you say I told you so, I will murder you," she says, a bitter tone in her voice tells me that however enthusiastically she greeted me in the house, she still remembers how we left things.

"I didn't say a word." I look back at her, but I can't help the smug grin.

"What are you thinking then? Because your face certainly speaks volumes today."

"Just amused you're so terrified of a spider."

"Of course you would be." She glares at me, wiping some of the dirt off her legs.

"Are you all right? You didn't break skin, did you?" I try to take a closer look, but she pulls back from me, and it cuts even though it shouldn't.

"I'm fine," she huffs defensively, starting to move to stand.

"Here, just wait before you hurt yourself worse. Let me get the kayak out of the way, and I'll help you up."

"Oh no. No way. Do not start with the Boy Scout routine," she mutters. It's another little dig. She used to call me Scout when she wanted to put me in my place. Farm Boy when she wanted to double down on it. Make sure I remembered she was older, wiser, and more experienced than me. "I can stand up just fine."

Except then she tries and nearly falls again. A blush colors her cheeks, and I can see the frustration on her face. I do what I probably shouldn't then, reaching down and grabbing her around the waist, hauling her up to her feet in one quick motion. She lets out an exasperated huff but no further complaint, and I'm going to count that as a win.

I bend down to right the kayak and then turn to look at her leg. She tries it and bears weight before she looks at me skeptically.

"It's fine. Stupid spider."

I try to stifle the laugh but a small one escapes anyway, and her eyes immediately meet mine.

"I'm sorry," I say pressing my lips together. "I just didn't take you for the type to be afraid of spiders."

"I'm human. I have phobias, okay?" She frowns, a wounded look coming and going. I almost feel bad. She's such an unstoppable force so much of the time it just hit me as strange to see a spider take her down—literally.

"And since things are already insanely awkward at this point."

She stands a little taller, and I wonder if she's about to point at the elephant in the room. The years that have passed. The way we left things. I'm not at all prepared for what she actually says.

"I need you to pose naked for some photos."

"No." I don't even need to think about it. It's no on so many levels. No, I'm not getting naked in front of a camera. Especially not for her camera. Naked alone with her would be begging for trouble I don't need. Then there's the fact my PR team would have a meltdown and my family? They would just plain fucking melt at the idea of me doing anything like that. We barely get along as it is these days, I don't need more fuel on the fire.

"You didn't even ask why."

"I don't need to. It doesn't matter. The answer is no."

"Because it's me or in general? Because if it's me we could

get a different photographer. I know you might not be comfortable with me given our history and—"

I have no idea why, but the tone in which she says it. Like it's a challenge, like I couldn't handle being naked in front of her—never mind that I do actually have serious concerns about it—I hate it. It needles me.

"I'd be fine. But it's still no," I cut her off.

"It's to save Harper and Alex. To help raise money for her museum. I mean, I haven't talked to her about it yet, but it would be the best way to make money. Leverage the celebrity of the team and do it for a good cause. I know a lot of the other guys would do it."

"You know? Because you know them?"

"I'm not saying there wouldn't be holdouts but let's be honest you all walk around half-naked in locker rooms and a million other public places. And since most of you can't keep it in your pants, half the women in Seattle have probably seen a Phantom dick in their lives."

"Yeah? Ask them then."

"You know it's you they'll want. Your celebrity would sell more, faster. What's the problem?"

"Getting naked in the locker room where there aren't any cameras is different than making a permanent record. And I haven't personally fucked half the city."

She follows me as I move to take the kayaks off the racks Ben has them stored on.

"We can place a towel or a ball strategically. No one's asking for full frontal."

"Still no."

"Again, a different photographer could step in for yours. I'm sure Violet has contacts."

If I was going to do what she's asking, I definitely wouldn't want someone else. She'd be the only one I'd consider, but I'm not about to let her have that information. Because that's playing with fire and with her I always get burned.

"Do you not understand the word no?"

"Not when it can help raise money for a good cause. I like to exhaust all avenues before I give up."

"It would be off-brand for me."

"To raise money?"

"To have photos done like that."

"Ah, still too wholesome. I get it."

"You're not going to bait me."

"You sure about that?" she says in a tone I remember. One that says she thinks she owns me and can get me to do anything she wants.

I pull the last kayak off its rack and set it down on the floor. I turn to her and lean down to meet her eyes with my own.

"Absolutely positive."

She blinks and her eyes flicker with the challenge, drifting over my face and then down my body.

"Don't do that."

"What?"

"Challenge me. I'm trying to play nice with you, Colton. It's not really in my wheelhouse, but I'm trying for Ben and Violet."

"I'm well aware playing nice isn't something you're capable of," I say it before I have time to think better of it. This is what she does. Pushes my buttons and gets a reaction out of me that no one else can.

"If this is about how we left things... I told you then and I'll say it as many times as I can. I'm sorry. I never meant to hurt you."

No. I know she never meant to hurt me. It didn't change the facts. But I'm not about to give her any ammunition. So instead, I laugh, shaking my head, and smile at her.

"This isn't about that. It's about the fact that it's not on-brand for me and it's just not something I'm interested in doing. I'll happily donate money, but I'm not stripping down."

"Fine. I think you should get a new brand. This Midwestern boy-next-door thing is played out."

"It got me where I am." I grit my teeth.

"True. I'm sure all the beer-belching, corn-chip-eating, aging former high school football stars would be horrified to see you naked. Worried their wives might finally have something to turn them on for the first time in years. Have them sneaking off to the laundry room and letting a rough cycle and thoughts of you take them to the only orgasm they've had this year."

"Well, they can't all be as perfect as you, can they?"

Her eyes light with anger, and I can see her grind her teeth, but she doesn't respond. A moment later something else flickers across her face, something I can't quite read. I want to ask her what it is. But instead, she stands straighter and looks me in the eye. There's hurt there, and more painted across her face.

I said I wouldn't take the bait, and I not only took it, but I turned around and stuck the knife in. Now I'm the asshole. I start to apologize but she charges on, acting like nothing's wrong.

"Fine. If you change your mind. Let me know. Looks like you've got this covered. I'm going to get the stuff out of the shed." She turns on her heel and hurries out the door.

FIVE

Joss

I SHOULD NEVER HAVE COME to stay here. It was a stupid mistake and now I'm dealing with the consequences of that impulsive decision. Standing in front of a shed, trying to decide what to do with resurfacing attraction to a man who clearly still hates me. I pull the latch and prop the door open with a small door wedge just by the entrance when I realize it won't stay open on its own.

Colton, for all his current dislike of me, would never hurt me purposefully. Not that I'm special. He has a heart of gold. Is probably the kindest person I've ever met besides Ben and Violet, and I pretty much have no business going anywhere near him.

Except that Ben had a point earlier. He wasn't a kid anymore, and neither was Colton. He'd grown up. Shed the insecurities he'd had before. Exchanged the awkward-college-guy style for all the trappings of an insanely attractive grown-ass man. Talks like he has a newfound confidence—not shocking given he's the captain of what Violet tells me is one of the best teams in the country—and looks at me like I'm ancient history. A mistake he made once that he won't repeat. In fact, if he hadn't shown a glimpse of his hand in the boathouse, I'd have assumed he barely even remembered that once upon a time he liked to fuck me. All of that—combined with the fact I'm fairly certain that underneath the new look he probably still has a body at least as good if not better—has me desperately wishing I wasn't a bumbling mess right now.

But such is life.

I lift up a tarp to try to find the volleyball and net, only to discover that the nightmare in the boathouse has followed me to the shed, and this time it's wildly magnified. There are hundreds of tiny spiders crawling everywhere. Under the tarp, over the tarp. I look up and see them climbing the wall and the ceiling over my head.

I take a step back, tripping and falling backward. I hit the shed door, managing to keep my balance but it slams shut. Locking me in with Spider Armageddon. I rattle on the door with no luck. So I do what every sane rational grown-ass woman who has her shit together does. I let out a blood-curdling scream and wedge myself into the farthest corner of the shed, trying to get as far away from the spiders as possible.

Violet, Ben, and I are going to have *words*.

I look up and see a can of bug spray on the windowsill and grab it. It's mostly empty which means it can only really be a means of last defense but better than nothing. When all else fails and they're ready to devour me alive, I can at least take a few of the fuckers with me. I clutch it to my chest and double-check the wall behind me to make sure that it's at least spider-free.

Just then the shed door pops open, and I see my superhero in the form of the man who hates me.

"What the hell is going on?" Colt steps inside, studying the way I'm cowering in the corner and then searching for the source of my fear.

"The door!" I yell, but it's too late. It slams shut behind him with a gust of wind off the water, and I hear the door latch slam behind it. "Fuck!"

He turns around and presses on the door, trying to fight the same fate I had. Because now we're both stuck.

"We're locked in, aren't we?" he says at last, pressing his forehead to the door.

"With about a million spiders who want to murder us. Please tell me you have your cell phone."

"Nope. It's in my car. Charging," he says, sounding as defeated as I feel.

"Fucking fantastic. This is exactly how I've always wanted to die. With you judging me while these spiders eat my heart out with their itsy-bitsy fangs."

"Joss..." He looks over at the swarm of spiders on the other side of the shed. "They're probably more scared of you than you are of them."

"I don't believe you. That's what they would want you to think. They're clearly closing ranks"

He looks at me and then looks at the bug spray I'm clutching to my chest. He extends his hand for it.

"No. There's not much left. It's a last line of defense."

"Just trust me."

"Ha."

"Fine. Don't trust me, but assume that since I don't have the same fear that I'm being more rational than you right now?"

He has a point. One I don't love but can't argue with. So I reluctantly hand him the can. He shakes it, testing how much is left, and then opens it. He sprays a line along the floor up the walls and over the ceiling, creating a small but not insignificant barrier between me and my worst nightmare.

I let out a relieved sigh, wishing I'd thought of that first.

"Okay?" He looks at me pointedly.

"Okay," I answer.

His eyes turn back to the door as he sits the can back on the sill.

"Did you see how it latched?"

"No. Not a good look. I just saw it wouldn't stay shut, so I used the wedge, but I knocked it when I fell, and you must have kicked it accidentally when you ran in here."

"Because you were screaming like you were being murdered." He grouches at me.

"I said accidentally!" I snap back in return.

"God dammit." He runs a hand over his face.

"Language, Colton," I say sarcastically because the man rarely swears, and I'd always tease him about it.

"Don't start."

"Start what? I'm just trying to kid around with you. Jesus. Did this quarterback gig come with a side requirement of being a rude prick?"

"No."

"Then why are you being so prickly?"

"Because I'm stuck in a fucking shed with *you!*"

"Oh, like I want to be stuck in here with you after the way you've treated me today."

"Treated you how? I've been nothing but civil with you despite multiple fucking attempts on your part to be anything but."

"Excuse me? I've been civil. I'm doing everything I can to be good for Ben and Violet's sake. I want to be here with them, spend time with them. And I want to help Violet's friend Harper while I'm here."

"So spend time. Help them."

"I am."

"Good." He looks back at the door, studying it like he might be able to fix our situation.

"Great."

"Fantastic."

"But just to be clear, you're the one being a dick. I'm just trying to be friendly."

He lets out a sardonic laugh and turns around to face me again, his eyes meeting mine.

"Friendly... I bet. I'd love for you to explain how I'm being the dick in the situation, when you show up to Ben's birthday party dressed like that, wrapping yourself around me the second you see me and then asking me to strip naked for a camera the second you have me alone."

I let out a puff of air as I glare at him. "I see the pros haven't affected your ego. At. All."

"Are you going to pretend like you didn't wear this dress and those heels to get my attention?"

"I don't know what you're talking about."

"What color is the bra and panty set you've got on?"

Who the fuck is this guy? This isn't Colt. Not *my* Colt. Not the sweet reserved thoughtful young man who had been so fucking earnest and giving.

"Is it green?" He studies me and he grins when he sees something there he likes. "More of a jade or an emerald shade?"

"Don't be insane." I roll my eyes. It was definitely fucking emerald green. This asshole.

"Oh, now I know it is. Is that what you thought? You'd wear this dress and those heels, put on my favorite color, and I'd just come when I was called. Get on my knees for you and beg for a taste?"

"You should be so lucky."

His fingers slide under my chin as we stare at each other, his thumb brushing over the small cleft there.

"I'm not your lovesick boy anymore. You don't hold all the cards, and I don't come when I'm called."

"You sure about that? You used to come pretty hard when I told you what a good boy you were."

His eyes go bright as they meet mine, flickering with amusement as a wry smile spreads across his face. His lashes lowering as his eyes fall to my lips. This man is so beautiful on magazine covers, but in person, he takes my fucking breath away.

But he's not my type. We don't even like each other. Fucking him would be a mistake of epic proportions. I literally just got to town. I can't be making mistakes like that already. Disappointing Ben before I've even been on the ground for a full twenty-four hours.

"I mean if we're being honest, I liked it better when you couldn't say anything at all because these lips were wrapped around my cock."

"You have a filthy mouth for someone they call a priest."

"I recall you liking my mouth. *A lot.*"

"You were always so eager to use it. Hard not to."

"Pull your dress up and let me see the color."

"Excuse you. I'm a fucking lady. I don't just hike my skirt up because some asshole tells me to."

"I can make you."

"I'm sorry?" I blink at him, feigning disgust. Because I wish he *would* make me. This new Colt, the one with the mouth on him who gives two fucks less about propriety and cordialness? I like him. He's even hotter than the version I remember. Which means I am in *danger*.

He leans forward, caging me against the wall, and whispers against the shell of my ear, "You know you would still like the way I make you feel... Just us out here. No one will know you spread your legs for the golden boy. That you have a secret fetish for quarterbacks. But if you want me to make you come, you have to let me see first."

Holy fucking shit. Forget danger. I'm downright fucked.

I take in oxygen. Remind myself to breathe. That I'm the one in control here. I'm older. Wiser. And I *don't* have a secret fetish for quarterbacks.

But I do have a secret weakness for him. For those eyes and that panty-dropping smile. For how good he is with his hands. So I grab the sides of my skirt and pull it up, higher and higher until he can see what's underneath.

He'd better fucking appreciate them too. They were expensive. I bought them in a little boutique in Paris right before I flew back here. I'd told myself I was just getting them for me. That it had nothing, absolutely nothing to do with the fact that it's his favorite color. That he used to tease me that I reminded him of the Wicked Witch and loved seeing me in it. But it was a lie. One he knows now as he stares at the deep emerald green strip of satin that's hand-stitched to two sheer pieces of hand-made lace.

SIX

Colt

HER BODY IS as gorgeous as it ever was. If anything, she's improved with age because her hips are a little wider and her thighs are a little thicker. It makes me want to rip this dress off her, so I can see what the matching bra looks like. The way it probably perfectly frames her lush breasts. See if the rest of her body has filled out with time too because it looks like it has.

The tattoo of a pirate ship still wraps its way around her right hip, and I see hints of some new ink that's harder to make out in this light. I'd always been jealous of Ben—that Violet had tattooed his number on her wrist. I wanted to tattoo mine on Joss. Sign my name across her skin so every time another guy saw her like this, he'd ask her why she had it, and she'd have to tell him. She'd have to remember that I was the best she ever had. She'd confessed that much. Laughed it off that it was my eagerness that turned her on so much just like she's doing now.

"Turn around," I order her, pretending like I'm just taking

in the scenery. Like I don't care, and she doesn't have any effect on me. Because I shouldn't actually touch her. We are nothing but a disaster waiting to happen. Cordialness and civility, while we were around Ben and Violet, were the only things we could hope for.

"No comment? No gloating about being right?" she asks as she turns around, and I look at the lace on the back that leaves almost nothing to the imagination. I run my finger along the edge of it, down from her hip until I skim over her ass. It's perfect. Gorgeous and pale just like the rest of her. She bends slightly at the waist, knowing exactly what she's doing. The way her muscles flex underneath, I skim my hand over her cheek and imagine what she'd look like riding me in reverse. Wishing I could bend her over and slide inside. Show her how much of me she's been missing.

Sex is usually low on my priority list. So low the guys call me Priest because of how long it's been. But she appears and now I'm hard and desperate to fuck her. It must cut both ways, or she wouldn't be dressed like this. Jumping me the second I walk in the door. Following me down to the boat house. Looking at me with flustered interest. We might hate each other after everything, but the hate sex could be amazing.

"I don't need to gloat when we both already know the truth. It's obvious you wore this because you were hoping to get fucked tonight," I say softly as my fingers skim over the surface of her stomach, sliding down until I slip them beneath the fabric and pause when I hear her breath catch. "And since you wore my favorite color, pretty simple to figure out who you wore it for."

"You never know. It's Ben's birthday. Violet's put in a lot of work today. She might be tired and need me to pinch-hit."

I laugh and shake my head because this was classic Joss.

Always deflecting and saying something ludicrous. "She loves you a lot. Not enough to share her husband though."

"If you think you'll get me to admit I want you, Farm Boy, you can keep dreaming. Or try to torture it out of me. The latter might be more fun than whatever you're doing right now."

I press her up against the wall, grinding my cock against her ass, and then I slide my hand lower, letting my fingers graze her clit on the way down to test how wet she is. But I don't have to go further to find out. She's so wet for me she's already soaking through her panties and coating my fingers.

"I always loved that about you. How fucking fast you got turned on for me."

"You assume it's for you."

"I don't see anyone else out here."

"You also can't see who I'm imagining in my head."

I start to pull away then. I always liked playing with her. I love how prickly she is because it makes me remember that it's that much sweeter when she comes for me.

But given how things ended between us there's a fine line between fun and fucked up where she's concerned. And I'm not thinking straight right now. She's baiting me down a short road to hell and I'm following like she still controls the lead.

Her fingers wrap around my wrist, stopping my retreat.

"I said you could torture it out of me," she whispers.

I brush the pads of my fingers over her clit then in gentle circles alternating the pressure just enough to let her have a taste of what she wants from me. She lets out a stuttered breath and rocks her hips forward just a touch.

"You miss that?" I ask her. Because god do I miss it. She might have ripped my chest open and torn out my heart when it was already bruised and bloody from the last owner, but the way this woman could make me feel like a god is unmatched.

Not that there had been a lot of contenders. But this is part of the reason why. She'd ruined me for most other women. I'm still hopeful I could find one. One who could make my heart beat this fast. Make my cock this hard. I didn't hurt for options, but so far, she's it.

When she doesn't answer I pull away again.

"Fuck. No. Please," she lets out a series of curses and tightens her grip around my wrist.

"Please don't stop. Do the thing you were always good at."

I can't help the smirk that comes then because she'd always been fair about that. Telling me how good I was. How much she liked everything I did. She wasn't shy when it came to things like this, and it made me weak as hell for her.

"What thing's that?" I know, but I just want to hear her say it. I give her another brush of my fingers, teasing her and a little growl of frustration comes from her throat.

"You know the thing, Colt. Where you finger me but still have that perfect rhythm on my clit with your palm. Like you always did under the blanket when we were pretending to watch movies with them. I need it."

"You need me."

"I need your hands."

A little laugh escapes me, and I press a kiss to the back of her neck before I slide my fingers inside her, keeping a steady rhythm until I can hear her breathing start to get heavier.

"Thank God you're still good with them. I was worried it wouldn't be as good as I remembered."

"Glad I can still meet your standards."

"I think they've exceeded my standards now. Violet said they're worth nearly half a billion these days. I like expensive things, but a half-billion-dollar fingering might even exceed my wildest dreams."

"Joss?"

"Yes?"

"I need you to shut the fuck up and focus on coming hard for me. I don't want to hear anything but the little whimpers you make when you're close. You think you can do that?"

"Yes, sir," her tone is half sarcasm, but she glances back at me over her shoulder, a little devilish grin playing at her lips before she turns away again.

As much as I want to see her face, watch her while she comes for me, it's better this way. Too much is still left unsaid. Too much bad blood and too many broken promises between us that we'd need to sort through before we could ever fuck the way we used to. Even then, we're doomed from the start because when it comes to relationships, we don't even come close to meeting in the middle.

But I could make her come—and I love watching her. She's a wet whimpering mess, keeping just quiet enough that no one outside this shed can hear her but loud enough I can still feel it in my cock. It makes me wish it was my cock and not my fingers bringing her down like this, taking her over the edge while she falls so desperately over it.

Her breathing's erratic as she leans up against the wall, panting like she can barely get enough oxygen. It's all I can hear until it breaks with the sound of someone's voice—Ben.

"Colt! Joss!" I hear him looking for us.

"We're stuck in here!" I yell to him.

"Where?" he yells back, and I see him pause on the hill through the window.

"The shed."

She pushes her dress down and brushes her hair back as she turns around. Her eyes dart off toward the window and I'm waiting for her to say something cruel or sarcastic before Ben gets here. Instead, she's uncharacteristically quiet. So I say something stupid. Bound to get us into a situation we can't unfuck. Just like the last time we agreed to exchange favors for favors.

Ben's closing in so it's my last chance to say something.

"I'll pose for the pictures on one condition."

Her eyes come to mine, and she gives me a curious look.

"What's that?"

"You go first."

"Meaning?"

"You pose for nude shots, and I'll do it."

"I don't think the target audience wants pictures of me."

"I'll buy them."

Something changes in her eyes, a look that comes and goes that I can't read. She turns away from me then, so I can't see the rest of her reaction, because Ben opens the door and we both turn toward it.

"I'll think about it," she whispers as she walks past me and then Ben.

"Thank God, Benny. We could have died in there. You have a whole fucking spider army you need to take care of. Barely held them off. One of them definitely had a tiny machine gun, and I think they were building a trebuchet. It's out of control, really." She jokes with him, acting like nothing at all happened between us.

But Ben's eyes float over her and then land hard on me, an eyebrow rising along with his suspicion.

"Thanks for the rescue," I mutter.

"Seems like I might have shown up a little late."

"Or too early."

SEVEN

Joss

THAT NIGHT after everyone is gone and Harper and Ben have gone to bed, Violet and I sit out on the deck with cocktails. We're curled up under blankets and staring at the stars on her Adirondack chairs.

"So you and Colton managed not to kill each other."

"No thanks to your husband and his meddling comments."

"True. He was just ready to start shit all over the place tonight."

"Just to be clear, Xavier definitely snuck off to fuck Harper, right?"

"I would almost guarantee it, yes."

"I think I like them together."

"Well, that's good. Since we are trying to help them and her museum."

"Fuck that Drew guy though."

"Yeah, he's an ass. Hopefully, we'll be rid of him soon. I

never did like him much, but Xander and Harper were always fond of him, so I didn't want to piss anyone off."

"Makes sense."

"Circling back to you and Colton though..." She looks over at me and smiles when I roll my eyes. "Did you ask him to do the photos for you?"

"I did. When we went out to get the kayaks and stuff ready outside."

"And?"

"And then we were almost killed by the spider army your husband has been allowing to muster in your shed."

"Ha. I'll talk to him about it. What did Colt say?"

"He said no, but then he said he wants me to go first."

"Go first?" Violet's brow furrows as she tries to make sense of it.

"He wants me to pose nude. If I do it, he'll do it. He thinks I won't."

"Whoa. Wait, for what?"

"Excellent question."

"I mean, is he getting the photos?"

"I made a flippant remark, and he said he'd quote 'buy them'. Whatever that means."

"Uh, pretty sure that means that Colt still has a thing for you."

"A thing for looking at me naked. Not necessarily a thing for *me*. He might just want to mount trophies on the wall or something."

"That doesn't sound like Colt." Violet frowns. "I know you have your own opinions of him, and I know you hurt each other. I hate that. But he's a good guy, Joss. Like he and Ben might be in competition for the Boy Scout award."

"I know. You're right. I just don't know what he's up to and it makes me nervous."

"A guy who makes you nervous? Someone mark the day on the calendar." Violet grins at me until I raise my eyebrow and then she has the decency to tone it down. "Fine. What do you want him to be up to?" she asks pointedly.

I slide her a sideways glance and she smirks.

"That's what I thought." She takes a sip of her drink.

"I can't help it. I shouldn't. I know I need to stay away but whenever I'm around him..."

"Uh-huh." She grins wider.

"Stop that."

"What?" She feigns innocence.

"You know what. I'm not you, Violet. The prince isn't secretly in love with me. We don't magically end up together and live happily ever after in our gorgeous castle on the water."

"You never know. I'm rooting for it."

"You remember you were rooting for it last time too? I've told you... Falling in love isn't a thing that happens to me. Falling in lust, sure. And if anyone's capable of causing that it's the second coming of James Dean. But love? Nope."

"Yes, but this time you're older and wiser. You've loved and lost. You know the difference between the jerks and the good ones now."

"I've always known the difference, just sometimes the jerks were better in bed. Also, loved? Let's not get carried away with ourselves," I scoff, but the word pings around inside my head, rattling against my insecurities and better judgment and then landing hard. Did I love Colt? I was pretty sure I was incapable of the emotion. I mean, I loved him. The same way I loved Ben and Violet—but love, like *in love*? That's not an emotion I'm capable of. I might still have strong feelings about the sex we had though. That couldn't be helped.

"Are you saying he was bad?"

"No. Not at all. Just a general observation." Because

anywhere Colt had been inexperienced, he'd been very eager to learn. But I don't share that. Not even with Violet because he was and is a very private person, and despite my loud mouth and our bad blood, I do try to keep his confidence.

"Okay then. You could give it a second try. Maybe it'd work out better this time."

"I'm not trying to give anything a second try. Other than maybe the sex. *Maybe*. But that will only get me in trouble. Also, I'm fairly certain if you want to give someone a chance at things you don't ask them for nudes."

"In his defense, you asked first."

"Touché. But still..." I fiddle with a piece of string on the edge of the blanket.

"So are you going to do the photos?" Violet asks.

"I mean, have you seen him? Are you aware of my inability to say no to him?" I raise a brow at her. "Plus, I told Harper I'd help. If helping means I trade nude photos with the hottest man on earth, that's just what I have to do. It's a sacrifice, but what choice do I have?"

She laughs and shakes her head. "You just want to see him naked again."

I pretend to glare at her until we both break out in laughter. I take a sip of my drink as we stare out into the night.

"This is all your fault you know. 'Come see me, Joss. You can stay with us, Joss. It'll be like old times, Joss.' Making me forget that he was here, and I'd have to see him five million times thanks to Ben."

"Well, we'll still have fun. Just get the photos and get out, like you do with any other client. Then maybe you two can learn to get along, be friends again."

"Maybe."

EIGHT

Colt

BEN and I have just finished up drills and are on the sideline recovering and getting some electrolytes back into our systems.

"We gonna talk about what I walked in on?" Ben asks, not bothering to look at me.

"I don't need a lecture if that's what you're asking."

"So it was what it looked like?"

"Did it look like we accidentally got locked in a shed, and she's terrified of spiders?"

"It looked like she was terrified, and you found a pretty specific way of distracting her." Ben smirks to himself and then squeezes a stream of water out of the sports bottle.

"I plead the fifth." I roll my head back and forth over my shoulders, trying to keep my muscles loose.

"And you're sure you don't need the lecture?" he asks, giving me a quick sideways glance.

"I know who she is."

"And yet you still walk straight into the fire."

"Do you lecture her like this?"

"Yes. I gave her specific directions to not start shit before she ever came here. That we love her but that I didn't want to see any bloodshed between the two of you."

"I'm trying. She just pushes every fucking button I have. Like she knows every single code and the exact order to push them to get maximum efficiency out of her torture. Staying a step ahead of her is exhausting."

"I know. She helped me wear down Violet's defenses." He smirks again.

"Try being on the receiving end sometime."

"No thanks. I'm very happy with the fantasy that I already have at home."

"Jesus. Where's Tobias when I need him? You probably would have made him literally throw up in his mouth a little with that, you know?"

"Just saying. You should try it."

I grunt in response because the sad truth is that Joss is the fantasy for me. I'd realized it yesterday the second we were arguing in the boathouse and confirmed it in the shed. Even when we're arguing she lights every tinder inside me. She's all I've been able to think of since, and the fact that she planned to get under my skin, wearing all my favorite things, just makes me that much more determined to prove to her that I'm not the blubbering kid I was when she ran the last time.

"I don't like the look on your face," Ben mutters, and I realize he's watching me.

"I made an ass out of myself the last time. I want a chance to show her I'm not a fucking kid anymore."

"I told her that."

"You what?"

"I just reminded her that I wasn't a kid anymore and that you aren't either."

"Fantastic. You tell her I graduated out of the Power Wheels too? Drive a real car now..."

"Listen. I'm just trying to keep the peace between you two. Last time it caused a lot of strain between all of us when you two decided to blow up like a fucking supernova. I'm not against the two of you together. Fuck... I wish you would work your shit out. I just want it to not kill everyone in the process."

"I can handle myself."

"I know you can—in any situation that doesn't involve her. When she's involved..."

"I can handle her too."

"I guess we're about to find out."

NINE

Joss

THAT EVENING when I'm back at the house, I find Violet in the kitchen getting a drink of water and I grab one and join her at the counter.

"So what are we doing tonight? Cocktails downtown? Dinner on the water?" I ask when I see her, grinning because I love that I'm getting to see my best friend this much. "Is Harper coming?"

"Harper and Scarlett are out doing something together tonight after they finish up at the museum."

"Dang. I was hoping to talk to her some more. I need to schedule some time with her to sit down and talk logistics and planning for the nonprofit. We have so much paperwork and stuff to file. It's going to be exhausting for a bit."

"Yeah. Let me know what I can help with. I'm glad you two have teamed up but happy to be an auxiliary member of the team." Violet smiles at me.

"Will do. So plans for tonight?"

"I rented out the aquarium for Ben's birthday. He doesn't know that though. I just told him I got us some tickets to an after-hours event there tonight and then I thought we could maybe get a late dinner. Not too late though because Ben has early practice tomorrow since they had a short one today."

"Okay. That sounds like a date though. Am I crashing your and Ben's date?" I frown.

"Crashing our date? Do we have a date?" Ben suddenly appears from around the corner, a sweaty wet mess in what appears to be running clothes. He leans over and kisses Violet, and her face contorts as she kisses him back.

"I love you, but you need a shower."

"That's where I'm headed. Colt and I just went for a long run."

And like it's an entrance announcement, Colt's in the room a second later looking just as sweaty and wet—his shirt plastered to his chest, his hair wet and slicked back, his cheeks flushed. He looks like he just had a marathon sex session. Flashbacks of him in my bed years ago come flooding back, and him sliding his hand between my thighs in the shed come right on its heels. I really don't need to be seeing this. Even in my imagination. It's going to destroy what little self-control I have left.

He nods at me and Violet briefly. "Mind if I get a glass of water?"

"Of course. Go ahead. There are some electrolyte packets in there too if you want them." Violet points to the drawer.

"So what about us on a date?" Ben asks.

"I have those tickets to that event at the aquarium. Part of the membership thing we got for donating, remember? I was about to call to see where you were. We'll have to hurry up and get ready if we're gonna make it. I thought if we were going to be downtown, we could go out for dinner. Joss is worried about being a third wheel though."

"Colt could go. We've got four tickets, don't we?"

My eyes lift to Ben's, and I see the devious grin on his face. I raise an eyebrow at him before I let myself look briefly—so very briefly—at Colt. His back is turned though, and I can't read his reaction.

"Colt?"

"Hmm?" He looks at Ben.

"You want to go to the aquarium and then dinner? We could see if we can get in at that one place with the cheesy fried rice ball things. God that sounds so fucking good after this run. If you're up for it, I mean."

I don't know what Ben is up to, but he's about to get kicked in the shins if he's not careful. I glare at him, but he just ignores me.

"Uhh... how soon are you going? I need a shower." Colt turns finally and waves his hand over his sweaty appearance.

"You could take a shower here. Guest shower's open," Violet offers.

This devious bitch. I can't glare now because he'd see.

"I have clothes in the car, but are you sure? I don't want to be in the way."

"Definitely not in the way. Then Joss doesn't have to worry about feeling weird either," Ben says as he heads down the hall for his own shower.

"It'll be perfect. Please, Colt?" Violet gives him an endearing look, and as the defacto mother of this little group they have, I can see him look at her and then fall into line.

"All right. As long as I can use your shower."

"Definitely. Joss, could you get him some towels out of the guest closet?"

"Sure." I plaster on a smile, hoping she sees how much she's going to pay for this in my eyes.

"Thanks!" She just grins at me pleasantly.

"All right. Grabbing clothes and I'll try to hurry," I hear Colt say as he walks away.

I grumble to myself as I walk down the hall and into the guest room, opening the closet to pull out a couple of towels for him.

"Hey Betty," I say, using the nickname I've given my phone assistant. "Text Violet 'Colt, oh please go with us on this double date. Please use our shower, Colt. Please strip down naked just across the hall from Joss. Because she doesn't already have self-control problems when it comes to him. Let's torture her. You and your meddlesome husband are lucky I love you as much as I do!' Send text, Betty."

I hear the phone mumble a response back in my pocket, and I close the closet behind me, walking the towels back to the guest bath. And of course, I'm not paying attention, so I nearly collide with the sweaty six-foot-four quarterback who somehow still manages to smell amazing despite his state.

"Sorry. Wasn't watching. Here are some towels." I hold them out.

"Thanks." He gives me a small smile.

"Yep." I turn and make a beeline for my room because the last thing I need to do is spend any time alone with him. I hear him shut the door to the bathroom, and I feel some relief that there's at least that barrier between us again. I have no idea how the hell I was going to survive this trip if I was going to have to see this man around every corner in addition to photographing him naked. Assuming I could convince him to do that. First, I have to find the courage to pose naked under this kind of pressure.

When I get back into the bedroom to change into something to wear out tonight, I pull my phone out to see if my trai-torous friend has responded. When I see nothing, I click my tongue. Thinks she can just ignore me. I see how it is. I pull up the window to text her again and my heart sinks. Because the last text sent is to Colt.

I feel sick. I flip it open praying that I did not do what I think I did.

But it's there, carved in virtual stone in the text message I sent, because I stupidly never deleted his number. I try to recall it, but I've waited too damn long to realize my idiocy. Betty must have missed the part where I said "Violet" And thought I said, "Text Colt."

The panic starts to set in then, the anxiety ricocheting around in my chest until it feels like it might make my heart burst through my ribs. *Shit. Fuck. Damn.*

He couldn't have seen it yet. Not when I handed him the towels. He would have said something. Been weird. Made a face. There would have been something to let me know he'd seen it.

I absolutely do not need Colt knowing all my inner angst about him. Every encounter since I got here with him has been one embarrassing moment after another, and I just need a break. One little break. Apparently, that's too much to ask.

He was in a hurry to get cleaned up. So maybe, just maybe, he still hasn't seen it yet. I'd bet money his phone's just sitting on the counter while he takes his shower. All I have to do is creep in and delete the message.

Unless he locks his phone. But he's from the Heartland, right? Some farm in the middle of a map dot. Where they leave their cars and their doors unlocked. Maybe that extends to phones. Maybe he's the last man on earth who doesn't lock it down hard so the woman he's out with doesn't find out about the other five on the roster. Especially since his roster seems to be pretty sparse if I'm to believe the rumors.

I could do this. I'd just slip in and out. Delete the text. He'd never see it, and I could stop having an anxiety attack.

I slip out my door, checking the hallway in each direction because while Violet would probably assist me in this endeavor, Ben would definitely stop me from busting into a bathroom while Colt's showering. My hand lands on the door handle. I say a quick prayer that thing is unlocked. Because again, he showers in a locker room most days a week. While the rest of us wouldn't leave it unlocked, he might... right? *Please.* Please say he would.

I press down on the handle and it moves, a second later the door creaks open half an inch, and I listen quietly. Making sure I can hear the water running. I pause again. Because he could just be letting the water warm up and the only thing worse than him seeing that text message is him seeing that text message *and* seeing me creep into a bathroom on him.

I take a breath, count to ten and then slide it open a little further, peeking around the edge to see if I can see him. But sure enough, the main part of the room is empty, the water is running, and the curtain's closed. I could get in and out.

I hurry through the door, pushing it most of the way shut so I'm not alerting Ben or Violet to what I'm doing. Then I look around frantically for his phone. I don't see it on the counter or anywhere easily visible. I look on a couple of shelves and then spot the bag on the floor in front of the shower.

That has to be where it is. So I sneak closer and crouch down, hurriedly patting the outside trying to figure out if there's a hard phone-shaped piece inside, and I finally feel one. I hear him move in the shower though. A small plastic clicking sound like he's pouring shampoo or body wash out of a bottle. And a second later when the room floods with the smell of my shampoo, I eye the closed curtain. That bastard. Stealing my shampoo. I'm guessing he didn't have any. But he could have asked first. So rude.

Fuck. *The phone.* I need to focus.

I pat around and unzip the pocket. Unfortunately, the sound of unzipping the bag sounds like it's being echoed through a fucking megaphone against the tiles in this room. I pause, again saying a little prayer to the gods that this man doesn't hear it. Maybe his head's under the water while he washes the shampoo out. Maybe fans chanting his name all the time have made him hard of hearing at a young age. Whatever it is, I'll take it.

I hear him clear his throat, the sound of another bottle being uncapped and then closed and set on a shelf follows it. I reach my hand into the open pocket, feeling around and finding socks, some energy packets, what I'm fairly certain is a condom —so maybe not a priest after all, my heart skips—and some kind of paper but still no phone. I reach the furthest part of the pocket and realize it must be in the inner pocket of the bag. I could honestly scream that this is so difficult. If he'd just left it out on the counter like a normal person, I'd have been in and out by now.

I go to unzip the inside zipper quietly, but it's the next sound that stops me dead in my tracks.

"Fuckkkk..." I hear him hiss, and I stop. Going stark-still and listening hard to see if I'm hearing what I think I'm hearing. Because Colt doesn't swear often. The rarity was always a reward for me to hear when we fucked.

The smell of my conditioner envelops me, and I hear another soft "fuck" come from behind the shower curtain, and I simultaneously want to die and melt into the floor. Because Colton St. George is very definitely jacking off using my conditioner about two feet away from me and has no idea I'm here listening. And it's the hottest thing that's happened to me in a long time. I can't decide if that's sad or serendipitous.

At least until I nearly fall and grab the cabinet to stop myself, making a loud noise that has him pulling back the curtain a second later. Where he has a full view of me, toppled over, hand in his bag, very clearly snooping and listening in on his little self-care session.

Kill. Me. Now.

I rarely blush. I'm not shy and there's very little at this point in my life that shocks me. But the look on his face right now? It's making my skin molten hot, and not in a good way.

TEN

Colt

"JOSS?" I'd been imagining her just now to be fair—but naked, wet, and willing with me in this shower, not on the floor rifling through my bag while she stares at me with her mouth agape. "What are you doing?"

Instead of answering, her face contorts, and her brow furrows and she starts rifling through the bag some more pulling out my phone a second later.

"Joss! What the fuck are you doing?" I repeat because I can't imagine she's in the bathroom stealing my phone for a good reason. I can't even begin to fathom why she's doing it though.

"Nothing. I'm doing nothing!"

She starts to stand, and I realize she's about to make a break for it, so I jump out of the shower, grabbing a towel in the process because I don't need her to see the state the imaginary version of her has put me in, and bolt after her. She stumbles over the rug as she makes for the door, and it gives me just enough time to stop her in her tracks. I reach over her, slamming my hand against the upper part of the door, shutting it, and holding it tight while she struggles underneath me to try to open it back up again. I can't exactly wrap the towel around me while I hold the door, so I'm stuck just holding the towel to shield the most crucial parts of my anatomy from her.

"Give me the phone back, Joss."

"No!"

"Why the hell are you stealing my phone?"

"I just need to do a thing and then I'll give it back to you. Just let me go and I'll give it back by the time you're out of the shower," she says it like it's a normal reasonable request all the while still fighting me and trying to open the door. The worst part is all her struggling in this close of proximity is making her body graze against mine over and over again and considering where I'd been mentally and physically when I was interrupted by her, this is *not* helping.

"What the fuck are you doing sneaking in here while I shower, going through my shit?"

She whips around then, an accusation on her face.

"What the fuck are you doing stealing my conditioner and using it to jack off? That stuff is expensive you know. I got it in Switzerland. It wasn't cheap!"

What I was doing was trying to take the edge off because she drives me insane, and if I have to spend the whole night around her, I needed whatever sanity I could buy. The conditioner was just conveniently located. Not that I'm about to tell her that.

"No. I don't think so. Give me the phone, Joss."

"I told you. I have one thing I need to do and then you can have it back."

"What do you need to do?"

"Delete a text message."

I'm surprised when she's so forthcoming but also confused.

"What?"

"I accidentally sent a text meant for Violet to you, and I need to delete it. It's embarrassing."

"Embarrassing?"

"Yes. So will you please just let me delete it?" She's messing with the lock screen on the phone now, and again, I can't stop her because I've got one hand on the door and the other on a towel covering my raging hard-on.

"How the hell is it more embarrassing than this?" I ask, so annoyed I could yell.

She looks up and glares at me.

"Well if you'd just stayed in the shower and finished yourself off instead of having to investigate noises, this wouldn't be happening. You can go back in there and do that right after you give me your password."

"I'm not giving you my password."

"Fine. You can stand there all dripping wet on Violet's floor while I figure it out myself. We'll be late to her event, but I'll just explain that you were having a marathon self-care session. I'm sure they'll understand."

"Jesus Christ, Joss. Put the fucking phone down and get out!"

She makes a gasping noise and stands up straighter. "Don't you swear at me! I'm the one mad at you right now!"

"You're mad at me?" I ask incredulously.

"Yes! Give me the stupid password. Let me delete the text, and I'll leave you alone."

"No." I can't give her the password. Because if I do, she'll figure out the meaning and then she'll have even more ammunition. Not to mention there are other things she could find on my phone—I don't need her seeing any of it.

Her eyes go dark then, and she whips around grabbing onto the door handle and pulling hard, shoving back with her ass as she does it. It knocks me off-kilter and she nearly gets the door open. Except I'm bigger and faster than her. I grab her and turn her around, pressing her up against the door until she's pinned. I lose the towel in the process, and it drops in between us, catching where our bodies are too close to let it fall to the floor, and she lets out a little gasp.

She looks up at the ceiling and then her eyes close, and she bites her lower lip like I've somehow scandalized her.

"Put the phone on the counter."

She complies finally but refuses to open her eyes. I grab the ends of the towel, still using my knee and body weight to pin her and wrap it around my waist before I lose it entirely.

"I'll delete the text—myself—without looking at it if you tell me what it was about." I offer a white flag, hoping she'll concede and we can break this stalemate. Because fighting with her like this is only going to lead to the same place fighting in the shed did.

"Sure, right after you tell me what thoughts you were jacking off over."

"Joss," I warn, although I suppose that's technically also the answer to her question.

"Fine! You, obviously. The text was about you. And instead of sending it to Violet, it sent it to you." She sighs.

"And it's more embarrassing than all of this?"

"At least this is mutually embarrassing."

"How do you figure?"

"You're dripping wet all over me, nearly lost your towel, and I reiterate, very clearly using my expensive conditioner for unintended purposes. I doubt you're going to tell them about the text messages now because then we'd have to tell this whole story and it doesn't look much better for you."

"I didn't sneak into a bathroom while someone was showering."

"I didn't leave the door unlocked."

"Holy fuck." I pinch the bridge of my nose. "You're infuriating, do you know that?"

"I assumed from the way you keep swearing at me."

My brow furrows as I stare and then I pull away from her, grabbing the phone and unlocking it to pull up the text. I can see part of the message in the preview as I go to delete it.

JOSS:

Please go with us on this double date...

"Do you not want me to go tonight?"

"You said you weren't going to read it!"

"I'm not but some of it's visible when I open the app."

"Give it to me." She goes to snatch the phone out of my hands.

"Joss!" I pull it back.

"Fine. It was sarcastic about you coming tonight and her offering to have you shower here and how I don't need to be thinking about you naked. And this right here, is exactly why. Now you've gotten me all wet and been pressed up against me. I heard you jacking off and I don't need all of this! I'm in a weak fucking state, and I don't need you being all James Dean with abs around me. Okay? So no. I didn't want you to go tonight. Or be showering here. Or be here at all frankly!"

I have so many things I want to say, but I need to be more careful with her than I have in the past. Because getting wrapped up in the hurricane that is Jocelyn Marks is the last thing I need right now in my life.

"Then why didn't you just say that when they invited me?"

"Because they love you. You're the good one. Their golden boy. The one who's always there for them and goes on runs and hangs out at their house on the weekend. I can't tell them they can't invite you out with us. Then they'll just think I'm a bitch and tell me I need to behave."

"Well, you do need to learn how to behave."

She rolls her eyes. "You wish."

Those words must make me lose my mind because the next second I'm hauling her up into my arms and dragging her into the still-running shower.

ELEVEN

Joss

"OH MY GOD!" I start to scream the words, but they come out muted when I remember I don't want Ben or Violet to come running. He puts me down directly under the spray of the shower head, and I could kill him. Right here in cold blood. Because now my clothes are soaking wet, more so than they already were and my hair is dripping. I swipe at my eyes because the mascara I put on this morning is definitely not waterproof, and I'm sure I look like a feral raccoon now. Just fucking great.

"Are you insane?" I yell as I try to open my eyes but fail when I feel the sting from the combination of water and mascara. I step out of the stream of water and gasp for air.

"No, but you are. Breaking into the bathroom. Rifling through my shit. Trying to steal my phone. Not giving it back when you're caught. Flipping out because we're going to an aquarium with our friends. It's an *aquarium*, Joss. There are a million other things to look at and do while you're there. You wouldn't even have to interact with me. And if you hadn't snuck into the bathroom, you wouldn't be seeing me naked either. So get a grip."

I manage to blink enough to see again, and he's standing just outside the stream of water on the other side of the shower glowering at me. His towel is hanging on by a thread and the deep vees of his hips and the light blond trail of hair over his abdomen are distracting the fuck out of me—leading my eyes down to where he's still obviously hard. I raise a brow at him because if this is turning him on, he really has changed.

"Oh, I'll get a grip." I push off the wall of the shower and slide my hand down the front of his towel. "Is this where you need me to get a grip?"

His blue eyes light with a warning look, and he pushes me back up against the tiles again, one hand on my hip and his other hand wrapping around a fistful of my hair as his eyes search my face.

"I don't know. Is this where you need mine?"

"Maybe." We stare at each other for a minute and then I finally break. "I hate that they like you so much. I never get to see them and when I finally do suddenly you have to be everywhere. At Ben's party. At the aquarium. At his games."

"At *his* games..." He lets out a derisive laugh. "I'm the fucking quarterback."

"It's annoying!"

"I'll be sure to tell them you think so."

"Don't you dare."

"You were going to tell Violet anyway when you texted her, right? So what's the problem?"

"Ben. He wants me to get along with you."

"So why can't we just get along? I've been playing nice."

"You're not playing nice. You're pretending to be nice

when it's convenient. The rest of the time you're glowering, slamming me against shower walls, and asking for nudes."

"Tasteful nudes." His eyes drift down over my body. "I just think if you're going to make me do it, you should know what it feels like first."

"Right. I'm sure. Is that your plan here with me being in the shower?"

"There was no plan here. You just drive me fucking insane."

"Trust me. I've learned my lesson. I won't accidentally text you again."

"You're being ridiculous. We're grown-ups, Joss. We had a thing once a million years ago. We can be normal and share time with our best friends."

"I'm being ridiculous?" I scoff. "You're the one running around half-naked chasing me."

"Because you're stealing things."

"I didn't steal, I just borrowed." I flash an innocent look in his direction.

"Borrowed..." A smug smile forms on his lips. "Don't borrow things from me, and we'll be fine."

"I'll take it into consideration. So what were you thinking about in the shower?" I smirk.

He grins at the space on the floor between us and then his eyes lift slowly to meet mine, with that half-lidded gorgeous deep blue stare that only he has. His hand tightens around the fistful of hair, and he pulls it back as he stands taller, narrowing the gap between us as he brings his lips to my ear.

"How much I'd like to see you on your knees. If we didn't have somewhere to be, I'd put you there now."

I feel my stomach flip and the flicker of want blooms in its place. This new Colt is dangerous. To my sanity and any hope I have of reformation. Because I just want to fall back into every single bad habit with him.

He smiles as he studies my face. "I thought you'd like that."

"There are other things I'd like."

"Like not getting caught by Ben or Violet?"

Shit.

He had a point. This is exactly why he is such a problem for me. He scrambles my better sense. Obviously, or I wouldn't be in this situation.

"Go get changed and fixed up. I need to finish my shower so we don't make them late. We can finish this later."

I search his face for a minute and then smile, a stupid giddy one because Colton St. George makes me feel like a girl with a crush rather than a grown woman who should know better.

"Okay." I push off the tile wall and move around him, glancing at myself in the mirror. I look a little drowned but a quick change of clothes, makeup wipes, and a round with the blow dryer should fix most of it. As I reach for the door handle, he clears his throat.

"And Joss?" he calls after me.

"Yeah?" I answer without looking back because if I do there's a good chance I'll go running back to him.

"Wear a skirt."

I grin to myself but walk out the door without saying anything.

TWELVE

Colt

I DON'T KNOW what magic she has, but she manages to look gorgeous by the time we're leaving for the aquarium a bit later. I smile when I see the skirt she has on, and she gives me a sly grin behind their backs.

When we're in the car she keeps a chaste distance, and we get sucked into several conversations about the team, Violet's work, and the plans the girls have for the nonprofit Joss and Harper are launching.

"You're going to have to get your board members lined up pretty quickly, so you can adopt your bylaws and get everything in order to start taking donations. The sooner the better." Violet turns to look at Joss in the back seat.

"I know, but I don't want to pick just anyone. The board's going to have to be good. Have a lot of reach in the community and enough standing that they can hit the ground running building partnerships. Ideally, someone who already knows some of the museum and arts organization directors because we need their buy-in quickly for this to have staying power."

"What about someone who knows a bunch of directors, the mayor, and just won the city keeper award for their involvement with the local nonprofits? Allegedly the last fundraiser they had raised over ten million dollars for the charity in one night," Ben adds from the front seat.

"Sounds like a magical unicorn who wouldn't want to work with a startup nonprofit. You've got a special in with them, Benny? Cause I'll buy you all the appetizers you want if you can get them interested." Joss grins at him through the rearview mirror.

"I think I could convince him. He'd probably want a prominent position though, where he had some real sway in the organization."

"I mean with those credentials I'd make him president. Well, they'd have to vote—the board. But if he is what you say, no way a sensible board would want anyone else in that seat."

"I think he'd probably agree to that."

"Don't get my hopes up, Benjamin." Joss gives him a look like she doesn't quite believe it.

"If we're talking president and it means I get to boss the co-directors around on occasion, I'd do it." I turn to Joss, raising my eyebrow and giving her a smug grin as she lets out a tiny, shocked sound.

"No." Joss looks to me with accusation but a hint of curiosity in her eyes.

"Yep." Ben looks incredibly pleased that he managed to walk her straight into that trap.

"Vi, I thought we were friends. You're just going to let your husband bamboozle me like that?"

"It was for your own good."

Joss folds her arms over her chest and gives me a sidelong

glance. She pretends to look irritated, but I honestly think she's a little proud. Like she's assessing me differently with the new information. I give her half a smirk, and I get a huff and a small smile in return.

WHEN WE GET to the aquarium the place is nearly empty, and Ben looks to Violet quizzically as he pulls the door open for her.

"So when I said it was an after-hours event, I actually meant we have the place to ourselves." Violet grins at him.

"What? The whole place?"

"Yeah. You've been saying you wanted to go, so I asked if it was possible to rent the place out, and they said yes. I might have namedropped you a bit."

"Violet..."

"I know. I use my powers wisely though. And you guys are under so much pressure this season. I thought it would be a good escape for a couple of hours. Calm your stress levels a bit. And we're getting a private tour behind the scenes." Violet turns to us. "I only asked about Ben and me, but I could ask for you all too. You're definitely welcome to tour the public areas though. I already asked about that."

"No. You should go on your private tour together, the two of you. I can wander around. Having the whole place to myself sounds amazing."

"Well, as long as you two can play nice." Violet looks between us.

"We can play nice. Right, Joss?" I grin at her.

"Of course." She grins back, a glint in her eye.

. . .

AFTER A QUICK INTRODUCTION and signing some autographs for family members of the employees, Joss and I are let loose in the aquarium while Ben and Violet take their private tour. We make our way through the exhibits for a few moments in silence, finding ourselves in an underwater dome when she finally speaks.

"Did you delete the text?"

"Yes."

"Without looking at it?"

"Yes. I told you I would."

"Thank you."

"Not gonna tell me what the rest of it said?"

"I told you enough. I'm sorry for breaking into the bathroom while you were showering. I just... can we be honest for a moment?" She stops and looks at me for permission to continue.

"Yeah..." I agree, wondering where this is headed.

"This is getting messy fast right?" She frowns.

"Complicated maybe. I don't know that I'd say messy."

"Yet."

I tilt my head because it's a fair possibility it will get messy.

"Nude photos, the idea of you on the board, whatever just happened in that bathroom... or the first night I was here. This is bad. We're older, more mature now. We can do better than the last time."

"Agreed that we can do better. Is it necessarily bad though?"

She eyes me skeptically. "That there's still a weird spark here? Yeah, I think that's bad given the way it blew up the last time."

I shrug, trying to make it look casual even though I feel the apprehension starting to creep in. "I think a lot has changed since then. And you're only in town for a few weeks. Seeing

Ben and Violet, getting Harper and the nonprofit set up, and then you're back on the road?"

"Right."

"So you won't be here to deal with me on the board. You photograph people all the time, so it'll be professional. And a few weeks of flirting never killed anyone."

"Nearly killed us both the last time."

"Yeah well, we were fucking. Not flirting. But I was a kid who'd just had his heart ripped out of his chest by the only girl he'd ever thought he'd be with. With the rival quarterback. I was in a pretty ugly place at the time that had nothing to do with you."

"And now, what are you? The guys call you a priest, but you certainly don't talk like it."

I'm not excited about getting into the weeds on this with her.

"They call me priest because I don't fuck around as much as they do."

"Why not?"

"What do you mean?"

"You're the quarterback. I don't know a ton about football, but I know it makes you the Queen Bee—"

"The Queen Bee..." I echo with a laugh.

"You know what I mean. You're incredibly attractive and you have that whole good-guy image. Plus, the money and the fame? You could have anyone you want. I'm sure actresses and models are lined up to put themselves in your way. Why not take advantage of it? I would if I were you."

"I love football. I love this team. And I want all these guys and this city to have the rings, the trophy. It's my main priority in life. I eat, drink, sleep, *live* the path to getting us there. Which doesn't leave time for a lot of other things. Most women don't want to come in second, understandably. And second place is all I have to offer."

She looks at me carefully, her eyes drifting over me and back to my face like she's considering that statement.

"Even still. I find it hard to believe at least a few wouldn't be willing to try."

I shrug again. "I've dated a few here and there. One I almost thought was going somewhere. But it is what it is. You're still single, so what's with the judgment?"

"I'm single because I don't have time for relationships either. I want to be on the road. Seeing new places and new people, whenever I can. I don't want to have to say no to new experiences because somebody sitting at home tells me I have to."

"I get it. Being on the road is where you're happy."

"Right," she agrees.

"So neither of us wants a relationship. So I don't think we're in danger." I give her a meaningful look.

"But we need to be careful around each other. So we don't make this messy on accident. You don't have time for it and neither do I. Ben and Violet definitely don't want to referee another round."

"Well, just keep your hands to yourself and stay out of the bathroom when I'm showering." I give her a playful smile.

"I can keep my hands to myself. You're the real problem." She shrugs.

"Me?" The laugh rumbles out of me before I can stop it. "Dollface, one of us definitely has impulse-control problems, but it's not me."

"How dare you!" She pretends to act pissed but cracks a smile a second later. "We'll see. I have more control than you think. I bet you crack first, *Priest*."

"I'm not cracking first."

"I guess we'll find out, won't we?"

"That a bet?" I ask, my eyes drifting over her.

"Maybe. Do you want it to be?"

"Maybe. Depends on the rules of the agreement. Like, do I get to torment and torture you to see if you'll break?"

"Sure. Do your worst."

I grin because I know so many of her favorite things. So many ways she likes to be touched and talked to. I'm fairly certain I could bring her down in one night.

"Keep grinning like that, Farm Boy. You forget, I taught you everything you know. Which means I know all your weaknesses."

I close the distance between us because I still remember everything she taught me. How much she liked finding those weaknesses.

"Like you didn't love every second of getting to teach a guy how to fuck exactly how you wanted."

"I never said it was a burden. I like a challenge." Her eyes glint with amusement as I take another step closer to her.

"So do I."

"I've noticed. This new version of you...the bossy-in-charge one. I think I might like it."

"You might need it."

Her eyes flick up to mine then, a sudden awareness in them and her hands go to my chest as she comes closer to me. Her lashes fluttering as her gaze lowers to my lips.

"Fairly certain touching violates the bet." I glance down at where she's touching me, her palms sliding over my chest.

"No touching rule then?" She pulls her hands back.

"Seems like that would be safer." I shrug, pretending to be nonchalant. Because if this woman touches me, I'm in danger. I have to build up endurance when it comes to her. Take her in slow doses. Because otherwise, I'm grabbing her and throwing her up against walls like some kind of depraved monster, desperate to fuck her into oblivion and show her how much she misses me.

"Seems like you're worried about your chances. Worried you might need me again. But I'll allow it."

"If either of us should be worried, it's you." I grin at her and her eyes flash to mine, fluttering a little before she turns away to look at the expanse of blue water and sea life beyond the glass.

"We'll see, Farm Boy."

THIRTEEN

Joss

I'M DEFINITELY WORRIED. He's all I can think about lately, and my mind is whirring with all the possibilities of what having the grown-up version of him could be like. Having him grab my hair and put me on my knees like he threatened earlier. Having him take me any and every single way he wants me. I would let Colt have almost anything.

I just can't have this turning into a mess again. Another situation where we can't stand to see each other, and Ben and Violet are trying to run damage control between the two of us. Where I spend years away from him because I can't handle seeing his face again.

His eyes search mine like he knows I'm doing the math.

"So we're getting along and learning to be friends again?" I ask, studying his deep blue gaze in return.

"I mean, I'll also kind of be your boss if I'm on the board."

"You're getting ahead of yourself."

"You said yourself, getting someone like me on the board would be like landing a unicorn."

"Is this your way of getting out of the photos? Because we still need them for the book."

"I told you. You do the photos. I'll do the photos. You can come to my house after the game this weekend and we can get them done."

"Why are you being agreeable all of the sudden?" I raise a brow at him.

"Because I remember how much I like hearing you whimper my name and the sooner I get you to cave, the better." A wry smile crosses his lips, and I want to kiss it off of him so badly.

"Who are you, and where's the sweet farm boy?"

"You only get him if you're really good."

"You're already fighting dirty." I glare at him.

"Good. Now turn around and look at the water again."

I raise an eyebrow.

"Turn around," he repeats.

I do as he asks, and he leans over me, placing a hand on the wall over my shoulder as he leans in closer to whisper in my ear.

"I'm glad you wore that skirt for me. Makes me so fucking hard knowing you listen and do the things I ask for. The more you do that while we play this game, the more I'll do for you. Sound fair?"

"Fair enough." I hope I'm maintaining a placid look on my face because inside I'm already falling apart for him.

"There are definitely cameras in here so we're going to have to be careful. I'm gonna pretend like we're just talking and watching the sharks swim by. But I need you to do me a favor."

"A favor?"

"Yes. The way you came apart for me in the shed the other

day. I want to hear it again. But if I can't touch you, you'll have to do it for me."

"Why would I do that?"

"Because I'm going to talk you through it, and that's going to torture me as much as it does you."

"Okay," I whisper.

"Slide your hand down your skirt for me. Did you wear another color I like underneath?"

"No. I didn't wear anything... for you."

"Fuck me. Malicious compliance. Missed that about you too." I smirk at the growly way he says it. "Touch yourself for me."

I'm staring into the deep blue of the water as his warm breath coasts over my neck, his lips hovering just above without making contact. My fingers slide under the waistband of my skirt and skim over my clit. The second I make contact I know it's not going to take me long to come because Colt is my secret weakness.

He's the one I see whenever I close my eyes, whether I'm by myself or with someone else. It's always him. I have no idea why he has such a hold over my imagination. He's gorgeous, exceptionally so, and how he's tall and talented with a voice that's sexy as hell is a lethal combination even if I don't care about football. But it's more than that—something harder to explain. His energy, the way he talks to me, the way he has this quiet stoic silence and only speaks when it's something worth hearing.

"You wet for me, Dollface?"

Speaking of. Hearing him call me by the nickname he gave me sends a whisper of want down my spine. To hear him say it now, makes me weak all over again like it used to. I nod in response to his question because if I open my mouth, I'm going to say so many things I shouldn't right now. Especially this early on in the game. I'll ruin it before we even really get started.

"I knew you would be after the way you looked at me in the shower. Those gorgeous green eyes so bright. Reminds me of the first time you let me taste you. You remember that?"

I nod as I brush the pads of my fingers lightly over my clit, just the slightest touch because any real contact is going to send me over the edge far too quickly. I want to listen to him right now. His voice is so deep when he talks to me, so thick with lust that I want to hear it every single night.

"I wasn't sure you were ever going to let me. The way you made me beg for it."

I'd never been a fan of receiving, until him. He didn't exactly know what he was doing at the time, but he was so very willing to learn and very good at listening to directions. By the time we were done, I almost hated myself for creating such a perfect monster I couldn't keep.

"I remember," I whisper.

"That was my favorite lesson you ever gave me. That first time I got to drag my tongue over you and hear you come—the way you tasted—I couldn't get enough. That still replays in my head. When you cave, you going to let me try again?"

"When *you* cave... yes." The last word comes out on a gasp because I'm starting to circle my clit in rougher strokes. Listening to him say these kinds of things to me is like being edged, and I need relief. I had no idea Colt was capable of this. We'd never done anything like this in public and while he would occasionally talk about something he wanted; it was never like this.

"You can definitely try to get me to cave. If it means more of you wearing all the things I love for me, I'll happily submit to torture. And I know you love torturing me."

"You make it fun."

"You having fun torturing me right now? Touching yourself and letting me hear you breathe like this?"

"Yes."

"*If* I caved, the first thing I'd do is pull this skirt up and fuck you up against the glass. Listen to you whimper about how good I feel. Take you up to the edge again and again like you used to like it until you begged. Feel your whole body quiver while you come hard on my cock. I know you must have missed that."

This man has way too many unfair advantages, and I'm a moron for volunteering this game. One that right now, I just want to lose. But I soldier on, pretending like I'm not as affected as I am. Staring out into the water as it fades into a blue abyss, while I start to fade into the edge of my orgasm.

He leans in again, his whole body millimeters away from mine. So close he's almost touching me and still so far away.

"Fuck..." he breathes out and it slides over my skin. "You're beautiful like this. Come for me, Dollface. Let me hear you, so I know what I'm missing."

I come apart a second later, pressing my hand to the glass as I try to keep my balance through the wave of white lightning that speeds through my nerve endings. He wraps an arm around my waist, pulling me back up against his body, whispering in my ear about how good and perfect I am over and over. Breaking the rules we just set. But I don't care.

"I love the way you sound when you come. It's one of my favorite things in the world." He turns me around as he says the words, studying me. He takes my hand a second later, kissing my wrist and then opening my palm up and kissing it too before he trails his tongue over my fingers.

"Right up there with how you taste."

My lashes flutter as I bring my eyes up to his, trying to catch my breath and my sanity again. I feel sated and devoid of it all at the same time because I want this man to wreck me. Take me and have his way with me any way he wants, however and whenever that is. And right now, I desperately want to make him come the same way I just did. But then I remember I can't touch him, and he shouldn't be touching me right now either.

"Cheating," I whisper.

"Well, if I'm already in trouble for it then I might as well use that to my advantage." He smiles at me and threads his fingers with mine. "Come on. We better explore some or Ben and Violet are going to be suspicious."

I tighten my fingers around his and smile. The way he can talk to me like that one second and then hold my hand like we're at the fairgrounds the next makes my heart do something that feels suspiciously like palpitations.

FOURTEEN

Joss

AFTER THE AQUARIUM INCIDENT, I decide the sooner I get these photos out of the way the better. It'd be a quick in-and-out affair. He offered to do it after this week's game, so I took it.

I watch Harper and Alex walk off together after the game as I make my way toward Colt, and I feel that little flicker of jealousy that I sometimes do when I watch Ben and Violet. Seeing them all together, so freaking happy and sweet and in love. It makes me wish I was capable of it. That I could fall for someone hard and feel all the butterflies and heart palpitations it must cause. Think about futures and houses and wedding dresses. But it just isn't for me.

What is for me, however, is the way looking at Colton St. George makes me desperate to be thrown up against a wall and fucked hard. He could do it too—with that height and those arms. Standing there after a game he won, watching me as I cross the lot to his side. I hear fans calling for him behind me and when I get closer, I raise an eyebrow.

"Not going to go sign some things?" I ask.

"I didn't think you'd want to wait, and I assumed your tolerance for all things football is probably dangerously close to having expired for the day."

"It expired the moment I walked into the stadium but was slightly renewed by watching you play. Harper's right about that much. Your asses do look good in those tight little pants you wear."

He laughs and shakes his head. "You willing to wait a few minutes?"

"Yeah, go ahead. I'll stay back here though. Don't want them getting ideas about us standing together."

"Can't have that."

I watch for a few minutes while Colt greets his fans and signs jerseys, posing for photos and generally keeping everyone happy and entertained as I hear laughter float across the parking lot. When he returns there's almost a skip in his step, and I can't help the smile that comes to my face when I see his boyish grin.

"Loving the fame then?" I ask, leaning up against the column of the parking garage.

"Less the fame, and more that people are excited about the team and how things are going. The whole city comes alive when we're doing well. It's a nice feeling."

"I bet." I look him over.

"You ready to strip for me then?"

"Depends. You ready to strip for me?" I raise an eyebrow in return.

"You first."

WHEN WE GET to his house, I'm a gaping mess as we walk in the door because it's massive. I expected some sort of penthouse suite or a fancy condo. I wasn't expecting this sprawling mansion for a single guy. But then this is Colt we're talking about, and he's probably planning ahead for his future like a responsible adult. And if he's the monk everyone keeps making him out to be, it makes sense he doesn't have a bachelor pad in the middle of the city.

Still though, it's a lot to take in and reminds me of the massive gulf between us. The aging apartment Violet and I lived in at his age compared to this place reminds me of how different our lives have gone.

"This is insane. Do you just get lost in here sometimes? Take a wrong turn and forget how to get back to your kitchen."

"No, I'm pretty used to it by now."

"But when you first moved in, it was a maze, wasn't it? You got lost in your own house."

"Not lost. Just turned around when they were still finishing it and all the walls weren't up. Once."

"Uh-huh. House so big you got lost in it." I smirk at him, as I hitch my camera bag higher on my shoulder.

"Do you want to put that in my room?"

"Is that where we're shooting?"

"I think so. We can take a tour and see what you prefer but the master is probably the best. Especially for the photos I want."

"Oh yeah?" I ask, suddenly curious about what kind of photos he thinks I'm willing to do for him.

"They'll be tasteful. You'll just need the room."

"Uh-huh."

"Listen, I'm going after you so you know anything I ask for will be couched in the idea that you could ask for the same or worse."

"I'm only asking for tasteful shots that could go in a coffee table book. All the most important parts of you will be covered. So keep that in mind with what you're dreaming up there, Farm Boy."

"Will it be topless though?"

"Mine or yours?"

"Yours. Obviously, mine will be." He gives me half an eye roll.

"I guess it could be. Depends on what you're planning to do with it."

"Put it up on the bedroom wall." He throws his bag down and turns on the light when we reach his massive bedroom. "Right over there." He points to a massive blank spot between two windows.

"Oh yeah? Life-size?" I laugh at the idea of being naked up on this man's bedroom wall.

"Hadn't thought about what size yet exactly. I wasn't sure if it would be one photo, or maybe a series that we could put up four or five of them in a row there." His tone is deadpan and after I sit down my camera bag, I look at him quizzically.

"You're serious."

"Yeah." His brow furrows.

"Colt you can't put naked photos of me up on your bedroom wall."

"Why not? No one but me will see them."

"Yeah, you and whatever women you bring back here. And God forbid your future wife sees them."

"Women don't come back here." He's terse when he answers.

"Oh god. Please don't tell me you're one of those guys who only fucks women in hotels. I mean... it's kind of hot. The high thread counts and the room service. The big bathtubs are a plus too, but it's so heartless. You're treating her like she's not good enough to see your house or something. I taught you better than that."

He's frowning hard until the last thing I say and then he looks up with a grin on his face. "You taught me a lot of things. Some I remember better than others, especially when we practiced them. So maybe we'll try here once and a hotel another time. Then maybe I'll learn."

Just like he wants I'm immediately imagining those playing out, and I glare at him.

"That is just poor sportsmanship. I expect better from you than that Mr. Quarterback of the Year."

He grins for a moment but then his frown returns. "How do you know that?"

"The QB of the year thing? I do spend a lot of time in airports. Which have lots of newsstands. With magazines that have your face plastered on them. Plus your besties are my besties if you remember right."

"Oh yeah?" A smug grin tugs at his lips that I know about his press.

"Yeah. A guy at the airport didn't believe me when I said I knew you. Not that I can blame him, we don't exactly look like friends."

"Or fuck buddies." He grins wider and it makes me realize he's gotten us way off track.

"So no women in your room? Or no women at all?"

"At all. Not lately." The terseness is back, and he leaves the room. I follow him as he makes a fast clip back toward the kitchen.

"Oh I thought you just meant no relationships. I see why they call you Priest now."

"Yes. You going to taunt me now too?" He turns away from me, looking in the fridge rather than at me.

"No. If I did, I'd be a hypocrite," I say, leaning on the marbled counter.

He glances up. "How so?"

"No men at all lately." I shrug.

His brow shoots up. "You expect me to believe that you don't have a roster right now?"

"I mean, I have a roster, but it's badly out of date and most of it is really just a phone sex roster."

"A phone sex roster?"

"Yes. I'm insanely busy. On the road a lot. Sometimes phone sex is all there is."

"Why do you need a roster for that? Wouldn't one guy be sufficient?"

"I mean, he might be busy. Or not into whatever I'm in the mood for that night. Or maybe his dirty talk isn't on point. You know?" I shrug. "You don't have a phone sex roster? Or just a roster a mile long, period? In case you decide to break your streak?"

"The fame means it's hard to trust most of the women I meet. Imagine what a phone sex recording of the highest-paid QB in the league would go for on the tabloid market."

"I don't think they care about how much you're paid. I think they'd pay extra for how sexy your voice is."

"You think my voice is sexy?" He looks at me like it's a strange thing to say, but his lip quivers with a smile.

"Uh yeah... You'd definitely be at the top of my phone sex roster if you were an option."

"But I'm not an option?"

I look down at the counter, pondering that. "I don't know. Would it violate our rules, or is that technically a loophole?"

"Technically a loophole, I think. We wouldn't be touching or having actual sex, so..."

"So maybe an option."

"Maybe?"

"We'll see how you do with these photos. Speaking of, do you want to get started?"

"Sure, but I need some dinner. I can order something and have it delivered?"

"That sounds good. I didn't eat much at the stadium."

He hands me some menus, and we pour over them for a few minutes until we decide on sandwiches and fruit. He puts in the order while I finish getting the camera equipment ready. I strip down to my panties in the process and put on a robe I brought with me, because the sooner we get this over and the more professional I act about it—the less likely this is to turn into a deep pit of temptation. As much as I want to use this opportunity to tease him and try to get him to break, I know if he doesn't, I definitely will. Because he's relentless and I'm not about to lose this game we're playing.

FIFTEEN

Colt

WHEN I WALK BACK into the bedroom after ordering the food, she's kneeling on the bed adjusting the cameras and lighting with her phone. She's distracted by taking a few test photos, so I get to lean against the door frame taking her in.

She's in a light pink robe, and apparently naked underneath already given how much I can see of her thighs and the way her nipple piercings press against the satin. I'm dying to see her without it, sprawled out on my bed. I wish it was with her underneath me but having pictures of her in that state that I can revisit whenever I want is the next best thing. Even if it is a form of torture.

"All right Farm Boy. You still haven't told me what you want with these pictures. I assume you want me on the bed, or you wouldn't have chosen a bedroom, but we can move things around if you like." Her eyes drift to me as she sets her phone down.

"The bed is good unless you think somewhere else is better. I want you laying down, naked, with..." I pause to bend over and pull a ball out of my bag, tossing it to her. She catches it and raises an eyebrow. "That covering the 'most important bits' as you put it."

She looks down at the ball and back at me, a small smirk forming on her lips. "You're so predictable. You gonna want me in your jersey next?"

"No. Just these. Although there is something else I want to add."

"What's that?"

"You'll see. Can you take photos like that, or do you need to show me how to do it?" I nod to her position on the bed.

"I can do it. I'll set a timer once I've framed the shot and it'll take a series of photos. I can move my phone out of shot then. Worse comes to worst, I can edit it out too."

"All right." I nod, watching her as her eyes flicker to me and then back to her camera. If I didn't know her better, I'd say she was nervous. Because there's definitely palpable tension building in the room. The air is heavy, thick with electricity like just before a storm.

It's not anything new really, for me to see her naked—and she's not exactly shy. She has a gorgeous body, and she knows it. But I still see her fingers hesitate when she sets the ball aside and goes to untie the robe.

"If you don't want to do this, we don't have to," I say suddenly, and she pauses, the robe falling partially open as she looks up at me.

"We do though. Because I need the photos of you. I promised Harper I'd get you in the book come hell or high water, so I have to pay my dues." She smiles at me.

"You don't have to do this. I'll do them," I say, feeling guilty that I've pushed her to do something she doesn't want to. That she feels obligated to do. I'd meant this to be fun, like part of the game we've been playing.

"I know you would." Her eyes soften as she looks at me. "But at least let me pretend like you wouldn't?"

I raise an eyebrow at her, and she just gives me a little grin. I frown in response though because it makes me nervous.

"I just don't want you to be uncomfortable Joss."

"I'm not uncomfortable. I just... even I have a flicker of nerves about stripping down for America's Most Eligible Bachelor, so I can take half-naked photos on his bed while he watches. I think most women would."

"Most women aren't you, Joss. No other woman has even come close. Why do you think I want you on my wall?"

"You're good at that, Farm Boy." Her eyes flash to mine, and she grins again. Like that bit of confidence boost is what she needed, and she pushes the robe off her shoulders, letting it pool around her knees on the bed.

Meanwhile, every drop of blood I have is pooling south with it because the glimpses I got of her in the dress and dripping wet in the shower were not nearly enough to prepare me. Somehow this woman looks better than every memory and fantasy I've had of her over the years. The soft swell of her stomach, the curve of her hips, the way her tattoos compliment her pale skin, and then my favorite part of her body—they're full and perfect, teardrop shaped with pale pink pierced nipples. I'm already remembering what it felt like to run my tongue over the metal as I watch them bead up from the cool air in the room.

"You want the panties off or on?"

"On," I answer immediately. I thought originally I'd want her stripped bare but I can't handle it. If she slips them off, I'm going to be on my knees in front of her begging for anything she'll give me.

"Okay." She smirks, like she knows what I'm thinking. "So you just want me laying back with this between my thighs? Kind of still make it look like it's covering things?"

She lays down on the bed, shifting around to get comfortable and her breasts sway with the motion. She moves the football into place and then looks over to me for a response.

"Yes," my voice comes out raspier than it should, and there's an answering smirk on her lips. She's loving that she has me rattled.

She fixes her hair and makes amusing faces at the camera as she tries to situate herself in frame.

"Come here and check the monitor image on my phone and see if you like it." She nods to her phone next to her on the bed, and I do as she asks, grabbing the phone to look at the image.

Fuck me. She's honestly better than any fantasy I've ever had like this, and it's not lost on me how lucky I am that she's willing to do this for me. There's just one missing element I want. One thing Ben got from Violet that I never got from her. A thing she'd never really give me because she doesn't love me the way Violet loves him, but she might be willing to play the part for this photo session. I try to compose myself, act more nonchalant than I'm feeling about all of this. Because she's got a sixth sense for weakness, and all it would take is a few of the right words for me to be begging her to break the agreement we made.

"One more thing." I reach into my pocket and pull out the Sharpie I'd been using to sign jerseys earlier.

She raises a brow in question but doesn't move. I uncap it and sit down next to her on the bed, moving to hover over her hip and looking up at her in question. Her brow furrows but she nods for me to go ahead.

I press the tip of the black marker to her skin, just above the lace band and to the inside of her hipbone, pressing the palm of my left hand to her abdomen. Goosebumps break out across her flesh, and I pretend not to notice because this is probably cheating on the agreement. Touching her far too dangerously close to how I want to touch her. Tempting myself to slide my palm lower. But I drag my attention back to the task at hand, signing her hip with a flourish until it reads "Colton St. George."

There's a little click of her tongue as she looks up at me. She's smiling but her eyes are still heavy with lust, and I want this woman so badly I'd give up almost anything to have her right now. Except I don't want her to see me as a boy anymore. I need her to see me as something more—an equal. It'd be the only chance we'd have. So I keep my mouth shut and smirk instead.

"I'm surprised you didn't want that across my tits."

"One, they're too fucking gorgeous for any sort of graffiti, and two, if it was real, I'd want this where any guy who gets this far has to see it and know you've had better."

"If it was real?" She raises an eyebrow.

"I've always been jealous of Ben. That his girl did that for him."

"And I'm *your* girl?"

"In some parallel universe, definitely."

SIXTEEN

Joss

I'M NOT BUILT to withstand Colton St. George. The fuckboys, musicians, artists, any athlete that isn't him—they don't even register. But this man somehow knows exactly what to say and how to look at me to casually reach inside my chest and wrap every vulnerable part of me up in lightness. He breathes life back into parts of my heart I'd forgotten exist. It's almost enough to break me.

Instead, I just whisper, "Ah, okay."

"Kind of looks like it belongs there, really..." He admires his work with the tilt of his head.

It does belong there, probably in permanent ink like he's hinting at because whether he knows it or not he owns parts of me no one else will ever get. Vulnerabilities and stolen moments in our past that I haven't been able to imagine having with anyone else. Which feels crazy because when you look at the two of us on paper you definitely wouldn't think we're the kind of friends who fit that way, but somehow, we fall together like we were always meant to be.

"Uh-huh," I mumble with a smile. "I'll do that as soon as I can tattoo 'Joss was here first' right over your cock."

"Don't say cock." He gives me an admonishing look.

"Why not?"

"It sounds dirty when you say it."

"And you like that?"

"Too much."

"Oh, Farm Boy, you shouldn't confess your weaknesses to the opposing team. We can use it to torture you."

"Maybe I like being tortured." He grins again, and I feel a flutter in my stomach. Because I imagine him tied up and at my mercy, slowly torturing him until he begs for me, and this whole scene is making me incredibly wet and desperate to have him touch me.

"I'll keep that in mind. Now you need to go and stand by the door again, so I can take these photos." I nod for him to move.

His eyes rake over me one last time, studying each curve on his way down until his eyes land on the football, and he turns it slightly, glancing at the preview image on my phone before he's satisfied with the position and stands again. I set up the camera to take the photos on a delayed timer and toss my phone out of frame before it starts. It snaps dozens of shots, and I reposition slightly for each one, changing my facial expression occasionally in an effort to give him some to pick from.

When it's done, I call him back over to look at the previews.

"This good?"

"Yeah. I think they'll do." He smiles as he flips through them.

"Any others you want?"

"Yes, but no..." I know what he means because now that I'm

thinking about us switching places, I don't know how I'm going to survive it.

"All right. Then you're up." I stand up next to him and grab my phone and robe off the bed, making a point of bending over right in front of him. Just before sliding the robe back on while he watches only a foot away from me. His eyes drop to my breasts and then back up to my lips and every thought is written on his face like he's not even trying to disguise it.

His eyes come up to mine and there's a question in them. Like maybe he's ready to cave or ask for some sort of temporary detente in our little war game. He starts to form a word, hesitating ever so slightly—

Then the doorbell rings, loudly, echoing through the house.

"Dinner," he says instead.

"Dinner," I agree, wrapping my robe and tying it around my waist. I follow him out into the living room.

"You can grab some plates and forks if you want. Cabinet there, and drawer there," he says and points to them as he walks toward the foyer to answer the door.

He returns a few minutes later with the bags and a couple of drinks to where I've already set things up for us at the counter.

"Don't think this gets you out of it." I point to the food. "You're still getting naked."

"Yes, ma'am." He nods.

WHEN WE'RE DONE and heading back to the bedroom, I frown at the scene because it's not what I imagine for him.

"I really think we need to get you into a proper studio. Where I can control the light and we can do some backdrops that will highlight your eye color."

"Don't tell me you're chickening out."

"I am not chickening out. But I want the best shots possible for this book. The light and the angles to be perfect. I've got one I've already toured, and I'm just waiting to hear back if I can rent the space for the next couple of weeks. Can we do it once I've got the studio now that I've held up my end of the bargain?"

"Sure. In the meantime, you going to edit those for me, so I can get them printed?"

"I'll get them printed and framed for you." I counter. "They can be an early Christmas gift from me."

He grins in response. "All right. I still think you should take a couple of test shots though. It'll help you figure out what you want to do when we get to the studio."

"I'm exhausted after the game, pretending to understand football, and then posing naked for my ex-fuckbuddy... That takes a lot out of a girl, you know? There's a deep soak in a bathtub that's calling my name right about now."

"I can draw you a bath here."

"Here?"

"I have a huge one in the master. Has a great view if it wasn't already dark out. But you can use it."

"Yes, but do you have bath bombs and bubbles? Because Violet has lots."

"Actually yes. I just got one of those grab bags from an event that's filled with bath stuff, so you can have your pick of bath bombs and bubbles."

"Tempting."

"I thought so."

"I feel like I'm being tempted into some inner circle of hell though. Trying to wear me down while I'm tired?"

"I just want another glimpse of you naked, and I figure there probably won't be another good excuse any time soon."

"Unless you cave."

"Which I won't."

"I think this is cheating a bit."

"I think you not wanting to see me naked tonight is cheating a bit. I think *you* can't handle it."

"I can absolutely handle it."

"We'll see."

"Go get the bath ready. While you do that, I'll pack this stuff up so your room isn't a mess."

He gives me a playful grin, and his eyes light up. "Yes, ma'am."

"And do not call me ma'am!" I call after him as he heads to the bathroom.

SEVENTEEN

Joss

"WHO IS THEO?" Colt nods to my phone when he comes back into the room and it lights up for the third time in a row. I'm not excited to tell him because I know he won't love the answer.

"A guy I met while I was traveling. We talk every now and again."

More like we have phone sex every now and again. We've never actually had sex. I was drunk the first night we met, and he was a gentleman, walking my friend and me back to our hotel room on the streets of Munich after a long night at Oktoberfest. He was hot as hell though and leaving the next day, so he offered to meet for breakfast. Except then I'd been violently hungover. He'd told me to keep his number in case we were ever in the same city again. So occasionally we check to see if the other is in the same town when we're lonely and bored. Once I missed him by a day, but that's just our luck. We commiserated over our loneliness on the road and that has turned into a friends-with-phone-sex-benefits situation.

"Talk?" Colt asks like he already knows the answer is more than that.

"About sex, usually while one of my toys is involved." I give him a pointed look in hopes he'll drop it.

"So phone-sex friends?" He sounds curious rather than annoyed, which is interesting.

"Something like that..." I eye him carefully.

"Is that what he's texting for now?"

"I haven't read them, so I don't know."

"Read them." It's his turn to give me a pointed look.

I eye him skeptically but pick up my phone and open it going straight to the messages.

THEO:

Up for a chat tonight?

Unless you're in Berlin or somewhere I can hop a train?

Miss hearing your voice.

I grin at my phone. Theo doesn't make my stomach flip and my heart race like Colt does, but he's a really sweet guy with an accent I can't resist which makes him a pretty damn sexy phone partner most of the time. The fact that he never gives up on us meeting someday is also strangely endearing.

"Must be good." Colt raises an eyebrow at me.

"Sorry. Yes, as suspected."

"He asked you to have phone sex?"

"Yes."

"And if I wasn't here, you'd say yes?"

"Maybe."

He gives me a look that tells me he knows the answer.

"Fine. Probably. But you're here."

"So tell him yes."

"Uh, I don't think so." I give Colt a brief look and return to packing the final few camera items back into my bag.

"Not in the mood?"

"I mean it's not that, it's just that..." I'm trying to figure out how to answer without admitting I want Colt too much to focus on anyone else right now.

"Because I'm in the mood to watch you."

"Watch me?" I ask, confused. "Watch me have phone sex?"

"Yes. I want to know what turns you on these days. I need that top roster spot once you're back on the road."

My stupid heart flutters in my chest, but I tamp it down and sit back on the bed, looking up at him. And suddenly I have an idea.

"So... Pretend we're having phone sex..." I smirk up at him. "Hello?"

He frowns for a moment, but then it morphs. Colt gives me a flash of that panty-dropping smile he always uses, and I feel my stomach somersault with nerves. I take a deep breath reminding myself this is just a silly game where we've made up all the rules. But I still feel like I'm walking a thin line.

He sits down in the chair across from the bed and mimes holding a phone. "Hello, Dollface."

I can't help the laugh that tumbles out, and he grins in response. I take a deep breath and continue on.

"I can't stop thinking about you. About the first time I went down on my knees for you. The look in your eyes when I put you in my mouth that first time. How much I liked it," I say in my sweetest voice.

His eyes widen, and he tilts his head back, staring at the ceiling and then closes his eyes on a groan before he speaks again.

"I still think about those red lips of yours. How pretty they looked while you sucked on me. Gets me off every time. But I can't wait to have you ask for it again. Hear you tell me how much you want it."

"I think about it too. What it would feel like to have you touch me finally. How your fingers would feel in my hair. How rough I could ask you to be."

I slide my fingers under the band of my panties as I look up at Colt because it's him I always think about anyway. Now, I just have the luck of being able to watch the live version in front of me. His eyes lock with mine and his hand runs absently over the front of his sweats.

"I'd have a fistful of it while I fuck you."

"Am I tied up while you do it?"

Colt raises his brow at the mention of me being tied up. It wasn't something we'd ever done. I'd wanted to but I wanted to ease him into it, and we never got that far before things fell apart.

"You like being tied up?"

"I like the idea of you tying me up. Torturing me with things you know I like," I confess.

The look he gives me in return, his blue eyes bright with want, melts every single part of me.

"Yes. Your hands behind your back. On your knees. Naked and willing." His hand slides under his sweats, and a stuttered curse comes out of him. "Are you wet for me?"

"Yes. Soaking wet, just hearing your voice," I answer him.

He smirks in return, pulling his sweats down and his cock out slowly. Making me watch what I can't have. He gives himself a rough stroke and something glints in the light. Something I can't possibly be seeing.

I jump off the bed without thinking, going for a closer look.

Colt's smirk just grows wider. Because Farm Boy has a Prince Albert. One that was definitely not there before.

"Are you fucking serious?" I look up at him.

He strokes himself again without answering. His eyes flicker with the taunt, and I feel like I might just give in right here. Fall to my knees and tell him he can have any and every fucking thing he wants. Because I want this new version of him, the one I've never known.

"You don't fight fair," I mutter, walking back to the bed because at least the distance will help. Two could play this game though. I slip my panties off and bend over to the camera bag I've left stashed at the foot of the bed.

I pull my vibrator out of it, and Colt's eyebrow lifts with the revelation. I just smirk in response. I turn it on and sit back on the bed, spreading my legs and teasing my clit with it while Colt watches.

"F-uck," I stutter as I hit myself just right.

I close my eyes and try to focus. Try to remind myself that I don't need him. I've done fine for years without him. There's no reason to cave to this now.

A second later though I feel Colt's hand on mine. My eyes pop open, and I give him a questioning look. He's stripped out of his sweats, completely naked, and I'm not about to tell him no. It's his hands and his body I really want. So if he's ready to call the bet already, so am I. But instead of touching me, he takes the vibrator—dangerously close to breaking our agreement.

He shrugs and gives me a devious grin. "Not technically touching you."

I can't help the small smile that comes to my lips as I scoot backward, and he climbs onto the bed between my legs. My eyes drift over his body, falling over the lean muscle, the way each sculpted part of him curves, dips, and flexes as he moves. Meeting his eyes again to find a self-satisfied grin on his face.

"Finding loopholes now?" I whisper.

"Whatever it takes to get you to admit it." Colt slides the vibrator in and out, and I brush my fingers in circles over my clit, coming closer and closer to falling over a cliff. One he pushes me over with every touch and word.

EIGHTEEN

Colt

I'M NOT REMOTELY prepared for what I asked for. Her spread out on my bed, looking so fucking beautiful it hurts, saying insanely dirty things I've missed hearing from her. All while I fuck her with a vibrator because I promised not to touch her.

It's the sweetest kind of torture I've ever imagined for myself. The only thing keeping me grounded is the way she looks at me, so soft and heated that I know it's me she'll be thinking of for the foreseeable future. Me she's thinking of now while she moans and writhes.

She's so wet at this point that despite my attempts not to touch her I still manage to get my fingers slick with her come, and the second she comes for me I'm using that to my own advantage. Because I'm so fucking hard, I'm leaking and my cock is desperate for any sort of friction, so much so that I'm grinding into the fucking comforter for relief as I bring her closer.

I want her more than anything I've ever wanted in the world right now except for one thing—the chance to show her I can play these games and handle this kind of sex without everything turning into a mess. But it's taking every ounce of willpower I have.

"Fuck... Yes. My god. Like that. It feels so good like that," she cries out, and then she picks up her speed as she rubs her clit, and I do my best to match the rhythm and pace. She counters each stroke of the vibrator with her hips and the mattress shifts with her movement. I bite my tongue hard, trying to give myself something, anything to focus on that isn't how badly I want to slide inside her.

She whimpers again, and it's one of the hottest things I've heard in my life. I'd forgotten how good she sounds. How perfect she looks like this. That she's every fantasy I've had come to life.

"Holy fucking Christ," I mutter and her brow furrows as she looks up at me, and it melts into an amused smile as she takes in how wrecked I am just from watching her.

"Too much for you?" she mumbles, rolling her lower lip between her teeth as she holds back another moan. In turn, I put the vibrator on a higher setting.

"Fuck me," she curses loudly, turning her head to the side and burying her face against her shoulder. A series of moans and whimpers leave her then, and she mutters she's coming as I watch her fully unravel in front of me. Her thighs wide, her pussy slick, her fingers curled around the edge of my comforter as her body shivers through the last of it.

She's gorgeous like this, and it reminds me of the hours we used to spend in her room. Her playful laugh and teasing smile as she let me explore every curve of her body until I knew how to make her come by heart. I want her again, like this and every other possible way.

She looks up at me with soft sated eyes and trails her fingers over her stomach. I turn the vibrator off and lay it down on the bed, my hand returning to my cock because after watching her, I need to come so fucking badly I don't care how desperate I look.

Her eyes fall heavy on where my hand meets my cock, and I imagine her crawling toward me and wrapping her lips around it. Looking at me with those big green eyes while I slide to the back of her throat. My fingers in her hair while her tongue cradles me. It takes me so close to the edge I start breathing heavily, and she sits up. Her eyes rake over me and land on my cock again, her tongue running over the edge of her lip.

"I've been dying to see you like this," she admits softly. I give myself another soft tentative stroke, not nearly the amount of friction I need as she watches. Her lashes fluttering as she takes me in, nibbling the side of her lip. "All you have to do is say the word."

I let out a muted groan and her eyes lift to my mouth. Her tongue slides over her lower lip and then she bites it. I glare at her for tempting me now when I'm so weak for her.

"Touch yourself," I say as I watch her hands slide over her thighs absently.

Her fingers slide down, dragging through the wetness still there and then drawing out a small circle over her clit as her eyes stay locked on me.

"You know it's you that I always think about. When I'm alone I mean..."

"Fuck... Joss..." I don't have better words. Not ones that don't end with me saying I give.

"I don't know if I can do this. Stick to the agreement. I think I might want you too much," she confesses.

"You can handle it," I say gruffly as I start to stroke faster. I want it to last, but I have to finish if I get out of this alive. "I'm close already. Listening to you. Fuck..."

She smirks and then grabs the vibrator, turning it on, and I raise an eyebrow.

"You trust me?"

"Yes." I give her a questioning look.

She leans forward and places the vibrating tip between my balls and ass, and I nearly come out of my fucking skin at how good it feels and how fast it takes me to the edge. I stroke harder then, feeling the edge of my release coming quickly. I look up at her, giving her a half-hooded glare and cursing her for being so fucking clever all the time.

"I thought you'd like that," she whispers. "You're so fucking hot, Colt. Hard to believe you're real sometimes." Her eyes drift over me, her body inches from mine. It's all it takes. With those words, I'm over the edge. Coming hard and fast. It sends a flood of fire through my limbs, and I swear I can feel the echoes of it in every single inch of my body.

She pulls the vibrator away, shutting it off, and I open my eyes. Her fingers slide along her thigh where I managed to catch her, swirling through my come and painting a trail down her leg. She presses the tips of her fingers to her tongue and licks, an evil grin as she does it.

"Not technically touching you." She shrugs one shoulder.

"Holy fuck," I curse as I collapse on the bed next to her.

"Vibrator would feel even better *inside*, you know, but I figured that's too much for you right now. We'll have to work our way up to that. I can order one for you."

"I don't know about that." I give her a skeptical look

because having something in my ass was not at the top of my list of things to try right now.

"Okay. But never say never. You might like it."

"Well I never thought I'd like pretend phone sex, but that was pretty fucking hot."

"And messy. Your poor comforter." She looks half despondent and half amused as she surveys the damage we've done.

"It'll wash out." I smile.

"About that bath..."

NINETEEN

Colt

"RIGHT. Let me go add some more hot water. It's probably getting cold, then you can get in."

I need a minute in anyway. A moment to remind myself not to make confessions to Joss that she's not ready to hear. I head to the bathroom, and sure enough, the bathwater is approaching tepid. I drain some of it and then restart the hot water.

"This bathtub is huge!" She gasps as she enters the room.

"Yeah. I wanted to be able to spread out in it and relax."

"Looks like it was made for two." She grins.

I wince internally because that had been a thought in my mind when I had it installed. I imagined a girlfriend or a wife. Someone I could come home to after games when I was beaten up and bruised. Climb into the tub with her.

Except every time I tried to imagine the beautiful blue-eyed blonde cheerleader who always flirts with me or one of the women I dated in the past in that role, she'd morph into a woman with black hair and bright green eyes. So I suppose it's fitting that she's the first to use it. Might as well permanently burn the image into the space.

"That too," I answer, staring into the water.

"So you'll join me then?" There's a hopeful tone to her voice.

I should say no. It's playing with fire. It's one thing to fuck her with a vibrator while I watch her have pretend phone sex. Another if we're climbing into the tub for an after-session. She must see the doubtful look on my face as I turn off the water.

"I'll keep my hands to myself. I promise. I mean I can't promise we won't touch. But I'll behave." She grins at me.

"Will you?" I give her a skeptical look because I don't know if I believe in my own willpower.

"Yes. I'll be an exceptionally good girl. I promise, Farm Boy."

"Okay." I fold like cheap cardboard. Because I want this girl in my bath. In my bed. Everywhere I can have her before she leaves me again.

I climb into the water, and she follows me, carefully lowering herself so our bodies touch as little as possible. She leans back in the tub and her eyes run over me like she's assessing me with newfound information.

"How the fuck do you get a Prince Albert and not tell me, St. George?" Her tone is accusatory but there's a smile on her face. "That's information I should have had before we started this. Unfair tactics. You should be penalized for that."

I shrug. "A woman told me once that it felt amazing, and it was worth trying if I ever wanted to ditch the Farm Boy thing."

"And you listened to her, but never let her enjoy it?"

"She was long gone by then."

"I still can't believe you didn't tell me." She splashes water in my direction. "That was worth a text. A telegram. An anonymous memo. *Something*. But I was right, wasn't I? I bet that's gotten you lots of extra points in bed. Not that you need them. What the hell was I thinking giving you more ideas like that when you already have such an unfair advantage? I swear. I need to be stopped."

"I think you were trying to help an awkward fumbling way-too-old-for-a-football-player-virgin figure out how not to suck in bed."

"You never sucked in bed, Colt. You were inexperienced sometimes, but there's a difference between inexperience and sucking at something. And there was very little fumbling. I was surprised. In fact, I thought you might have been lying at first."

"Lying about being a virgin? Why the fuck would I do that?" I'd been horrified at having to admit it to her the first time—explaining that my ex and I had been waiting for each other until we weren't—but was too afraid she'd figure it out not to.

"Get me to sleep with you. You weren't my type at all—you know that. I thought maybe you just wanted to brag to your friends you got an older alt girl to fuck you, but the more you talked... You were just so kind and sincere about everything. You'd have been a sociopath to carry on like that if it wasn't real."

"I wanted to brag. You were so fucking gorgeous. And patient with me."

"I know, so much patience... The number of times I had to teach you proper technique with your tongue. Such a burden. You owe me if we're being honest." She's sitting back now, her fingers dancing over her knees as she runs the soap over her skin.

"Yeah, what do I owe you?" I can see her nipples beading up and her legs starting to fall open, just that tiny bit wider in the bath. This is the other thing about Joss. When she wants something, she doesn't drop it.

"A taste. A chance to run my tongue over it. Feel it hit the back of my throat. And if I do that well enough, then..." Her fingers drop down from her knee, sliding over her thigh, down into the water between her legs and she bites her lower lip.

I'm out of my depth with her. Most of the women I've dated, since we went our separate ways after our failed experiment, weren't nearly as confident as she was, or as willing to speak their minds so bluntly. They'd been shy and quiet, and while it had sometimes been nice to be around someone who could just sit in silence, I miss Joss's confidence when it comes to the way she asks for things. So much so, I'd skipped out on more than one date because they didn't measure up to the ghost in my head.

Joss is in a league all her own. Bemused and understated confidence most of the time, and all the right words when I want to hear them most. Her arm moves again, and the water ripples above, her eyes closing for a moment before they reopen and latch onto me again.

"Then what?" I ask.

"Then you could fuck me like you promised to in the shower."

"I didn't promise to fuck you."

"You promised to put me on my knees."

"But then I promised not to touch you."

TWENTY

Joss

"RIGHT, and I'm supposed to be behaving." I sigh.

"You did promise." Colton gives me a chastising look before it breaks into a smile.

I forgot how dedicated to carrying out a task he could be. Sometimes it's to my advantage. Sometimes less so. Apparently, right now it's the latter.

"All right. Let's talk about something less sexy then."

"Do you like being tied up?" he asks, sliding his hand along the edge of the tub, coming dangerously close to touching my knee.

"That is *not* less sexy."

He shrugs. "I'm just curious. You never mentioned it when we were... in our previous arrangement."

"Because that's slightly more advanced and you were still learning the basics. Needed to conquer the first set of ropes before you could conquer the second." I grin and give him a playful wink, dragging my toes along the side of his hip as I do it. Testing the bounds of our agreement under the water.

"Clever," he deadpans with an eye roll to match. He takes my foot and brings it up to his chest, massaging my instep. "You still didn't answer the question though."

"Yes, I like being tied up in theory. Ropes. Handcuffs. All the usual things. But I haven't done it many times, so..." I trail off as his fingers reach my ankle, sliding along my Achilles tendon.

"Why not?"

"Because... like you know, I only do casual. Doing that sort of thing requires trust and while I like pushing my comfort zone, I don't fuck with the trust part of things. You know?"

He nods.

"If I was serious about getting into it beyond the casual pair of handcuffs, I could probably find someone through a members-only club or something where it would be vetted and safer, but that would involve being in the same place for more than a minute. Another thing I'm incapable of." I give a half smile and shrug.

"Would you trust me?" He lets go of that foot and reaches for the other, resting it against his chest again.

"Of course. But you'd have to touch me, and we just agreed we're not doing that," I say while he's actively massaging his way up my calf and we're both ignoring it like it's not actually happening.

"There's still time for one of us to cave." His eyes lift from his task, and he flashes a smile at me.

"Is that a fantasy of yours?" I pull my foot back and shift in the water, sitting up on my knees and straddling his lap. Water splashes over the edge onto the tiles below with the movement.

There's barely enough room for it, and I'd guess there's half a centimeter between me and his cock this way. His face contorts at the position, a furrowed brow and a questioning glance coming and going in rapid succession. I rest my hands on his shoulders for balance and then start massaging them in slow circles.

His eyebrow lifts, reminding me I'm not supposed to be touching him.

"If you can massage my feet, I can massage your shoulders. I'm just being a good friend."

"Right," he says doubtfully, his eyes landing hard on my breasts which nearly graze him as my fingers slide over his traps.

"You still didn't answer the question."

"I'm having a hard time remembering what it was." He grins as he pushes a little tuft of bubbles off my nipple with his thumb.

"That's cheating for sure, but I'm going to allow it this once... I asked if tying women up is a fantasy of yours."

"Tying women up? No. Tying you up? Yes."

"Because I'm a pain in your ass and run my mouth too much?" I laugh.

"Because I imagine how hot it would be to tease you to the edge over and over until you were begging me to put you out of your misery and then have you ride my face. I think about how wet and desperate you'd be, how rough you'd ride me, how good you'd fucking taste like that."

My jaw drops and my fingers still. I just stare at him for a long minute. "I really did create a monster. The things your mind comes up with, Farm Boy..." I shake my head, smiling at him.

He smirks, but his eyes fall over me again. "I know whatever I could come up with, you'd find something beyond. So why do you like the idea of guys tying you up?"

I take a breath, closing my eyes and trying to decide if I confess to him the thing I really want. What I would only trust him with. I open them again a second later to see blue eyes locked on me, and I know I shouldn't tell him, but I do anyway.

"I like the idea of you tying me up and using me. Showing me how good you've gotten at all the things I taught you."

"Using you how?" I'll give him credit that he keeps a poker face when he asks, but the way his eyes light at the suggestion lets me know it's something he wants.

"Any way you want."

His chest rises with an intake of breath, and my hand slides down over his chest. His lids lower as his gaze drops to my mouth, and I move an inch closer, tempting him to kiss me like I know he wants to. But a second later he closes his eyes, leaning his head back and when he resurfaces and opens them, they're crystal clear and bright blue again. We stare at each other for a long moment, unsaid words between us, and then he clears his throat.

"We should rinse off."

"Right," I agree even though I don't want to.

It takes every ounce of willpower I have to lift my hands and get out of the tub. He follows close behind, and turns on the shower, letting the water heat before we slide under it. There are two shower heads side by side so we can rinse off at the same time. Because like the tub, everything in this house was built for two—for him and his wife.

He turns off the shower after he's done, grabbing a towel, and then scrubbing it over his hair and body before wrapping it around his waist. He walks over to the side of the tub, grabbing another towel from the heated bar there, and motions for me. I turn off the water and walk toward him slowly, giving him a curious look.

He gently pats me dry with the towel and then holds it out so I can wrap it around me, grabbing me another towel for my hair that I use to get most of the moisture out of the ends. I've managed not to get it too wet, but I hadn't exactly been using caution in the last few hours.

"Do you have any lotion?" I ask softly because this time of year if I don't use some my skin turns into a desert in record time.

"Yeah. There's some that came with the bath soak." I watch him go into a cabinet and return with it. But instead of handing it to me, he squeezes some into his palms and motions for me to turn for him.

I do and slide my hair off to the side as he puts it on my back and shoulders. His palms gliding downward, over my upper arms, across my elbows, and all the way down to my wrists. His hands move back and forth over my skin, swirling little circles in their wake and making my whole body light up for him. I look at him, imagining I'll see a devious grin, but I don't. Just the furrowed brow of a man concentrating.

"Legs?" he asks, and I nod. I should point out to him that this is dangerously close to the hundredth violation of the agreement we made in as many minutes. That he's well over the line considering he's touching me, massaging me, making me want all over again even though what we just did should have sated me. At least taken the edge off for a short while. Would have if it were anyone else. But with Colton, I don't think anything is ever enough.

His hands run over my knees, down my calves, and over my ankles, massaging tender circles as he works his way back up. He stops on my lower thigh, where the towel hits, and grabs more lotion, switching to the other leg. As he works his way up this time, his hand goes up the back of my thigh coming to rest just below the curve of my ass under the towel. He looks up at me for permission to go further, and I smirk.

"I think we're approaching cheating territory."

"And you don't want to cheat?"

"What I want doesn't matter."

He stands then, rising to his full height and when I take a step back, he takes one forward. He's switched again from the sweet caring guy with the boyish grin, back to the man who chases what he wants. He's quiet but his eyes say everything for him.

"It matters."

My heart thuds in my chest as I stare up at him, lost in his deep blue eyes. Because I want him so badly. Want to drive him to the point that he hauls me up against a wall again and this time doesn't stop himself. But then I'll crave him constantly. We'll be out of this limbo and into the next. This one is where we just play a game over sex. It's fun, harmless, and sexy as fuck. The next limbo? That's the problem.

"Crossing this line is one thing. Of course I want to cross it. But the next line... the one after we do this and try to define *us*. That's where our hearts get involved. That's where things can break. I don't want us to break. I've missed you so much, Colt. So much I didn't realize because I didn't even want to let myself feel it." My voice quivers with the words because I feel vulnerable admitting them, but I need him to hear it.

"I missed you too." His face softens and he wraps his arms around me and pulls me close to him. I follow his lead.

For a moment I feel content again. Whole. Because sometimes I think Colt might just be one of those people for me. Just like Violet and Ben are, where they make up pieces of my soul, and when they're missing, I'm not a whole person anymore.

"Stay here tonight. Sleep in my bed." He brushes the hair

back out of my face and studies me for a moment. "We won't cross any lines, but I want you here."

"Okay," I agree because I don't want to say no. I'm not ready to leave either. "But only if I get to pick the show we watch before bed. Cause Lord knows I'm not watching sports highlights."

I feel him tighten his grip, and I can hear the amused tone in his voice when he speaks, "If that's what it takes."

TWENTY-ONE

Joss

I TRY to sneak in through the front door to the hallway, but I'm in far too close proximity to the kitchen not to be heard, and just when I think I'm home free, there's a throat-clearing sound. I turn and Violet's standing there in her pajamas, coffee mug in hand and eyebrow raised.

"If you're going to make me worry about you all night, then when you come home in the morning you at least owe me the juicy details."

"Shit. I'm sorry. My phone was in the kitchen, and I was in the bedroom—" I stop abruptly when I realize what it sounds like I'm confessing.

"Uh-huh. When Ben tried to get ahold of Colt and he didn't answer either, we assumed you two were together. Catching up. Revisiting old times. Bad habits. You know." Her lips quiver and a smile flits over them before she takes another sip of her coffee.

"It wasn't... We didn't."

"You just were in his bedroom, too busy to answer your phones for hours, and then didn't come home until morning."

"Yes, something like that."

"Remember in grad school when you told me there was no way that Ben and I were just watching TV in my room?"

"Okay well. It was... exactly like that actually."

"Uh-huh."

"I'm serious. Exactly like that. We didn't do anything together. I just took a bath. He took a shower. At the same time, as friends do on occasion. Then I was tired and we fell asleep. In his bed, but there was a pillow wall between us. It was all very above-board, Violet, so take your judgy eyes and shove them up your—"

"Sounds like you were up late and didn't get enough sleep. Would you like some caffeine before you say inexcusably mean things to your best friend?"

I make a face, then mimic what she just said like I'm a freaking child because it's all I've got right now. I'm cranky as hell, not so much over the lack of sleep as I am the lack of sex. This thing Colt and I are doing is torture. Pure and simple. The slow drip of torment, all the hints of things that could be. The way he looks at me. The way he sounds. Watching his hand run over his cock until he came.

"I'm going to take that as a yes." She gives me the side-eye.

I follow her into the kitchen, figuring it's time I come clean to her because at this point I need an outside opinion. A sounding board. Someone to tell me that I've waded in too deep and that I need to get myself back out. Because right now, I just want to cave to our little bet and call it a day.

She fixes my coffee just the way I like it with extra cream and sugar, a routine we perfected for each other when we were roomies. Whoever was more conscious in the morning was the one who handled the coffee making. This morning, judging by her perky appearance, that's definitely her.

"So, shall I interrogate you or would you rather just fess up?"

"Depends on what I'm fessing up to."

"Sleeping with Colt."

"I didn't sleep with him. The tension is high, and we agreed it would be an epic mistake to get involved again. Given that it ended so badly the last time and there's no chance for us now either."

"Why is there no chance?"

"He's a quarterback who lives and breathes this city. I'm a photographer always on the road. Those things don't mesh."

"Well, it wouldn't be easy..." She shrugs as she stares at me over her coffee cup.

"It would be awful. And that's assuming we could work through all our shit from the past, and that's a big assumption."

"But..." She looks at me expectantly.

"But... I can't be in the same room as him without wanting to fuck his brains out. Okay?"

"Okay, Ms. Cranky."

"Sorry. I need my caffeine." I take a chug of the lukewarm coffee and glance out the window. "So we made this agreement... Bet. I don't know. Whatever you want to call it. I feel silly explaining it, but basically, we agreed we wouldn't get physically involved. But now it's turned into a game of brinksmanship as to who can get the other person to cave."

"I see."

"Do you?" I flash her a look.

"It certainly sounds *interesting*."

"Well, it's had some *interesting* results. Anyway, I went to his place yesterday to do the pictures—"

"Did you get naked for him?"

"Topless, not fully naked. I put off doing his pictures though. I need to find a studio. That's one of the things I need to nail down today. Can you get in touch with your friend and see if we can confirm that space, so I can get the guys scheduled? Time is running out."

"Of course, but topless photos with him there and that didn't end in the two of you fucking each others' brains out?"

"No. But only because we had other kinds of fun—solo fun."

"Solo fun together?" She raises her brow.

"Yes."

"And?"

"And now I just want him more. It's awful. I'm going to have to avoid him for a while I think, or else I'm definitely going to be the one to cave."

"Well good news, they get on a flight in a couple of days because they're playing their Thursday night game out of town. He didn't mention that?"

"No. But that's good. If I can just make it a few days avoiding him, maybe I'll get out of this alive. Maybe I find a good cougar bar, find a look-alike, and fuck this out with them. I don't know. It's bad, Violet. It's very bad."

"First, you're not a cougar. A mini cougar maybe, and that's a stretch. Second, you definitely do *not* fuck this out with someone else." Violet gives me a grumpy look.

"I'm not serious. Not really. I just don't want to fuck this up with him again. I like him, just generally. As a person, as a friend. I like having him back in my life to talk to and joke with and spend time around. I like that the four of us can hang out again. If we get involved again, that all goes to hell."

"Or you fall in love and end up happy like Ben and me."

"That's exactly why I haven't been talking about this with you. I *knew* you would say that. You and your toxic cesspool of optimism. Being in a happy relationship has really rotted your brain Vi."

"I mean, isn't it a possibility?"

"It's a possibility in the same way that it's possible according to quantum physics for a fully formed and functioning unicorn's heart to magically pop into existence floating in the air in front of me. *Possible* but so absurdly unlikely that it's not worth entertaining."

"I see we're in that kind of mood. But you remember how badly I protested that Ben and I could never work, and now look at us."

"Ben was obsessed with you and willing to do whatever it took to get you. And you are far more well-adjusted than I am."

"Colt's obsessed with you."

"Says who?" I eye her carefully because I do want to know if he's been talking to Ben.

We said we'd try to keep them out of it, but here I am spilling my guts to Violet anyway. I wouldn't be surprised if he and Ben had their own version of morning coffee. Probably morning sports drinks and drills or something football-y. Who knows.

"Says anyone who looks at him. Says the fact he wanted nude photos of you when he's otherwise a celibate monk. Did he tell you what he wanted the pictures for by the way? As if we all don't already know."

"Violet! Have some class."

"Oh, come on."

"I'll have you know, he wanted to frame them and put them on the wall. Of his bedroom. Where he's definitely not going to use them as you're implying." I take a sip of my coffee far too soon and end up sputtering it and having to grab a napkin.

"Jesus, Joss. Then stop being obtuse. What was it you said

to me, 'He's a good boy. Give that poor boy what he wants.' I think it was something like that."

"Yeah, he is *not* a boy anymore." I raise my brows and smirk as I think of the way he looked last night. "And after last night, I've discovered he's definitely not good all the time."

"I'm *aware*."

"Oh yeah? Does Ben know?" I tease her.

"Ha. Ben knows I have eyes like every other woman in this city."

"In this country if all the features and advertising deals have anything to say about it."

"Is that what you're worried about?"

"I don't know. Not exactly. I know I'm his type. For whatever reason I won that lottery. But the rest of the world would probably think it's a weird choice for him."

"You never know. They might like it. Him choosing someone less conventional."

"Or I get accused of cradle robbing their favorite quarterback."

"The age gap is not that big Joss, ask me how I know. Plus June was older than Johnny, remember? And look how they worked out."

I sigh. I knew Violet would do this. Make it seem like Colt and I could be together. That we had a chance in hell of making this work. I'm not the cold-hearted bitch I was when I was younger. I've somehow softened with time and experience. Or maybe just with missing him in my life. I don't hate the idea of a relationship anymore. Especially since the last year has given me a lot of time alone to reflect. But there was a difference between a relationship theoretically and the reality of a relationship with Colt.

"What's with all the gear-turning going on?" She gives me a meaningful look.

"Nothing. Just thinking about what you said. Trying to decide if you're crazy for thinking it's possible or if I'm crazy for not giving it serious consideration. One of us is definitely crazy though."

She rolls her eyes.

"Just finish your coffee and get some rest. We can revisit it when you're not a zombie. Harper and Scarlett want to get together later. So maybe they'll have thoughts."

TWENTY-TWO

Colt

AS I WIND up my cooldowns on the field, Tobias comes and sits next to me to do his own.

"I'm going to get naked for your girl tonight. She's even taking me out to dinner after." He grins at me as he stretches his leg out.

"She's not my girl." I shake my head, stretching my arm across my chest.

"Oh yeah? So you don't mind if I shoot my shot with her then? See if she likes the preview enough to want the whole thing."

"The fuck you will," I snap at him.

Tobias stops his workout and turns to look at me slowly, devious amusement spreading across his face.

"That's what I fucking thought."

"Stay out of it and stay away from her."

"Listen. You're Priest for a reason. You show this kind of

interest in a woman, especially one who seems to be the opposite of the sweet soft-spoken blue-eyed blonde fifties-home-
maker type I expected to see you with, and I get curious."

"Why does it matter?"

"Cause you're not one of us. You're not me and Xander.
You're a get married, have babies, and the picket-fence type."

"Or you just think I am. Also, Xander is looking like the
picket-fence type these days."

"Always happy to be surprised. And true. Now that Xander
is down bad, I can always use a new wingman. There are a
couple of places where the women in the VIP sections are
always hot as fuck, we could check them out if you're up for it."

"No thanks."

"Because you're already involved with a tattooed
photographer?"

"You're not gonna let this drop, are you?"

"No. I think I like her for you. She's feisty and loud. I bet
she drives you insane. It's perfect."

"I'm glad I have your seal of approval."

"You should be. I'm shit at finding someone myself, but for
other people? I can spot them a mile away. Xander and Harper.
My brother and his wife Wren. The second I saw them
together I knew. Took a little longer than expected with Xander
and Harper, but they got there."

"Yeah well, like Waylon and Ben said, Joss and I have been
there. It didn't end with us walking down the aisle. Obviously."

"Why not?"

I give him a deadpan look because I don't know why I've
suddenly landed in Westfield's sights. "Because I'm a quarterback and she's an internationally renowned photographer.
We're both already married—to our jobs."

He gives me a skeptical look.

"When are you planning to get married? Or are we just

waiting on a woman who can tolerate you for more than a night?"

"Don't start. Xander already has."

"I bet he has." I laugh. "Before you know it you two are gonna have kids in the same preschool and be going on family vacations to the beach together. I'm gonna laugh so damn hard that I'm the last one standing."

"We'll see about that. And don't scare me with that shit, all right? It already scares me he's all in on it. I was all about seeing the two of them get together, but now he's got little hearts in his eyes wherever he goes. It's fucking frightening, honestly. If I lose my mind like that too... fuck. Something's seriously wrong in the world."

"Or maybe you've just finally grown the hell up."

"I'm as grown as I want to be now."

"The non-stop parties, lavish spending, flowing liquor, revolving door of women. That's maturity?"

"I work really fucking hard every week. I deserve some downtime."

"If that's what we're calling it now."

"I'm serious though. I know a couple of places that are fun. You could try making an effort to come to my parties instead of avoiding them like the plague."

"They just seem like places to get into trouble."

"You must like trouble deep down, or you wouldn't be obsessing over her."

"I'm not obsessing," I grump. It's a lie. I'm definitely obsessing. She's on my mind every waking hour and haunting my dreams too. I've actively tried to give myself a cooling-off period the last few days since the photo session at my house because I'm in way over my head with her.

"What's he obsessing about now? Jones not being able to

hold the line during practice?" Ben asks when he overhears part of the conversation.

"A woman and not the game for once," Tobias answers.

"Well that could be good for him." Ben grins at me as he sits down to stretch with us.

"Don't start," I grumble, and they both laugh.

WHEN WE'RE out of practice I'm anxious to go see her. I haven't since we got back from out of town and while I think there's an unwritten rule that would keep her and Tobias from doing anything, the idea of the two of them alone together while he gets naked isn't my favorite. He's more her type than I am, and they're closer in age. Add in their views on life, tattoos, people, parties, sex, and both of their outgoing personalities, it seems like the recipe for the perfect no strings hookup. I can feel the hint of jealousy creep up my spine just thinking about it.

There's no reason I can't go and visit her at the studio though. Claim I want to see what it's like to make me more comfortable when I have to go under the lights. God knows I've already seen a naked Tobias in and out of the locker room more times than I can count. So maybe I'd just surprise her, claiming I want to get dinner with her and check out the studio. It's true after all. I pull up the text message where she gave me the address and put it in my GPS, hoping that it's a good surprise and not a bad one for both of us.

When I get there and knock on the door, it's Harper's friend, Scarlett, who answers looking surprised and flustered to see me on the other side of it.

"Colton St. George," she blurts out.

"Scarlett—I don't know your last name," I counter, smiling at her because this is a reaction I'm not entirely unused to getting from people. She's technically met me before from across a room with brief introductions, but never actually spoken to me face-to-face.

"Edgar."

I raise a brow.

"That's my last name. Sorry, you don't care. I assume you're here to see Tobias?"

"Joss actually."

"They're in the studio taking pictures. I'm helping out until Harper gets here. You want me to ask if it's okay if you go in?"

"Oh, I'm sure it's okay."

"He's um... not fully dressed though, so..." she hesitates, and I can almost see a blush on her cheeks.

"Yeah, we share a locker room every day, so I've seen it all already. Not to mention he'd probably run around naked if it wouldn't get him arrested."

"I noticed." Her eyes flash in the direction of the door.

"That where they are?"

She blinks and recomposes herself as if she's coming out of a fog, but she's at least treating me like I'm a normal person now, so I'll take it.

"Yes. I was just on my way to grab some clothes for him to wear for another short shoot we're doing for the museum. You might work for it too. Would you be interested if one of the uniforms fits?"

"Uh... maybe. Once I get a chance to talk to Joss we can chat about it, okay?"

"All right." She nods and then hurries past me out the door.

I knock on the door before I open it and then slide inside.

"Scarlett, you can just come in and out without knocking.

Just make sure you shut the door. Okay, Westfield, pull the shirt off but do it slowly. Like you're trying to seduce me, okay?"

I glance across the room where Tobias sees me and smirks. Joss is still too focused on getting the right angle with her camera, and she hasn't looked up yet.

"Seduction. Not smugness, Westfield. There's a difference. I hope you know it."

"Oh, I know it." He's incredibly amused that she hasn't realized I'm here.

"You're pretty damn good in front of the camera. You have some magic. I bet the team photographers love you."

"Everyone loves me."

"Oh yeah, everyone? The rumors aren't all bullshit then?" Joss smiles at him as she looks up from her camera and that right there is enough to make the ember of jealousy bloom into a fire.

"Absolutely not." Tobias grins back at her. "Happy to give you a chance to find out."

Joss raises a brow and shakes her head, a smile flitting over her lips. "That sounds like a terrible idea."

He pulls his shirt all the way off and tosses it to the floor and she takes a few more shots of him.

"How so?"

"Because I don't need that kind of trouble in my life. I have enough. Let me get another battery for the camera. This one's getting low, and I don't want to miss a shot if it goes out. In the meantime, strip out of those jeans. Or wait—do you have something on under them?"

"Yes ma'am." He gives her a cheeky grin.

"Okay, then yes. Strip out of them and don't call me ma'am again. Before you get completely naked, we probably need to make sure Scarlett is prepared, so she doesn't have a heart attack."

"I don't know. I like seeing all the different shades of red I can make her turn. See if she can live up to her name."

"You're bad. Don't let him get to you, Scarlett." Joss shakes her head and then turns in my direction and nearly bumps into me. "Holy Fuck! Colt! I thought you were Scarlett. When did you get here?"

She grabs her chest as she blinks at me and takes in my presence, her eyes traveling up my body to my face.

"A while ago. You were busy, and I didn't want to interrupt —*the magic.*"

Her brow furrows and then she gives me a sly once over. "What are you doing here anyway?"

"Tobias mentioned he was doing his photos tonight. I was in the neighborhood, and I figured it wouldn't be a bad idea to see what to expect."

"I see," she answers me, but her eyes are on the bag in front of her as she roots around for a battery.

"Am I interrupting?" I ask, trying not to sound as jealous as I feel.

"I don't mind if you're here as long as Westfield doesn't mind. Might do Scarlett some good because he's attempting to scandalize her."

I glance over at him, and he's down to his underwear and scrolling on his phone while he waits for her.

"Sounds like he's attempting to scandalize you," I say, watching as she plugs the new battery in.

Her eyes flick up to mine. "Are you jealous, Farm Boy?"

"Should I be?"

TWENTY-THREE

Joss

COLT LOOKS SURLY as hell standing in front of me, and I can't help the small laugh that tumbles out which doesn't help matters at all.

"Are you normally jealous of him?" I finally ask when the pout threatens to turn into a glare.

"No. I don't fucking care what Westfield does."

"Then why would you be now?"

"He's your type, and the two of you are flirting a whole fucking lot."

"Colton," I tsk at him. "Using the f-word. What's happening to you?"

"Spending too much time around you." He turns and looks over at Tobias. "You give a fuck if I stay here while you parade around in your underwear?"

"Nope," Tobias calls back from over his phone.

The way Tobias doesn't even react to hearing Colt's voice

tells me I was played by the guy who was supposed to be helping me.

"He knew you were here the whole time, didn't he?"

"He saw me walk in, which is why he turned up his fucking act by ten degrees."

"Well, he's been mouthy since Scarlett got here, so I didn't notice."

"She seems rattled by him. He being an ass to her?"

"He was a little rough with her earlier. I think he's in a mood over something. He keeps looking at his phone and pacing around. I don't know what they said to each other because she was asking his measurements to see if she had a uniform he could wear and who fucking knows."

"He doesn't seem moody with you."

"I'm his type. That's why we get each other." I grin back at Colt, and he frowns again when I use his words against him.

"Now you're trying to press my buttons." His eyes darken as he looks at me, his lashes lowering and his jaw going tight.

"Is it working?" I grin at him for another moment before I turn back to the task at hand. Whatever has Westfield in a tizzy, I want to get him in and out of this shoot first before his mood sours more than it already has.

"You ready?"

He nods and sets his phone aside, and we work for several more minutes until I get a few good shots. I coach him through a few poses and adjust the light once or twice to get the right angle. He's not Colt. Not by a long shot. But he's got the body and the tattoos that would normally make my knees weak. And he looks like a fucking rockstar under these lights. I can't wait to get my hands on the edits.

I hear the door open, and I look up to see Alex and Harper stepping in.

"I know we're super late, but his charity event ran late. I'm sorry, Joss!"

"No worries."

"You still have time for me, or you want to reschedule?"

"How fast can you strip?"

"Is Harper doing the stripping? Because then, pretty fucking fast."

Harper punches his arm. "Don't embarrass me in front of my co-director."

"Ow! Fuck. Okay. She doesn't strip me at all. Saint here's practically a nun." He laughs as she glowers at him. "You and Priest could start your own outpost."

"Very funny, Xavier." Colt flicks him a look.

"You strip down today too?"

"Nope."

"All right, Xavier. Strip down and get over there. Westfield, go get geared up for the shoot Scarlett needs. And Scarlett, do you have a replica that'll fit Xavier?"

She takes one look over his form. "Uh, no. Can promise I don't."

"Hear that, Saint? I'm too big for her."

"Oh my god. Go get naked, will you?"

"Anytime you want." Alex kisses her and then takes off behind the wall to get undressed.

LIKE TOBIAS, Alex has done plenty of photoshoots for magazines and he knows the ropes well enough that we can peel through a series of photos pretty fast. By the time we're done, Scarlett's close to having Tobias ready, and we're on our way to being done with this whole day. And given that I'm exhausted and everyone else looks it as well, that's probably a good thing.

"Wow. Does that line usually work for you?" I hear Scarlett snap at Tobias as she puts the finishing touches on his uniform. Colt has opted out of playing dress up today, and I can feel his mood souring as fast as Westfield's the more the night wears on. I need to hurry and wrap this all up, or I feel like I'm going to have an actual war that breaks out.

I get the last few photos I need for the exhibit Scarlett's working on and then rattle out instructions for everyone to wrap things as I start packing up. When we're all done, Scarlett wanders up to Harper and me.

"Thank you so much for doing those photos for us. I'm super grateful."

"Of course. Any time. I was gonna go grab dinner, do you want to come?"

"Oh um, I am hungry but I don't want to impose." Her eyes drift between me and the surly quarterback.

"No imposition. You can tell me more about the museum and we can see what else I might be able to help with. Harper's filled me in on a lot but now that she's not there day-to-day anymore it's probably good if you keep us up to date. That way we can make sure we're doing everything we can to support you."

"Yeah, you should come, Scarlett." Harper nods.

"Okay." She smiles and nods. "Did you have somewhere in mind? There's a fun little dive bar down the street that has good pizza."

"That works for me."

"We going to dinner?" Westfield asks as he appears out of nowhere and wraps an arm around my shoulder. I flash him a look, but whatever bad mood he's in has moved to a sort of manic happiness.

"Are you sure you don't want to head home? It's been a long night."

"Nah. I need some food and good company." Westfield grins again.

Scarlett looks at him with disgust, but I don't miss the way her eyes stutter over his chest and arms. And neither does he apparently because he raises a brow at her.

"You coming too, Spitfire?"

"Yes. I'm going, and I have a name," she says shortly, flashing a reassuring smile at me when I give her a questioning look.

I look over at Colt. "You coming, Farm Boy?"

"Would love to." I ignore the sarcasm in his voice.

TWENTY-FOUR

Colt

THE ONLY TABLE they have in the place is a U-shaped booth we all have to squish into. These tables were definitely not made with guys our size in mind, and Joss's warm body's pressed against mine. I can feel every little move she makes—every breath, every laugh, and her fingers graze my leg more than once in accidental contact. Between that and the agitation I feel over Tobias's attitude, blooming jealousy, and the constant reminder that she's not actually mine to claim—I'm grumpy as hell. I also probably need food. Really hunger is probably an underlying problem for most of the people at this table.

"So what's the state of the Drew situation?" Joss asks Harper pointedly.

"I don't know a lot, haven't spoken to him or anyone related to him since Alex told him to leave us alone. Just the bit that I've heard from a couple of mutual friends we still have with him. Although, most of them have cut ties too. Apparently, he's selling the place he just bought and our old house to try and create some cash flow."

"My lawyers are going after him for multiple breaches of contract but that's going to take a while to work itself out in the courts. I guess he's trying to lawyer up with the money," Alex adds. "Frankly, I don't give a fuck what happens to him as long as he stays away from us." Alex shrugs, and Harper wraps her hand around his arm.

"Apathy is the best revenge." Harper smiles up at Alex.

"Agreed." Joss holds up her water glass in a mock toast.

Seeing Alex and Harper happy makes me stupid. They give me the smallest, silliest glimmer of hope. Because if they could make it work after all of those years apart, after she was married to his best friend, then maybe Joss and I have a chance in hell. *Maybe.*

Except then I look to my right and Tobias is leaning over and whispering something to Joss, and the soft giggle that floats out of her a second later makes that bloom of hope return to simmering jealousy. I'm tempted to drag her out of this place, only I'm the calm and collected one so I can't afford to overreact.

Tobias looks up and his eyes lock with mine, a devious grin spreading across his face when he sees me. He has the decency to pull away from Joss though, leaning back and draping an arm behind Scarlett. Her eyes flicker over him and the little twitch of irritation over her lip reminds me of what we're more likely to end up as—mortal enemies who make all their friends worried they're about to cause a scene.

"Do you want to split one of these pizzas?" Joss leans over to me and interrupts my thoughts, her hand on my thigh to get my attention.

"Sure. What do you want?"

"Whatever you want is fine. I can pick the toppings I don't like off."

"Sausage and green pepper?"

"That's perfect." She grins at me.

I stare down at her where her fingers linger. "Pretty sure that's cheating."

"Seating in here is tight. I don't think it can be helped. Might have to sit in your lap if Scarlett and Tobias don't take things down a notch," she whispers. "Not that I would complain."

My heart flickers with hope again as she grins at me, and I try to ignore it this time. I could find peace if I just tried to keep logic on my side rather than lust.

THE REST of the dinner is quiet. Mostly discussions about the nonprofit and the state of the museum, and a little shit-talking between the guys about next week's game. A few fans come up to greet us just as we're wrapping up, and we sign autographs, much to Joss's amusement. When we go to leave Tobias wraps her in a bear hug and spins her around.

"Thanks for taking nudes of me, gorgeous. Can't wait to see what they look like when they're ready. Try not to fall in love with me too hard though, okay?"

"Oh fuck. Too late." She frowns and her palms rest on his chest a little too long for my liking.

"Colton, are you parked back by the studio?"

I nod, still listening to Tobias and Joss.

"Would you mind if I walked back with you? I just don't want to walk alone this late." Scarlett looks at me and I nod again, even though I hate the idea of leaving Joss with Tobias.

It's stupid jealousy on my part. I know that neither of them would act on it, but the easy way she flirts with him and touches him when I want her for myself is wearing on what little resistance I have left. And I'm half certain she's doing it on purpose for that reason alone.

When Tobias hears Scarlett ask me to walk with her he turns to her, and she glares at him.

"I got you, Spitfire. You can keep me safe. That fucking glower of yours is bound to scare everyone off." He holds an arm out for her, and she gives him a brief once over that finds him lacking.

"If your cologne doesn't just make them pass out on site," she mutters. She refuses his arm, but she starts to walk with him all the same.

Joss gives Harper a hug and exchanges a few more words before she joins me again, and we start walking a few paces behind Scarlett and Tobias.

As we get closer to the studio where our cars are parked, she's unusually quiet and the tension is rolling off both of us in waves. I feel like I'm waiting for something to bubble to the surface. Like we're about to combust right here on the sidewalk.

"We going to walk in silence the whole way?" She breaks the silence first.

"Seems that way."

"Are you pissed at me?"

"Should I be?"

"Just say what you want to say."

I stop dead in my tracks and give her a knowing look.

"Stop fucking touching Westfield. Stop flirting with him. And maybe don't eye-fuck him every chance you get."

"Or what?" she taunts me, the ghost of a smile on her lips.

"I'll fuck you so hard you forget other men exist."

"Do it." She grins.

"So you *are* doing it on purpose?"

She shrugs, and I can feel her getting under my skin. Pressing all the buttons as she always does.

"If you want to break the agreement, you can admit it instead of trying to torture me. I'm not taking the bait, Joss."

"Yet." She flashes a self-satisfied grin and somehow, I manage to resist the urge to fuck her up against a brick alleyway by counting back from ten all the way back to the cars.

TWENTY-FIVE

Joss

LATER THAT WEEK it's Colt's turn at the studio, and after lengthy negotiations with his PR team, I've been told that under absolutely no circumstances am I allowed to have him fully naked. That they'd consider underwear, but they want the last say. I've been stewing about it all day because while I don't exactly want all the women of the world seeing him naked either, he is the ultimate bait to get people to buy this book.

Tobias, Alex, and most of the rest of the guys who agreed to be photographed for it have already been in various states of undress for other fashion and ad campaigns. Colt is the one who everyone will want to see. But an idea just hit me, and after a quick text to him, now I'm just hoping he shows up in twenty minutes with what we need to do this justice.

When he walks in there's a storm cloud over him. He's irritated, and I don't know if it's with me or the world.

"You ready to be a centerfold?" I joke trying to break the tension following him.

He tosses his bag down and his eyes drift over me, a small smile dancing on his lips when he sees I'm wearing a dark jade green skirt for his benefit.

"Still trying to bait me?" he asks in return.

I uncross my legs, spreading them slightly and giving him a devilish grin. "Is it working?"

"Honestly, it might today. It's been a rough one, and the idea of being buried inside you, listening to you come from how much you like my cock? I'm tempted."

I cough, sputter, and sit up in my chair. "I'm sorry. Who are you, and where is Colt?"

He leans over and whispers against my ear, "I can play too." He's grinning again when he pulls away from me, and it's unfair how easily that smile melts me every time I see it.

"I'm not sure you deserve the gift I got for you then." I pretend to scowl at him.

"You got me a gift?"

"Yes, as a thank you for doing this despite the fact your PR team has been a nightmare. I'm sure they're giving you a lot of pushback on even being here. I hope that's not part of the reason for your bad day."

"They'll get over it. I'm sorry we can't do it how you'd like."

"It's okay. I have an idea for how we keep them happy but do something that could be even hotter."

"Oh yeah?"

"Yeah. But we'll get to that in a minute. First..." I reach into my bag and pull out the black box.

"What's this?"

"Open it."

He undoes the box, sliding the top open and pulling back

the insert, unveiling the pale teal oval and remote inside. He puzzles at it and then looks up at me.

"What's this?"

"An apology for torturing you. I'm not promising I'll stop, but this might even the field a little bit."

"How so?"

I pull it out of the box and hold up the two sides. "It's a remote-controlled vibrator, and it has a little magnetic piece here so it can be used with whatever pair you want to see me in. This is the remote. But there's also an app it can connect to if you want *remote* access."

His eyes lift to meet mine, and a smug smile tugs at the corner of his mouth.

"And when are you wearing this?"

"If you're good? Tonight."

He grins at me and takes a step forward but stops. Frowning at the box and then at me.

"Fuck you make this hard, you know? Right now, all I can think about is kissing you."

The burst of honesty from him about something so sweet takes me off guard, and I feel a flutter in my chest, the slight dip that makes me feel like I'm off my axis and able to spin off course any second.

"Me too," I admit.

"Good. Then I *know* I'll get to torture you with it." He glances back as he sets the box on a side table.

"I suppose I deserve that."

"So what do you need me to do to get started?"

I snap back into business mode then, working him through the first set of photos I want to take. Most of them are just of him being his handsome self, relaxed, and doing his sweet Midwestern charm thing. Black and white in his street clothes and in his uniform, and then slowly shedding those clothes to reveal his chest and abs. As long as I stay behind the camera, I can forget how very real and gorgeous he is. How much I want him. But when I pause to look up... That's when I fall apart. So I try to limit it, going through my paces as quickly and professionally as possible. Treating him just like any of the other guys.

Until we get to the last round. The one I'm not sure how he'll react to.

"All right. Now for the hard part."

"What's that?"

"Did you bring the gray sweats with you?"

He pulls them out of his bag and holds them up.

"Perfect. Strip out of everything else and put those on."

"Okay..." He gives me side-eye. "I don't see why this is difficult."

"Oh, my sweet summer child..." I grin at him.

I regret my taunting a moment later when I have to watch him change, and every muscular line of his body is on display as he slips into his sweats. They're tight, and already hugging him in most of the right places. I set my camera aside and pull them lower on his hips, making sure we get a good view of his Adonis belt.

I step back and take a few photos, a shiver running up my spine when I see how good they are. It's silly that he still makes me feel this way, but I can't help myself.

I put him through the paces, doing different poses and angles, teasing and taunting him to get some of the photos I want. After another twenty minutes or so, I finally call it. I flip through the previews and grin as I see how they've turned out.

"That bad?" He smirks.

"Just remembering what you looked like when I first met you. You had on a pair like this. And yes. They're good. Shit hot, honestly. I can't wait to edit them."

"You remember what I was wearing?"

"They were gray joggers so yes, I remember. The one thing you athlete types could really teach musicians to embrace more."

"Huh. I don't remember what you were wearing the first time I met you, but I definitely remember what you wore when you saved me at that party."

"I should hope so since you peeled half of it off me."

"You weren't exactly complaining when you were straddling my lap."

"It was a nice lap." I shrug one shoulder as I flick through more of the photos.

"Yeah?" He wraps his hand around a fistful of my t-shirt and pulls me down onto his lap as he slides back into the couch I have in the corner of the studio.

"This is touching, a.k.a. against the rules," I say as I reach over and set my camera down on the table before it breaks.

"Nah. This is just revisiting a memory. I wish you had that corset on again. And those garters... You were so damn hot that night."

"Because I was supposed to go to a club after. Not stay at a frat party trying to save your ass."

"Again, not what I remember you saying when you were grinding on my cock and whispering dirty things in my ear."

"That frat punch was strong."

"You blaming the punch for wanting to fuck me now?" He gives me an incredulous look.

"No. I blame you being shirtless like this and how soft your skin was for wanting to fuck you. The size of your cock didn't hurt either."

"Jesus, Joss."

"I'm just being honest. You had a good personality too."

He laughs and grabs the box off the side table, takes the remote out, and sets it aside, handing the rest to me.

"Go put this on."

I raise a brow in defiance because I know I promised he could torture me but straddling his lap like I am now already feels like the start of that. I'm not sure I can handle more.

"I was good for you. Did all your photos the way you wanted tonight. So go put it on and come back and sit on my lap." His brow matches mine as he reminds me that our agreement is based on favors. So I take the box silently and walk to the small studio bathroom, trying not to smile until I've shut the door.

TWENTY-SIX

Colt

SHE ACTS nonchalant when she reenters the room, even as she sits back down on my lap straddling me. All the way until her eyes catch on the remote in my hand. That's when they snap to mine.

"This *is* cheating you know."

"Nah. You're just sitting on my lap. Several layers of clothes between us. We're good."

Her green eyes narrow, and she makes a face like I'm being ridiculous.

"Cheater," she whispers.

So I press the tiny turquoise button on, using a medium setting, and hear the faint hum a second before she gasps and doubles over.

"Colt! Holy. Fuck."

I turn it up another notch and she buries her face in my

shoulder, little mewling gasping sounds come from her as she digs her fingers into the couch cushion beside me.

"Unfair, unfair, unfair..." she mutters into my skin.

I hit the pause button, and she pulls herself upright again, glaring at me but staying silent.

"What did you call me again?" I mock her.

She stays silent so I flick it back down to the lowest setting and turn it on. She closes her eyes, tilting her head back. Trying hard not to react as her fingers run over her thigh, trying to keep her calm. I turn it up another level.

"Fuck..." she moans. "I hate you. So-fucking-much, St. George."

I watch her as she rolls her lip between her teeth and her eyes shutter, lost in the moment. I'm torturing myself doing this, watching her react like this without really being the cause of it—unable to touch her.

Her eyes half open again and study me, unamused when she sees the grin on my face. I reach forward even though I shouldn't, running my thumb over her lower lip, pressing against the plump curve of it as I turn the setting up again and she gasps. Her tongue darts out and she licks the pad of my thumb, her hips starting to rock forward. She slides her lips around the tip of my thumb and sucks for a second before a moan rumbles free from my throat. Her eyes search my face and she grins as I pull my hand back a safe distance.

"You should cave and fuck me. Put me to good use instead of just teasing me to death."

"You want me to fuck you?"

"I want *you* to want to fuck me."

"Cave, and I will." I shrug like I'm unaffected, turning the vibrator up another notch.

"Oh my god..." A series of curses rip out of her, and her

eyes narrow on me. A glare there like I've never seen before just before a smug little smile flits across her face.

She slides forward, her legs spreading wider as she lines her clit up with my cock, making me feel the vibrator through my clothes. I drop the remote and grab her, pulling her close against me, and she starts to rock her hips again.

It feels like fucking torture, the vibration and the friction of her through the fabric. Making me dig my fingers into her thighs as she moves just to try to stay grounded. The look on her face lets me know she's loving every second of this. She reaches down, pulling the hem of her shirt up over her head and tossing it to the side.

"Jocelyn..." I warn her as I see her hands going for her bra straps. She ignores me and pulls them down, unsnapping the clasp and letting it fall off. "Jesus Christ, what are you doing?"

A wry smile dances over her lips as she leans forward just that touch more, the movement giving me more contact with the vibrator, and my cock can barely take it given how hard I am right now. Her lips go to my ear and her heavy breathing has goosebumps breaking out across my skin.

"Revisiting a memory," she whispers as her hands go to my shoulders.

"This is beyond cheating," I warn her.

"Your fault for starting it," she counters.

My hand slips back over the curve of her hip and thigh, wishing desperately that I could have her naked right now. I lean back and slide further down, too stupid and desperate to stop. It only gives her more access.

A thing she puts to good use immediately, grinding over me in slow torturous circles of her hips. She grins at the admission of weakness on my face as I stare up at her, sliding over me again, her hips rocking and her breasts swaying with the motion. I let out a frustrated groan as I close my eyes, trying to stay sane.

"All you have to do is say the words. Tell me to get on my knees, or strip down and ride you. Anything you want I'm yours. Just say it," she taunts me mercilessly.

"You're fucking evil." I fumble around and feel for the remote again, cranking it up to just shy of the last setting.

I slide my hand between us, finding the hard little disc and press it flush against her clit until she starts to quiver. I need her to come because this version of her on the edge isn't something I can withstand. Not when she's writhing on my lap and promising me anything I want. I refuse to lose though. In the long term, I know I will. I realize that much now. But I have to at least pretend like I can hold my ground against her.

She moans and buries her face into my shoulder. Her body is shaking as she comes hard, too overwhelmed to hold it off any longer. When her grip on my arm loosens, I release the pressure. Reaching over and turning the vibrator off as I hear her take a deep breath, seeking the oxygen she's denied herself buried against my skin. I slide my hand over her hip and up her bare back, tracing the long line of her spine. Because if I have the opportunity to touch her—I'm taking it.

Her face is still pressed against me when I feel her hand move, searching in between us and going to the waistband of the joggers I have on. I'm still so hard and desperate for her to do anything—touch me, suck me, fuck me—I literally don't care what it is as long as she's involved, and she calls the game first. But she doesn't say a word as her fingers start to slip under the fabric, and I grab her wrist.

"You have to say the magic words first."

"Let me make you come?" She grins against my shoulder.

"Ha. The real ones."

"Farm Boy, you made the fatal error of letting me come first."

"By design."

She sits back and studies my face. "You're really this determined?"

I stay silent but give her a smug smile in return, one I don't really feel right now because I'm still desperate for her.

"You don't want me to touch you?"

"We agreed. It was your idea if I remember right." I raise a brow at her, bluffing my way through this. She watches me, her eyes locking with mine for a moment and then drifting over my face down to my lips.

"Fine..." She frowns. "I'm not caving on the *whole* thing. But I'm caving on one part of it. I want to kiss you."

"So you can torture me some more?"

"No. Because I miss it. I miss you."

The simple words twist the organ inside my chest, and I nod without considering the consequences. She leans forward, her lips brushing over mine in soft teasing strokes. She tastes like the lemonade she's been drinking while she works, sweet with just that touch of sourness. I miss her. The realization floods every sense I have—the smell of her conditioner, the feel of her lips on mine, the way she tastes, the little way she flicks her tongue over my lower lip to tease me.

I go under her spell. Kissing her back like I'm desperate to feel her again and getting dragged under by the touch of her lips against mine. I run my fingers along the edge of her jaw and slip them back into her hair as I push it back from her face. She melts into me like she's been starving for this kind of affection and missing it for far too long. It's all too-fucking-much. Reminding me of what I had and lost. Wishing I could take it back and lie to her then like I'm lying to her now.

Maybe I would have never lost her in the first place if I'd

been able to pretend I can just fuck her and not feel. If it means I get another taste, another touch out of her—one more chance to feel like this—I'd take it. Even if it means it all burns down in the end.

A moment later she pulls back, looking dazed and almost drunkenly happy as she smiles at me, and I stand us both up and give her a swift pat on the ass before I say something stupid too soon.

"We should get packed up and get some food."

She blinks, like she's coming to and nods her agreement to my plan. "Right."

TWENTY-SEVEN

Joss

"HE'S GOING to die when he sees that." Violet shakes her head at the fact I'm wearing a Westfield jersey as I sit next to them in the box for the Thursday night game.

"It's not her fault. Tobias made it a condition of letting her have the ticket to sit with us up here," Harper defends me.

"She could have just asked Colt for one," Violet argues.

"Colt doesn't have any because his family never comes, and he doesn't date," I say, watching as the man launches a throw downfield that Ben catches and takes off with, being tackled just short of the end zone. I assume this is still a good thing when the entire crowd goes wild over the play.

Violet pauses to scream and clap for her man and then turns back to me, raising an eyebrow and giving me a look like I'm dense.

"He's the fucking quarterback. He could say he wants ten

tickets, and they'd find a way, Joss. You're baiting him, and you know it."

"I mean if it bothers him so much then why didn't he offer me a ticket?"

"Because you hate football, and he assumes you'll say no would be my guess."

"I don't hate football. I enjoy seeing tight asses in those little pants and watching them all wrestle each other to the ground. It's the scoring and all the stats and nonsense I don't care about."

"So... just the things that matter then."

"I think we have different definitions of what matters in life, Violet." I slide her a side-eye, and she shakes her head at me, laughing as they set up for another attempt at the end zone. A moment later Colton tosses Westfield the ball for an easy touchdown, and the stadium loses their minds again.

"Touchdown!" I yell, throwing my hands up. "See, Violet. I understand the things that matter."

AT HALFTIME we're eating a snack, and I'm sharing my funnel cake with a little blond-haired boy with bright blue eyes who's so damn cute he almost makes me think I want kids.

"May I have some more strawberry sauce please?" He looks up at me wide-eyed.

"Way, I've told you twice now that her funnel cake is *not* your funnel cake." Mackenzie's business tone is enough to put anyone in their place, but he gives her sad eyes.

"I asked nicely, and she said it was okay!" His lower lip rolls under.

"It's okay, really," I mouth the words to Mackenzie, the little boy's mom. She sighs and gives me a half smile and nods, looking exhausted.

"You want some more strawberry sauce, here you go." I hold the cup down for him to dip his piece of funnel cake in.

"Thank you very much, ma'am."

"Ma'am." I cough. "Okay, little guy if you want more strawberry sauce we need to move to a new name. I'm not ready to be a ma'am yet even if I look it."

"My daddy says I should call all ladies ma'am. He says it's proper to talk to ladies like that."

"I'll bet he does." I laugh and look at Mackenzie who's shaking her head. "You like watching your daddy play football?"

"Yes...yeah. Yes. He says life is all about football, women, and the great state of Texas. I've been to Texas you know. To see my Gammie. She lives down there. My uncle doesn't though. Not anymore. He plays football too."

"Oh does he?"

"He does. He told me when I... when I..." he pauses for a moment, distracted by dipping his funnel cake in the strawberry sauce again. Grabbing a giant glob that threatens to drip off the end before he catches it. "He, my uncle, he says when I'm big I'm gonna play football too and get all the ladies. Or I mean all the ma'ams."

We all burst out into laughter then.

"I'm gonna have to have a talk with your uncle if that's what he's telling you." Mackenzie sighs, but a grin erupts in its wake.

AFTER WE FINISH the funnel cake, and his impressionable ears are a safe distance away, I look up at Violet and Harper.

"So are you coming to this party too?"

"I might go for a little bit if Alex is up for it."

"I doubt it. Ben is not a fan. He likes to just chill out when his games are over, and he's not into the whole public debauchery."

"A curmudgeon already at his young age. Look what you've done to him, Violet."

"Yeah, well he's very into the private debauchery, so I don't mind." She smirks.

I sigh. "I just need some debauchery, period. Public. Private. I don't care."

"And Colt's still playing the priest?" Harper looks at me with pity.

"We said we wouldn't. Given our past."

"Oh, I think you should tell her the whole story." Violet side-eyes me again.

"I *was* promised a backstory. Is this the backstory or a new story?" Harper perks up at that.

"A remake. They're playing a game of chicken. Seeing who caves and asks for sex first." Violet rolls her eyes.

"Um excuse you, no. We agreed to keep our hands to ourselves and not get involved physically again because it ended so poorly last time."

"And that's what you've been doing... *not* getting involved —physically?" Violet's brow goes sky-high, and she says it in the most obnoxious tone possible while Harper stifles a laugh.

"Listen... I haven't had a good hookup in... Let's not even say how long because it's embarrassing. So I can't help it if temptation is constantly at my door. That's why I said, tell me what's going on at this party. Maybe I can have some fun there." I laugh because there's no way I'd do it, and Violet knows it.

"So Colt can get arrested for murder? No, thank you. I like the Phantom's chances this year and my husband needs his quarterback."

"Yeah, I don't think I would want to see Colt mad. He's always so calm and quiet," Harper adds.

"He'll be fine."

"Famous last words."

TWENTY-EIGHT

Colt

WHEN I GET out of the game, I start to head straight for my car. I'm fucking exhausted. The game was hard fought, and I'm thankful we won but it wasn't without me hitting the turf one too many times. We desperately need new linemen, especially on the outside. Prescott and Slader are doing a solid job, but they can only do so much. Daniels had been a mistake just like we all predicted and ends up on his ass so much that he's virtually useless.

As I pass by the area where the families meet up with the players, I see someone wearing a Westfield jersey. Someone that looks distinctly like a black-haired, green-eyed woman who spends a lot of her free time attempting to torture me. She's amused, and she spins around in the jersey as Tobias watches. My blood runs cold when she leans into his shoulder laughing.

If she's in with the families, it means she has a player's family ticket, and it definitely wasn't mine or Ben's. My heart rate ticks up, and I start walking in her direction. I have no clue what I'm going to say or do when I get there, but I'm ready for this weird flirtation she has going with Westfield to be snuffed out for good.

He sees me coming before she does, and I watch him give me an amused once over and then haul ass out of there before I can get close enough to say anything. She looks up a little dazed, her eyes searching for where he went and why. She starts to walk out and down the hall, presumably back to her car or to find him. I stalk behind her, grabbing her around the waist and hauling her into one of the side hallways that leads to the stadium seats. Pulling her into a space where there's an alcove and pressing her against the wall.

It's late and all the fans are gone. The stadium's dark and even the cleaning crew is starting to pack up, so it's just the two of us here. A small squeak comes out of her at being startled and then she looks up at me confused.

"Farm Boy, you scared the shit out of me. Jesus." She presses her hand to her heart.

"What the fuck are you doing?" I rasp, pinning her up against the wall.

She looks at me wide-eyed.

"Walking to my car?"

"I mean what are you doing with the families and whose fucking jersey are you wearing?"

"Oh. Yeah..." Her hands go to the jersey as she looks down at it. "Tobias gave me a ticket on the condition I wore his jersey... So I did."

"Tobias gave you a ticket?"

"Well, technically I asked. I wanted to sit with Violet and Harper, and I didn't want to make them sit down in the stands. Especially since Harper is semi-famous after that little stunt Alex pulled." She looks up at me like she's done absolutely nothing wrong, blinking innocently with a faint smile on her face.

"Why didn't you just ask me?"

"I heard them say you don't have tickets, since your family isn't out here often. And I was already planning to go to Tobias's party tonight, so I just asked while we were talking."

The mention of my family alongside this discussion of Tobias's party is pressing my buttons again, frustrating me, and making me worry at the same time.

"How much are you talking with Tobias now? I thought you said nothing was going on there."

"Nothing is going on there. We're just friends."

"Just friends. Like us?" I give her a pointed look.

"No. Not like us."

"You're not going to that party. It's nothing but sex and alcohol fueling a bunch of insane shit that Tobias shouldn't even be participating in. But then he refuses to grow up or listen to anything I say. The same way he thinks it's hilarious to give you family tickets and put you in his jersey. And you just fucking play along." My tone is laced with contempt, and I watch as her face shifts as she takes in the fact I'm legitimately pissed off.

She reaches out and her palm slips down my chest.

"Or maybe you just need to have some downtime and a chance to relax. Not have all this weight on your shoulders."

"Relax," I scoff.

"You're right that Tobias probably needs some grounding. But you need some... whatever the opposite of that is, maybe just fun? I'm sure that's why he's teasing you. You're still very young, Colt. You have your whole life ahead of you. You don't always have to be this reserved—strung this tight."

"I'm fine."

"Then go to the party with me. When I was your age, I

would have died to be invited to parties like this one. So I can pretend to be young again and you can take the night off from pretending to be old."

I don't know how the hell she does this. Turns the whole thing around and makes it seem like a reasonably good idea. Like I'm the one being ridiculous about the situation. I know I can't talk her out of this party though, and if she's going... I'm going.

"Fine. I need to go home and change though."

"Me too. You want to pick me up, or I can meet you at your place?"

"Come to my place, and we'll drive from there." Because while I haven't admitted defeat yet, I fully intend to have her in my bed tonight. "Ben and Violet not going?"

"No. Violet says Ben doesn't care for them."

"Because he's smart."

"Okay well, you can join him in being a curmudgeon tomorrow. But tonight you're mine, and we're going." She grins as her eyes drift over me, and I want to kiss her so badly. I almost do, my lips a hairsbreadth away from hers before I pull back.

"Whatever you wear tonight better be for me." I smack her on the ass playfully. "Now let's get you to your car."

WE'RE NOT at the party long before the music is insanely loud, and half the people here are already drunk. Joss is enjoying every second though, flitting around making friends, and chatting with everyone she meets. I watch her from a barstool when Tobias comes up and throws an arm around me.

"Can't believe you came, but I'm glad you're here. You want a drink?"

"Nope. I've got something." I hold up the glass of flavored soda water I'm sipping.

"Did you see your girl after the game?" He grins.

"Yeah, I saw your handiwork." I shake my head.

"And nothing?" He looks at me, disappointment staining his face.

"What did you expect would happen?"

He runs a hand over his face. "Listen I am trying fucking hard here to give you the excuse you need to just take what you fucking want and you drop the ball at every-fucking-turn."

I frown at him. "Are you drunk right now?"

"No, I'm not fucking drunk. Your girl, she wants you. But she wants you to want her, okay? And I don't mean you sit around and wait for her to make the fucking move. *You* make the move."

"You don't know her. We agreed not to get involved while she's here."

"I don't know her well. But just the few conversations we've had about you... The way she looks at you when you're around. You're dense as fuck if you think she doesn't worship the ground you walk on. She's just trying to give you your space if you want it. She told me she hurt you before, and she regrets it."

I don't love the idea of them having heart-to-hearts about me, but now I'm a little curious. I shake my head though because I can't imagine Tobias is a good source of information.

"Because you're so fucking good at relationships."

"Relationships, no. Sex. Women. Figuring out what they want? I could medal in that if it was an Olympic sport. Fuck... Listen to me. Women like her are in charge all fucking day long. They make all the moves. All the decisions. Smile at assholes more times than should be humanly possible. When it comes to sex, sometimes they just want to get fucked hard against a wall by someone who knows what they're doing to forget for a bit."

"I'm well aware of what Joss likes. I just don't want to fuck shit up where she's concerned." I can't afford to lose her, not now that I have her back in some form.

"Well, bad fucking news. You're fucking it up as we speak. She's over there, chatting up Danvers and Oliver while you're sitting here sipping a soda."

"I'm letting her have her fun."

"She didn't come to this party to chat while you babysit her. She came to this party for the same reason most of these people do. She brought you here to be that reason. I suggest you go take care of it. Cause if you don't, I'm not gonna let someone like her go to waste on Danvers or Oliver." He grins in a way that actually makes me want to punch him, and I clench my jaw. He laughs in response. "Yeah, that's what I fucking thought. Get. Your. Fucking. Girl!"

TWENTY-NINE

Joss

I'M in the middle of hearing some diatribe about rules and referees when I suddenly feel a hand around my wrist. I look up to see Colt standing over me.

"Come with me." He nods his head.

"Oh um, I guess, excuse me," I say to the two guys I'd been talking to.

One starts to protest but when he sees it's Colt standing behind me, he just gives a lift of his chin and goes back to talking to his buddy. Colt's grip around my wrist tightens as we weave through the crowd, and I follow him.

"Thanks for saving me from that shitshow, but is there a fire or what's...?" I trail off when I realize I'm not getting an answer, and I'll just have to wait to see what my fate is.

We come to a set of double doors, and he opens one up, ushering me inside and then closing and locking it behind us. My eyes have to adjust because this room is darker but as I blink, I realize it's a library. A substantial one, with a spiral staircase that leads up to a second floor and reading tables that actually have open books on them.

"What in the other world is this?" I stare at the massive space.

"Yeah, Tobias is a giant nerd. It's his dirty secret. This isn't where we're going though."

"No?"

He takes my wrist again and leads me up the staircase and over a catwalk, up another set of stairs to a mezzanine area that sits just in front of a massive window. Moonlight pours in through it, and I imagine this is how the library is lit indirectly during the day. There are a few big leather chairs sitting in front of the window alongside a telescope, and a bar cart. Whiskey tumblers and bottles are scattered over the top of it.

"I feel like we're entering his secret lair where he plots his evil plans or something."

"Just a place where you can get a birds-eye view of the party. And I can get some quiet," he says as he walks me up to the glass.

I look down, and I can see all the people outside in the heated pool and hot tubs. It even has a very interesting angle into the pool house. I raise an eyebrow when I can see the view in there.

He shrugs when his gaze follows mine to the couple there. "You wanted to enjoy the debauchery."

"Is this your usual spot?"

"I don't usually come to these parties."

"But you must have at some point, or you wouldn't know this exists."

"I used to. Trying to be a team player and keep an eye on Tobias because I always worry one of them is going to get out of hand. I can't afford to lose him."

"Right." I nod, listening but partially distracted by the scenes out the window. "So you'd just sit up here and... watch?" I bite my lip, trying not to smile at the idea of Colt up here like a voyeur, sipping whiskey and people-watching.

"Yep. Until I got tired of watching."

I don't miss the change in his tone, and I can practically feel the heat of his body as he presses closer behind me.

"I love watching you... come apart for me while you were angry in that shed, taking those photos for me, moaning while I fucked you with your toys on my bed. If you want to keep playing those games, I'll play as long as you want."

He drags his knuckles down the length of my spine that's exposed by my dress and a shiver breaks out over my skin. I don't speak because I want to hear him out before I say anything.

"But we don't have a lot of time left, and there are so many ways I could take care of you. Give you the fantasies you need for those long nights on the road. Ones I need for when you're gone. Things you know I'm the only man you'd trust to do for you. Things you're the only woman I can imagine doing them for."

His palm slides its way back up, taking my hair and brushing it to the side, before he presses a featherlight kiss to the base of my neck.

"I'd do anything for you... So you can have the obedient boy you remember, or you can have the man you want to fuck you how you deserve. But you have to choose."

I close my eyes because I can barely breathe. He brings his lips closer to the shell of my ear when he whispers the last bit.

"Just know either way, for the rest of the time you're here— you're mine."

I smile and dig my teeth into my lower lip in an attempt to stifle it. Because everything in my body's pooling warm and low, and I've won the fucking ultimate prize somehow because the sweetest boy on earth has turned into my darkest fantasy realized. I turn around and his blue eyes are focused on me like I'm the only thing in his world.

"Fuck me. Any and every way you want, Colt. *Please.*"

He kisses me then, his lips and tongue on mine in deliberate strokes. His hands wrap around me, and he pulls me tight to his body. His cock is hard against my stomach and a flash of the piercing comes to mind. I nearly beg him to let me suck him off. I keep my mouth shut though because I want him in charge of what comes next, taking everything he wants, when and how he wants it.

"I'm gonna give you what you want first, and then I'm going to take what I need."

His hand wraps around my hair a second later, tightening his grip and his tongue runs over his lip as he looks me over.

"Get on your knees and take me out."

I hit the wood floor hard and my hands scramble for his belt. I'm so desperate to make him fall apart that I almost feel like an inexperienced teenager, trying to remember the right way to do things. His hand goes to my wrists, and he slows me, his eyes watching me with careful interest.

"Slower."

I take my time then. Undoing his belt and his pants, palming him through his boxer briefs, and taking him out slowly. I stroke him gently, taking long painfully unhurried passes from base to tip as I stare up at him, and he watches me. His eyes fixate on my hand until I move my tongue into place, licking the tip and sliding over his piercing where he's already starting to leak for me. The taste of metal and him melting on my tongue.

"Put me in your mouth."

I take him eagerly, swirling my tongue along the underside,

using one hand to slide over the base and the other to cup his balls as I work him over.

"Fucking hell, Dollface. I forgot how good you are at that."

I take him deeper then, letting the tip slide just past the edge of my throat and holding for a moment before I pull away again. The stuttered groan that he releases has me looking up, and his eyes are closed. I miss the deep blue, but he still looks like a fucking dream like this. His fingers tighten in my hair and his hips thrust forward, using my mouth and tongue like I'm his. I'm wetter than I've been in recent memory, and all I can think about is how good his cock's going to feel inside me. How perfectly that piercing is going to hit.

He pulls back a little, and I use my tongue to cradle him as he takes shallow thrusts, sucking and humming as he fucks my mouth. His eyes open then, and he watches like he can barely believe how good it feels.

"Christ, Joss... You kill me. You are the most perfect thing I've ever known in my life."

I take him as deep as I can then, but when he sees the tears starting to form at the corner of my eyes, he pulls me back. Another stuttered moan leaves him, and he pulls out of my mouth.

"Up," he barely gets the word out, and I reach to touch him again after I stand, but he stops me, pulling himself together. And as he lets go of my hair, he speaks again, "Turn around and pull your dress up."

He palms my ass, grabbing a handful and squeezing hard. He kisses the side of my throat as his hand slips between my thighs, and he mutters a curse against my shoulder because I'm soaking wet for him.

"I've mentioned how much I love how wet you get when you really want it, right?"

"When I really need you."

"Take the panties off and pray I have a fucking condom."

I slide them off and a second later I hear a little sound of gratefulness before I hear the foil wrapper open, and I grin as I hang them on the edge of the bar cart. He doesn't waste any time after I bend over for him, spreading further as his fingers dig into my hip. He slides in slowly and out again once, twice, until he's sure that I'm ready for him.

"Put your hands on the glass."

I do as he asks, and I hear the groan of approval that comes out of him as he watches me.

"Spread wider for me," he whispers against my ear, teasing my clit as he does it, and I follow his directions. "Perfect. Just like that. I imagined you like this so many times. Spread for me. Dying to have me inside you."

"I am. I need you."

"Beg for it then."

The words turn my skin hot because it was the last thing I'd expected him to say. I hesitate for half a second before I realize this is what he meant when he said he'd take what he needed. My punishment for leaving him and then taunting him mercilessly the last few weeks. So I apologize the only way I know how—with the truth.

"You're all I can think about. All I've wanted. It's you whenever I close my eyes, and I need you so much. Please, Colt."

"Fuck me," he whispers under his breath and slides inside me a second later.

I moan and fight for purchase against the glass as he fucks me rough and deep. Less like the boy I knew and more like a man who's tired of my taunts and wants to teach me a lesson. Reminding me that he's the only one I'll ever want.

One hand wraps around my chest, dipping under the line of my dress and into my bra. His thumb swipes back and forth over my nipple, the other still working my clit to the edge as he fucks me harder.

"I missed hearing you. How good you feel. Your body's so fucking perfect. Fuck. It's been too long," he curses as he buries his face against my neck.

My orgasm hits out of nowhere, taking me by surprise, and I feel it melt through my nerve endings while I gasp through each wave of it. He fucks me harder then, cursing as his fingers dig into me, pressing me into the glass as he takes himself over the edge a few moments later. He stays still for a few moments, kissing the back of my neck and shoulders as we both try to come down. I blink at the view through the foggy glass, a pane we've left thoroughly marked.

He pulls out, handling the condom and clothes before turning to watch me put myself back in order as a smirk grows on his face.

"Don't be smug, Farm Boy." I grin, teasing him in return.

"Hard not to be when you look like this." He smiles and wraps a hand around my neck, bringing me close and kissing me. It isn't the sweet gentle kiss he'd given me the other night, but one that reminds me of what he said before—whatever happens, I'm *his*.

"So I guess we'll call it a tie?" I ask, not that we ever said what the consequences of the bet would be. Other than the possibility of an ending we've experienced before.

"I guess we can. Although you did beg for it." He grins and grabs my hand pulling me down onto his lap in the chair. I curl up there, resting my head against his chest and watching the party carry on out the window while he toys with the end of my hair, and I start to drift off. Content that I'm finally back with him, however short and sweet it might be.

THIRTY

Joss

WHEN I COME HOME from the latest round of meetings with potential donors, I'm ready to cry, scream and throw things. It'd been hell on earth and one smug jerk after another. Bow here. Kneel here. Kiss this ring. Kiss that ass.

Then the worst part of all, is that after all of that, we're still only a couple of donors richer than we were before I started the day. I told Harper I'd handle this part if she handled the board and some of the other technical things that needed to get done. We still need to hire an accountant and a lawyer, but I was hoping before we finished recruiting the board that we'd have a clearer picture of what our potential endowment and participation levels were going to look like.

Right now? Both look dire. Like I've way overpromised and wildly undelivered. I'm furious with myself and with the entire situation. As I walk into the living room, I can hear Violet meeting with a client in her office, so I sneak quietly upstairs.

I'm gonna take a long hot shower and wash this day off, and hopefully be better off for it. Then I'll talk to the bestie, and maybe she'll have some inspiring words. I can rally. I can do this.

Except twenty minutes later, I'm sitting on the bench in the shower bawling my eyes out. It's all more than I can take right now. The pressure of everything with the foundation is overwhelming, and now on top of that, I've given in to things with Colt.

It felt good to be with him again like it was right in the moment. But now that we've crossed the line I feel the anxiety like I'm just waiting for the thing that's gonna blow us up again. The shoe that drops and means he's ripped out of my life, and I lose him another time. It makes my whole life feel like a house of cards that's just teetering on the edge here. In a place I don't really belong. Trying to do more than I'm probably really capable of. All while attempting to pretend that I'm still the person I was years ago. The one who doesn't feel anything but pure joy and happiness. The one who only wakes up and does whatever she feels like in the morning. The one who everyone counts on to be the life of the party and make all the jokes.

I lean my head back against the tile, trying to wipe the tears away and compose myself. I need to finish this shower and talk to Violet. See if I can at least start by being honest with her.

WHEN I GO DOWNSTAIRS AGAIN and peek around the corner into her office, she's sitting at her desk and the rain's pattering against the windows as she works to make a storage mount for one of the objects she's preparing for loan.

"Do you have a minute?" I ask quietly, trying not to make her jolt.

She looks up at me and gives me a small smile. "Of course. What's up?"

"I need to talk with you about some things. A lot of things, really."

"Okay." She sets the tools down on the table and walks over to the cushioned bench in front of the bank of windows, patting the spot.

I wander over and curl up across from her, staring out at the water as I start my confession.

"I'm just having a rough day, and I think I just... need to talk to someone. Tell someone the truth and see where that gets me."

"Okay. I'm listening..." I can hear the concern in her tone, and I take a deep breath.

"I came back here because I missed you so much, but also because I was a little lost. I still love my work and getting to travel and see all the sights—don't get me wrong—but I think maybe it's taking a toll. Never having a home. Never having friends to spend every weekend with. All my connections are through the phone, and I honestly just feel disconnected sometimes."

"That's understandable."

"Then when I got here, I just saw this whole life you and Ben and Colt have. This whole little community you all have built up and how you all rely on each other. I just wanted to be a part of that, feel like I fit in somehow even if it's only for a few weeks, you know?" I glance at her, and her brow is furrowed, but she's nodding.

"I understand. I'm sure it feels like we've moved on without you. But, Joss, you know we miss you and love having you back here. You're my person, you know, and no matter how long you're gone anytime you come back it's like no time has passed as far as I'm concerned."

"I know. I mean I know you guys will always love me and let me back in, but it's hard not to feel like I'm on the outside looking in. Especially seeing you all married and happy, with your football family."

"You can always be a part of it, you know. You just have to decide you want to be here. I know I'm not the only one who would be thrilled about that idea." She gives me a meaningful look.

"Well, I want to make sense here. Be useful. And now I think I've bit off more than I can chew. This whole foundation thing. I'm sucking at it. I can't get the donors I thought I could, and my magic wand is rusty. I used to be really good at this but given I don't live here, and people don't know who I am..."

"No one's expecting you to work miracles, Joss. And frankly, you've already done a lot. Just the inspiration and boost you've given Harper. She was so defeated, and you've given her hope again."

"But what if I can't deliver on it?" I feel the tears start to come again.

"Joss. You are delivering on it. You're busting your ass. You got the football players organized and donating. You're doing the photos. I know those books are going to sell. It's gonna take a bit to get donors. You're a brand-new foundation. No one expects it to be an overnight sensation. It takes work."

"I guess."

"You know. You'd be giving me the same lecture if this was you on the other side of it."

I nod, staring out the window as the rain splashes against the deck making miniature puddles that shift and morph with each new splattering of droplets.

"I also caved with Colt. Well... I didn't cave so much as I taunted him mercilessly until we both did."

"Ah. So that's what's got you extra anxious." Violet knows me better than anyone. Probably even better than Colt.

"Yes. I don't want to fuck it up again. He's changed—a lot. But so have I, and I don't know if that means we get out of this unscathed or if there's just the potential for this to be even worse this time around."

"I think you've both matured a lot. I'm not worried."

"Ben is."

"Ben has extra worries because he wants Colt's head in the game."

"And I take it out?"

"I mean, he's not unaffected by you. But I wouldn't say you take him out of it. I think you just give him other things to give a fuck about. He's got to figure out how to have something in his life other than football. It's all he does, and it's not healthy. He hangs out with Ben and me plenty and goes to team events sometimes too. But from time to time, I really worry about how narrowly focused he is."

"Yeah, I can see that. He's kind of a workaholic like I am. He gets lost in the pursuit of it. There's a lot of pressure on his shoulders though."

"That's true. And I think you make him forget a little bit of that. Remind him there's more to life than playing flawless games with great stats."

I laugh, and she smiles at me.

"I think with the weather I need some chai. Want to get some with me?"

I nod and follow her out to the kitchen. The relief of having told someone floods me and the tears start to come again.

"Joss?" She looks at me with worry.

"No it's... it's okay. I'm just... whatever happens, I feel better I at least told you about it. You know? Having you listen.

Saying out loud that I'm worried about being a fuck-up. It feels better than just keeping it all inside."

"Well I'm glad." She rubs a hand over my back, and I jolt a little as we hear the sounds of footsteps down the hall, looking up to see Ben and Colt there. Which is fantastic timing because now he's going to have questions, and I don't know how many blubbering confessions about feelings I can make in one day.

THIRTY-ONE

Colt

THAT NIGHT after practice I follow Ben back to his place. He's got a new project he's working on in his boat house that he wants me to look at the details of, and he's offered to have me over for dinner. I'm pretty sure this is just another attempt on his part to play matchmaker between Joss and me, and I'm not really strong enough to fight it at this point. Not after the way she came apart for me. Definitely not after I remember all the reasons I wanted her in the first place, all of which still stand and then some. So if he wants to give me more excuses to see her, I'm taking them.

As we get into the house though and Ben goes to set the food in the kitchen, we're greeted by a scene of Violet rubbing Joss's back while tears fall down her face. I can't make out what she's saying, they're mumbled words that are too hard to hear from this far away, but it's obvious she's upset.

"Ben," Violet says, looking surprised and then giving him an uneasy look before she glances down at Joss.

Joss looks at us then, surprise on her face when she sees me standing next to him, and she stands abruptly. She swipes at her tears and smiles.

"You guys are back early," she says with forced brightness in her tone.

"They cut practice a little early today. I texted Violet."

"Oh, I missed that. Sorry." Violet shakes her head, and Ben walks over and wraps an arm around her before he kisses her cheek.

"And you brought dinner." Joss continues to grin despite how blotchy her cheeks are, and uneasiness stirs in my stomach. "I'm just gonna run and get cleaned up before dinner." She looks at the two of them and then starts moving for the stairs.

"Hi, Colton." There's another forced bright smile as she passes me, and I return the greeting, staring at her as she goes, before I look back at Ben and Violet with a questioning glance.

Once her footsteps are clearly up the stairs, I walk over to them and raise a brow at her.

"She's having trouble with the nonprofit stuff she's working on. And you know how she is... So she's taking it hard that it's not going well at the moment."

"What's the problem?" I ask.

"You should ask her. I don't want to overshare and upset her, but I'm sure she'd tell you if you asked."

"I'm gonna go and talk to her."

"She's in the blue guest room," Violet calls after me as I hurry up the stairs.

When I get to the door, I knock on it lightly.

"Be down in a sec!" she calls through it, and it's obvious she's still crying.

"Dollface, let me in."

There's a long pause, and the door finally opens. She's tried to brush away her tears again, but they're still pooling in her eyes. I've rarely seen this woman cry. Only one other time comes to mind, so I know it must be bad.

"What's wrong?" I ask softly, stepping into the room and closing the door behind me.

A little gasp comes out of her followed by a sob, and she wraps her arms around me.

"It's stupid. It'll be fine. Everything's fine. No one's dead or anything, and I can't even believe I'm crying. *Again.* I just fucking stopped. God, I'm a mess. It's just been a rough couple of days with the nonprofit Harper and I are working on."

I rub my hand over her back and kiss the top of her head. Her arms tighten around my waist, and she takes another deep breath as she buries her face in my chest.

"What's rough?"

"Oh god. What isn't? I think I've just overpromised things to Harper about what I can do here. I wanted to help her, and I thought I could. I'm trying with the book and stuff you know, but I just... The donor stuff isn't going well."

"How so?"

"Well. She's handling the board stuff. Between her and Alex they have some ideas for people who are well-qualified to run that side of things. So I've been trying to get some high-profile donors while she works on that. I mean hopefully, the board members are donors too, but we really need people beyond that group."

"Right." I nod, pulling her over to the bed and having her sit down next to me.

"So I've been working the contacts I have here, and some through Violet. No one's interested in a startup though. They'd rather donate to established funds in the city. One older woman even lectured me on how I was probably just going to split off more donors and muddy the waters and make it worse for everyone. I tried to explain that we're trying to create a pot of money all the museums and cultural centers could pull from, but she didn't want to hear it."

"Well, fuck her."

"Colton," she chides as she wipes a tear away. "Your language."

"I told you. I'm spending too much time around you."

She shakes her head and then leans it against my shoulder. "So now I have to figure out how to tell Harper I'm failing her."

"You're not failing her. You're just hitting some bumps in the road. It was bound to happen. Anytime you start something new like that, it can't go perfectly. You know that," I say softly, running my fingers over her upper arm as she leans into me.

"I'm supposed to do better. Be better. Violet counts on me, you know? She sold me as this magic fairy godmother who could help fix everything. And I'm failing both of them."

"Joss, you are not failing them. It's only been a few weeks. It usually takes months or even years to get this kind of thing off the ground."

"We don't have that kind of time though. I leave in a few weeks, and Harper's old museum needs the money. I talked to Scarlett the other day, and it's getting dire."

"Okay. Well, we can triage this. You find out how much they need and maybe I can help buy you more time."

"It sounded like a lot. And all the guys on the team have already donated what they pledged. It's how we've managed to have any funds at all."

"I can afford to donate more. A lot more really. I could just talk to my accountant about shifting what charities the money goes to this year."

"Colton, no. I'm not taking your money. Especially not at the expense of other charities who need it. I'm just complaining to you because you're my friend." She sits back away from me and scowls.

"I'm a donor the same as any other person, and I'm willing."

"I need more donors. Not to bleed one dry. That's not how this works. Or at least it's not how we build a successful nonprofit. We need to spread out where the money comes from. Lots of little donations from people invested in the cause will be better than a few from high profile donors. It's just doing a fundraiser, contacting all of those people, and getting them on board. That all costs money."

"Okay, so let me pay for that then. I'll front the money to help you get the advertising for new donors."

She's still scowling, but I can tell she's at least thinking about it now.

"Maybe."

"And I know you're not fond of the idea, but you should put me on the board."

The scowl deepens to a glare, and she glances at me and then the floor.

"You're right. I don't like it. At all."

"Why not?"

"Because you're still young, Colton. You're a wildly successful athlete. You should be out, partying and getting wild. Not sitting on the board of a nonprofit using all of your free time trying to cultivate donors. Violet's told me how many you're already involved in."

"Or maybe the board should have some younger opinions on it. With fresh ideas and different leads."

Her lips purse together as she looks at me again. "Stop making it sound reasonable."

"You just don't like that I'd have power over you." I smirk.

"No. Well, I mean, I don't love it. But the bigger issue is

that I feel like I'm taking advantage of you and your celebrity and relying on you to fix problems."

"That's what friends are for, Joss."

"Friendships are supposed to be reciprocal. I'm supposed to be able to help you in return and there's literally nothing I can do for you. You have it all at your fingertips. I don't like that kind of imbalance."

There's a whole host of things only she can do for me. But telling her now while she's crying her eyes out over her work project is not the time.

"I seem to remember you taking in a heartbroken college guy who had just broken up with his girlfriend after she cheated on him and listening to him rant and rave about how awful everything was. And then when he practically cried his eyes out to you—and Jesus Christ is that embarrassing in retrospect—about being a virgin with no game, you spent weeks building his confidence back up and teaching him every single trick you could think of. So I'm pretty sure I owe you a lifetime of favors." I slide my hand under her chin and tilt her face up gently, so her eyes meet mine.

There are still tears on her cheeks, but she cracks a small smile.

"Yeah, but that wasn't completely out of the goodness of my heart. I'd seen you in gray sweatpants without a shirt first."

"Yeah, well this isn't completely out of the goodness of my heart either. Don't worry. I have ulterior motives."

"Expecting repayment for your donations?" A smile flits over her lips, and I can't resist any longer.

I lean down to kiss her, and she melts into me. Kissing me back like I'm her lifeline in all of this. Her lips brushing over mine in eager passes and then she crawls onto my lap, pinning me back on the bed, pushing my hands over my head, and grinning as she straddles me. She grinds down and then leans forward to kiss her way down my neck.

"What kind of repayment would you like St. George?" She grins, the brightness returning to her eyes, and I smile back for a second before I remember that there's food and two people waiting for us downstairs.

I groan.

"What?"

"They bought dinner for all of us. They're waiting downstairs."

"Raincheck?"

"Raincheck."

She stands and holds out her hand to help me up, but I use it do drag her back onto my lap one last time, kissing her again, and grabbing her up into my arms as I stand.

"I could get used to this whole guy-who-can-pick-me-up thing. You think you could throw me around a little more too?" Her fingers latch around the back of my neck as I carry her out the door and down the hall.

"I think that could be arranged," I say as I sit her down at the steps and start to walk down them.

She stops though, pausing and grabbing my arm.

"Colt..."

I look up at her as I watch her face flicker through several emotions and then her eyes run over me, soft and reflective.

"Thank you. *Truly*."

"Of course, Dollface." I smile and grab her hand, lacing my fingers with hers and pulling her down the stairs alongside me.

THIRTY-TWO

Joss

AFTER DINNER we're curled up on the couches watching movies in the living room like old times, only the furniture and the TV are much nicer than what we had in grad school. Violet and Ben are snuggling on their couch, and Colton and I are sitting a chaste distance away from one another on the opposite couch.

Although Violet and Ben are barely watching the movie, and I keep seeing the blanket they're sharing shift and soft little laughs coming from Violet.

"Starting to wonder if we should give them the room," Colton leans over and whispers under his breath. "I'm about to fall asleep anyway."

"Hopefully they eventually find theirs. In the meantime though..." I smirk and then lay back, putting my head in his lap. "Me too. You make a nice pillow"

A smile flits across his lips and he brushes the hair out of my face, wrapping a strand around his finger and playing with the ends. The tender way he looks at me makes me melt inside. I glance up at the screen because I can't bear it anymore, not without wanting to kiss him, and it's one of my favorite scenes.

"I miss this. All four of us just hanging out and watching movies together. Eating takeout. Those were the good old days."

"They're the good days now too when you're here." His voice is soft, and his tone is warm. His fingers still thread through my hair, and his lids are heavy from his long day.

"Because I'm visiting. If I lived here, we'd all be busy and never have time to get together. That's the only good part about living away, when you come to town people actually make time for you and you make time for them. When you all live in the same city, it's like there's always a tomorrow and no one wants to slow down. Everyone's lost in all the hustle and bustle of their adult lives."

"We'd make time. *I'd* make time."

"You trying to convince me to move here, Farm Boy?"

"I'm just saying if the road isn't as appealing as it used to be, all your good friends live here."

"Are we friends again?" I look up at him because I know what he'll say, but I need to see his face to know what he truly means.

"Of course." He gives me an honest smile. "We could have been the whole time if you'd just given me a minute."

There's another giggle and this time I raise an eyebrow and clear my throat because Ben has disappeared under the blanket.

"Some of us are trying to watch the movie, lovebirds." I give Violet a pointed look.

"Sorry. Sorry...." Violet apologizes, looking like she's been caught red-handed. "I'm actually pretty tired. Do you mind if I go to bed?"

"Not at all," I answer because I wish she would. She could take Ben with her.

"Me too." Ben emerges from under the blanket and gives a dramatic yawn.

"Goodnight you two," Colton says in a tone that lets them both know we know they're not going to bed.

"If there are any noises that sound like screaming or moaning, it's just Violet. Sometimes she gets nightmares as soon as she goes to bed."

"Uh-huh." I smirk at Vi.

She shakes her head before she slaps Ben on the ass. "Let's go, sweet cheeks."

"Vi, not in front of company. I told you."

The two of them stumble up the stairs laughing and tickling each other along the way. The second they're out of sight, I breathe a sigh of relief.

"Thank God." Colt sighs.

"Yeah, now I can do this." I climb onto his lap, straddling him, and run my fingers into the short hair at the nape of his neck, teasing his scalp with my fingernails and kissing a trail up his neck.

"Holy hell, Joss..." His hands go to my hips as I grind over his lap and kiss my way over the stubble on his jaw.

"Too public for you? We can go to my room. It's on the other side of the house from their room, so we'd be okay. Might have to sneak you out in the morning like teenagers if you don't want questions though." I rock my hips as I feel him going hard underneath me, and he closes his eyes and leans his head back against the cushion. I run my hands over his chest and slide my tongue over his Adam's apple while he lets out a low groan.

His arms envelop me, and he stands as I wrap my legs

around his waist. "You're an evil woman. My whole body hurts from the drills we ran today, you know that?"

"I can do all the work. You just have to lay there and look pretty."

He laughs as he starts carrying me up the stairs, and I lean forward to kiss just beneath his ear, trailing another round of kisses down his throat and his fingers dig into my ass. I smirk as he sets me down on my feet again when we get into my room and start stripping out of my clothes, tossing them on the floor while he watches.

"Come on. You're not playing fair." His brow furrows as his eyes drift over my body. He groans as he falls to the bed.

"Fine. Fine. I'll let you sleep. I'm just getting ready for bed." I unhook my bra and toss it onto the chair. His eyes track my every movement as he sheds his own clothes, throwing them from the bed to the chair.

He slides under the covers and then makes room for me. "You let me get my sleep, and I'll let you do whatever you want to me in the morning."

"You're saying that 'cause you know I'll be dead to the world in the morning, and you'll just sneak off to practice before Ben and Violet find you." I pout as I get into bed next to him.

"We'll see." He kisses my cheek and curls his arm around my midsection, dragging me close to him. I tuck my head under his chin in turn, throwing one arm over his waist.

I could get used to this. Sleeping with him at my side. Knowing he'll be there in the morning. It's one side of domesticity I don't find entirely frightening.

THIRTY-THREE

Joss

I'M HALF-AWAKE when I feel a gust of cold air over my body, and I reach blindly for the covers to pull them back over me. Instead, my palm comes in contact with a warm bicep, and I lose the edges of reality that were seeping in. I fall back into the dream I was having. One where Colt was fucking me sense-less on every surface in his house and during the breaks in between we eat white chocolate raspberry cake—the one dessert I can actually make—and watch episodes of chateau restoration shows. I really need to make that dream a reality and soon.

Dream Colt's mouth returns to my nipple, his tongue sliding over the piercing there and I arch my back to meet him as his other hand palms my right breast, his thumb stroking over the matching piercing. I spread my legs to accommodate him, and his cock slides between my thighs, grazing me through the cotton of my panties, and I hook one leg around him to urge him on—willing them to mysteriously disappear as they usually do in my dreams.

"Oh my god... How are you this hard constantly? You're like magic," I mumble as one of my hands creeps up his arm, over his shoulder and my fingers drift over the nape of his neck.

A laugh rumbles out of him, and I frown at his amusement. It's an honest question, frankly. I know he's young and athletic and all the things that should make that easier, but we'd already fucked half a dozen times. He should be nearly spent. Another laugh comes, and apparently, I mumbled that last part out loud to him too. *Whoops.*

It doesn't deter him though; his hands and his tongue are focused on turning me into a puddle. I bury my fingers in his hair as his tongue travels down the center of my body. A soft moan escapes me as he kisses me through the fabric of my panties, and I curse the fact that I'm not already naked for him.

"Tell me to take them off," he says quietly, nipping at the inside of my thigh. "Let me eat you for breakfast."

"Okay." Because who the hell am I to argue with that?

"Are you awake?"

"Hmm," I mutter because barely opening my eyes I can tell it's still dark outside. No one should be awake at this hour. Not even our dream selves, and I turn to go back to sleep.

"Joss..." His tone is more insistent.

"Hmm."

"Tell me it's okay to take them off, Dollface. I wanna know you're awake enough."

I frown because this man still doesn't understand the lack of bounds to my obsession.

"Take them off. Rip them. Burn them. Whatever you want. Just fuck me, Farm Boy," I mumble, running my foot along his side.

A laugh rumbles out of him again, vibrating against me, and

his fingers slide under the band and tug downward as he moves with them. He slides back up the bed then, hooking one of my legs over his shoulder as he kisses his way up the inside of my thigh. The warmth of his body against mine and the gentle way he touches me sends me drifting back to the edge of deep sleep, where this dream meets the dark oblivion of nothingness.

Except then I feel his mouth on me, soft exploratory kisses at first and then a full long drag of his tongue over my clit that tears me out of the abyss I'd been drifting into. I thread my fingers through his hair and rock my hips up to meet his face. The real version of him had been amazing at this, and I'd invested time and effort into making him damn near perfect. I just had to hope the dream version could live up to the real thing.

"Oh fuck. You're so fucking good at that."

"I had a good teacher," he mumbles, and I feel two fingers slide inside me as he swirls his tongue over my clit. My nerve endings light up under his touch and flood with warmth, so much that it takes me out of the dream again. I want to cry because I want to stay in this one forever.

I open my eyes, blinking just as he starts to suck on my clit, and I gasp loudly, nearly choking on the sound. My fingers tighten in his hair as I try to reason with this version of reality. Because apparently, I'm *not* dreaming.

"Holy fuck, Colt." I barely get his name out before he's bringing another moan out of me, his tongue and fingers relentless as I writhe underneath him searching for more and less all at the same time.

I try to breathe, think, reason—anything resembling normal function and I can't. All I can feel or see is him as he brings me closer to the edge. His hands knead my thighs and ass as he pulls me toward him, and I turn into a mess underneath his touch.

I've never come so fast in my life, but he's utterly fucking perfect in his execution—of his technique, my clit, and my fucking sanity. I have to grab the extra pillow when I finally come because I remember we're in Violet's house.

I have no idea where they are in the house at this hour, and I doubt they want to hear me. And while it's not exactly a secret that we're fucking—I don't want to rob Colt of the chance to keep it a secret that we're doing it in their house if it's what he wants.

When I can finally breathe again, I pull the pillow away and look up to see him laughing at me, kissing his way up my stomach.

"That is one way to wake a girl up in the morning."

"I thought it might make you less grumpy." His eyes drift over my face before he kisses me, and I wrap my legs around his waist.

"Fuck me, and we can both be less grumpy," I mumble against his lips as I kiss him back.

"No time. I gotta get up and get food. Practice."

I groan. "This is the downside of fucking athletes, isn't it? Amazing fucking bodies but they have to spend all their time on upkeep."

"Something like that." Another laugh rolls free from him and then he grips me tight and pulls me out of bed with him, setting me on my feet.

"I don't have practice." I look at the time on the clock and debate getting back under the covers for a few more hours.

"No, but if I have to walk out and greet Ben and Violet this morning, so do you. You can do all the talking if they have questions." He gives me a look as he slips his clothes back on.

"What are we telling them?"

"That you have an insatiable appetite and I've fallen victim to it again."

"How dare you! Like this is all *my* fault?" I toss a pillow at him, giving him a mock pout.

He tosses it back to the bed when it lands on the floor and then stares at me, his eyes going soft for a moment before he runs up and grabs me, pulling me up into his arms and pinning me against the wall.

"You are so fucking sexy. I just want to stay here and watch you come over and over all day." His lips are on the side of my neck, kissing a trail downward, and I slide my arms around his neck.

"So stay and do that." I tighten my legs around him.

"I think they'd notice the guy who throws the ball is missing."

"Nonsense. Just have a decoy. Ben can put your jersey on and say Farm Boy things. It'll be fine."

He laughs and slaps me on the ass as he puts me back on my feet again.

"Come to my place tonight?"

"I suppose I could be convinced."

"This morning didn't convince you?"

"It was a good start. Some dirty texts throughout the day could seal the deal. A few shots of you in the locker room showers. That will get you anything you want."

He shakes his head at me like I've lost my mind. "Put some clothes on and let's go get breakfast."

WHEN WE WALK OUT into the kitchen, the smell of coffee and pancakes is already permeating, and Ben adds blueberries to the top of the latest batch while Violet sits at the counter on her phone. He looks up from his task to see the two of us but doesn't bat an eyelash at the fact that we're slinking out together.

"Pancakes, Benny?" I run up to his side. "Enough for me and my gentleman friend here?"

He grins. "Yeah, I can make a couple extra. Your gentleman friend needs to eat fast though because we're gonna be late for practice."

Colton reaches into the cabinet to grab us two extra mugs and plates, acting like this is a completely normal routine for all of us. And a few moments later we're sitting down to fresh blueberry pancakes with real maple syrup and a side of bacon.

"Is there a way to stay at this B&B permanently?" I ask as I take a bite and the pancakes practically melt on my tongue. It's not the white chocolate raspberry cake I was dreaming about, but it will do. "Your food is so good, Benny."

"Hey! What am I, chopped liver?" Violet looks up from her inbox.

"Your food is good too, Vi. Delicious in fact, you just have the unfortunate fate of being married to someone who is also magic in the kitchen so like I said. Do you have permanent move-in options?"

"It'll cost you. Especially if you're gonna sneak gentleman callers in the place in the middle of the night." Ben teases me.

"To be fair. You technically called him. I just took advantage of what was available last night. I thought he was part of the turndown service."

Colt makes a scoffing noise as he puts a plate in front of me. "Where's my tip then?"

"Your tip? Your tip is coming later when I do that thing with—"

I'm silenced by Colt's hand over my mouth which he follows with a kiss to my temple. "Do you want cream and sugar in your coffee?"

I nod my yes and he grins in response, making his way over to the coffee machine. Violet looks over at me, raising a brow and then giving me a knowing grin before she returns to her emails.

THIRTY-FOUR

Colt

"I NEED YOUR HELP," I say as Ben and I pack up in the locker room at the end of the day later that week.

"What's that?" Ben asks, glancing up at me before he continues to toss things in his bag.

"I bought a place for Joss. It's a studio with a couple of offices and an apartment upstairs. It's for her to have a place to stay when she's here, give her and Harper a home base, and somewhere she can work without having to rent studio space. My realtor found it."

"Okay..." He looks up at me with a furrowed brow.

"I need you and Violet to gift it to her."

His lips go flat, and he gives me a skeptical look.

"If I try to give it to her, she won't take it. But she won't say no to you two. You know she could use the boost right now."

"I don't know if Violet will want to do that."

"You can convince her."

"Are you sure it won't be better coming from you? The two of you have been getting along really well lately."

"That's exactly the reason I don't want to rock the boat with her. And an expensive gift like that? Her mind will run wild about what it means and why I did it. I just want to help her without stressing her out."

"And you already bought it?"

"Yes."

"Fuck... I guess I'll ask Violet tonight. I can't make any promises though. She's not going to be keen on any kind of deceit where Joss is involved, even if it is for her own good."

"I know... I mean we could make it legit. I could sell it to you." I smirk.

"How much was it?"

"A couple million."

"Yeah, no. I think I'm good with the deceit at that point."

I laugh and toss my bag over my shoulder. "Okay just... let me know what Violet says? Tell her she can call me if she wants to talk about it."

"I will. You and Joss... is that headed somewhere?"

The smile on my face fades, and I shrug. "She leaves in a couple of weeks, and I have no idea when she plans to come back through town."

"But you're buying her a place..."

I can't look Ben in the eye because I know what he's asking.

"So she has somewhere when she's in town. They need the HQ for their nonprofit. A place for their board meetings. The apartment upstairs is just a bonus that's there if she needs it. Fuck, maybe Harper would want it now that she's selling her house."

Ben laughs, "Like Xander would ever let her out of his sight. You know how fast he picked her up from our place?"

"Well... Then maybe it sits empty, or they rent it out for

some extra money. I don't know. The option is there if she wants it."

"I just don't want to see things go down like they did last time."

"We're adults. We've been crystal clear with each other about where things stand generally speaking. I just don't want her to read into this. Think I'm trying to talk her into staying or that I don't think she's capable of getting her own place if she wants. I'm just trying to make things easier on her. She always tries to do everything on her own."

"Yeah. She and Violet both have that stubborn streak."

"So like I said, better if it comes from a fellow stubborn friend than from me."

"I mean you're stubborn in your own ways."

I shake my head. "Yeah, yeah. I know."

A MOMENT later and Alex walks up to me, showered, and dressed, headed out for the day.

"Hey. So Harper and I had a chat after she and Joss talked about the donor situation. I have some prospects in mind. Some friends of my father's who are also football fans that I think we could pull in. I've reached out to a few of them, and they're up for a dinner if we show up. I promised you and me. Figure we can take the girls and they can work their angle while we work ours."

"Sounds great. Just let me know a date."

"One night this week. I'll nail it down with Harper and Joss and check in with you. I'm just warning you though, these guys are old school. Kinda assholes. But they're old money and when they move, their friends move with them, you know? They have deep pockets and have supported my dad's campaign for years."

"Got it. So Joss is going to hate them then."

"I'm guessing yes. Harper is not a big fan but said she's willing to meet if it means saving the museum. She's more motivated than Joss so..."

"I don't know. Joss is insanely motivated on this. It's all she talks about, and she's terrified of letting Harper down."

"Harper won't be let down. She knows Joss is trying to do the impossible."

"I mean we all do, but that won't stop her from feeling like she's got to take on the world."

"Sounds like someone I know." Alex smirks at me, and I hear Ben chuckle as he finishes at his locker.

I shoot them both a look in return.

"Just send me the info, and we'll see what we can do."

"Will do." Alex nods and then heads off.

THIRTY-FIVE

Joss

THE SECOND we get to the donor meeting I can tell this is going to be hell on earth. Harper and Alex are already there trying to make polite small talk, and Colt and I walk around the table to our seats. The entire time the two women, I assume wives of the men Alex's father knew, glower at me like I'm the most disgusting thing they've seen this century.

I'm dressed conservatively. Most of my tattoos are covered, and I'm wearing a simple sheath dress with sleeves that nearly hits my knees. The only bit of personality I currently have on display is the black heels that have a row of spikes down the backs. But they can't even see those from where they are. So it's just me they hate, apparently. The two men give me a lascivious once over I don't appreciate as Colt pulls my chair out for me.

There's a loud round of introductions and boisterous small talk before we finally order our food. It's quickly obvious that they see this as less of a business meeting and more of an opportunity to be seen out and about with Alex and Colt. Punctuated by the fact they stop several people passing their table, one a business partner, another a golf buddy, then an accountant, to make sure that everyone knows who they're sitting with. I cringe a little internally that Colt and Alex are being rolled out like circus freaks for entertainment just to try and help us.

But what really makes my nails dig into my thigh under the table is when the one with the graying mustache, one who doesn't deserve a name, decides to make his opinions on our foundation known.

"All right. I guess we better do a bit of business so we can enjoy dessert in peace," Mustache announces.

"We'd love to hear your thoughts on the foundation now that you know a little bit about it. If you have any questions, Jocelyn and I would be more than happy to answer them." Harper flashes a gorgeous smile in his direction.

"Well, that's just the thing I wanted to discuss with you. Who is going to be running this foundation? Because while I think it's sweet that you ladies got things going with your grassroots interest in culture, I think it's important you've got real business acumen at the top. Someone who knows how to manage money, make wise investments, and really see this thing through."

"We'll be co-directors of the foundation. But we're planning to have a board with lots of oversight from various parts of the community—making sure representation is diversified and we're not missing communities or partners we could be serving." I do my best to mimic Harper's cheerful disposition.

"You two women will be heading it up?"

"Yes."

He chortles to himself, and I'm tempted to chortle his ass into the stratosphere.

"Again I think it's lovely you ladies have done what you've done. Even that little photo book you've got going. I know my wife didn't approve. Thought it was rather scandalous when you heard didn't you, Gladys?" He looks to her with red-faced amusement and she only offers a silent sneer in return. "But I thought it was clever. Get your money where you can from those people who want to get their jollies from your guys. Thinking outside the box. I like it. But I think you need a stronger hand steering the ship. Don't you boys want to be involved?" He looks between Colt and Alex, and my blood starts to boil.

"Oh no, I'm planning to be hands-off. Harper is a thousand times smarter than I am, and these two pretty much single-handedly saved the history museum with their brains and willpower alone. I'm smart enough to know the best thing I can do for them is what I'm told," Alex answers.

Mustache Man frowns and turns to Colt for what I'm sure he thinks is going to be a better answer, and I'm also interested in hearing it.

"I agree with Xander. These two are the brains of the oper-ation. I've agreed in theory to serve on the board if they'll have me, but other than my celebrity I doubt there's much of substance I can contribute that they don't already have in spades."

This man was getting any kind of sex he wanted when we got home.

Mustache Man starts with a wheezing sigh of disapproval and a shake of his head. "I'm not sure how I feel about investing then. While I am impressed with what you've done, I'd much rather see someone at the helm I can be confident in. Have you thought about bringing someone else on? I can give you several recommendations from my club who might be a good fit. Guys with lots of experience." The question isn't even aimed at me and Harper but at Colt. Like we don't exist.

I send him a murderous smile across the table. I hope it looks less fake than it feels—so that when I rip his balls out through his throat, he has no idea it's coming, and he chokes on them. I start to open my mouth to respond when Colt knocks over his water glass and it spills directly into my lap. I gasp as the freezing ice water seeps through the fabric onto my thighs and push my chair back abruptly.

"Oh god. I'm so sorry." Colt dabs me with a napkin. "Damn. Here let me help you. Let's go back to the bathrooms. See if we can find a dryer or some more napkins." He stands and holds out his hand for mine and when I raise my eyes to meet his, I realize this is all a ruse. I grit my teeth but follow his lead.

The restaurant's fancy enough to have one of those lounge areas just inside the restrooms and Colt pulls me into it, locking the door behind us as he reaches for towels out of the basket near the sink and blots my dress again.

"I'm sorry," he apologizes again—a sincere one this time. "He's an asshole, Joss, I know. But he's a powerful asshole in this city. He knows a lot of people. Even if you don't want his money, you don't want to piss him off."

"Someone should put him in his fucking place."

"Agreed. But you ripping him a new one over dinner is only going to convince him his opinions are correct. He won't see reason that way."

"How will he see reason?"

"When you and Harper make this the foundation everyone wants to be involved in. He'll come running back to see his name on the donor wall because everyone who's anyone will want to be on it. When he has to apologize to you for not believing in your vision."

"That's a lovely thought, and currently very speculative fiction. There's not a great road to get there from failure city, population me."

"Alex and I need to leverage our celebrity more for you. Get the word out. Because you were right the first time, Joss. You don't need whales. You need a million little minnows who love you and your cause and will donate every month because they want to feel involved."

"Oh. Can you say that again?"

"What? About the minnows or the celebrity?"

"No the other thing. About me being right." I hold the towels tight to my dress as I grin at him, trying to squeeze the last of the water out.

"You were right, Joss," he repeats it with the flourish of an eye roll.

"Fuck that turns me on." I step forward and grab his tie, pulling him closer until our lips almost meet. "Do you know how hot you are?"

"You've mentioned it once or twice." He gives me that boyish grin, and I kiss him.

"All right. Let's hurry up and deal with these assholes, so you can take me home, rail me, and make me forget this whole night."

He laughs and wraps his hand around mine as we head back to the table, and I'm grateful that I have this guy who keeps me off kilter and balances me all at the same time.

THIRTY-SIX

Colt

THE GUYS and I are all sitting in one of the side rooms at the restaurant they've put together, so we can all eat together the night before this away game without being a giant distraction to the whole space. Tobias is sitting across from me, grinning with amusement as he eats his steak, and I raise an eyebrow at him.

"What?"

"Your girl sent me the edits of the photos she took of me today. She spent a lot of time on them."

I shake my head. "She already admitted you guys were conspiring, so it won't work anymore."

"Did it work at the party though?"

I give him a look, and he laughs.

"What?" Waylon asks when he looks up.

"Colt is down really fucking bad over a woman, and it's fucking beautiful to watch."

"The photographer?" Waylon asks.

"The very one." Tobias grins. "And now he has to sit around knowing she's seeing all of us naked."

"True. I have my shoot with her this week after we get back. Mac's excited about it." Waylon wears a massive grin on his face because the man's wife is obsessed with him. I feel my heart twist a little. It's a lot like watching Ben and Violet. The easy way the two of them seem to make things work. Wishing it was that way for us.

"I bet Joss is too. Especially if she's seen that drone shot the tabloids got of you and Mac on the beach."

"Tobias." Ben sighs.

"Oh, come on. I've waited forever for this. And that it's her? It's too fucking good to resist. Let me have my fun," Tobias grumps in return.

"Like I've said before... the payback for this? It's going to be painful." I glare at him.

"Worth it to see you squirm over a woman."

I shake my head and take another bite of my food because I wouldn't take the bait.

"You guys are good though?" Ben asks, glancing up at me and I can already guess what's going through his head.

"We're good. Better than, honestly," I say with more confidence than I feel because I have to be.

"And what about for this game?"

Ben knows what a lot of the other guys here don't. That tomorrow we're playing a divisional rival, but also the quarterback who took my spot at the college I attended before Highland. The same one who took my ex-girlfriend and then married her.

"Good."

"Kate working?" He raises a brow.

"Who's Kate?" Tobias asks, and I hate Ben a little for mentioning it now.

"A reporter," I answer, the shortness evident in my tone.

"An ex?" He grins.

"Ancient history."

"Like the photographer?"

"Nothing like the photographer."

"Interesting..."

It will be. Because Kate had been leaving comments on my social posts all week and making little comments after our interviews in the past that left me thinking she wanted more than that. And while it's satisfying to know she regrets her mistake; I don't want drama. The rivalry between our teams is enough without having to worry about layering that with more complications. And I definitely don't want anything that's going to rock the fragile new ground Joss and I have managed to cover. I just want to put this team down and this game behind me so that we're one step closer to bringing a trophy home, and I'm another day closer to having Joss again before she leaves.

THIRTY-SEVEN

Joss

I WAIT NERVOUSLY on the counter as I hear a car pull up in the distance. I've kind of broken into the man's home with Violet's spare key, waiting for him half naked with cupcakes like some sort of unhinged stalker, and suddenly this all seems like a very bad idea. Because I don't know what the fuck romantic is. Things Violet and Ben would be wildly amused by might be less than stellar in Colt's eyes. Even if it should be hot. Especially when it's been a long day for him.

When the door opens and he makes his way into the house, turning on the overhead lights, I make myself known.

"Surprise!"

He jumps back, his hand on his heart but it's the second voice that makes me jump off the counter.

"Holy shit!" Another male voice shouts, one not that dissimilar to Colt's.

That's when I realize there's a second person trailing

behind him. One who has the same sandy blond hair and blue eyes and is about an inch shorter than him. And right now, I'm thanking my lucky stars that I opted to wear the robe instead of just sitting here naked. I pull it tighter around me, covering my cleavage but that won't help the fact that my nipples are still showing through the thin fabric, and this robe barely covers the tops of my thighs.

"Holy hell, Joss. You scared the shit out of me."

"Well, I meant it to be a good surprise. I didn't realize you'd have company." I rub my hand over my heart where it's still beating a mile a minute, and he stares at me for a second.

"You know her? Thank fuck. I thought maybe you just had these kinds of women show up for you." The younger guy's eyes flick over me with subtle interest before they return to Colt.

"No, well I mean it's happened before but—"

"It's happened before?" I interrupt because I don't like the idea of naked women waiting for him. That's a new surprise fact because I thought I was all right with the idea of Colt and other women in theory. Turns out, no. Absolutely not okay with it.

"That's why I have the security system." He gives me a meaningful look.

"Oh."

"So is this your girlfriend then? You didn't tell me you had a girlfriend."

I see Colt's face go blank and his brain is struggling to catch up because he doesn't know how to define this.

"A good friend." I offer Colt some cover.

"A *very* good friend by the looks of it." The younger guy smirks as he looks at me.

"Cody!" Colt barks.

"Sorry, fuck. I'm just saying none of my friends wait for me looking like that."

I suddenly realize who he is, now that Colt has said his name. Everything falls into place.

"I didn't know your brother was coming, or I would have stayed at Violet's. I just wanted to surprise you. I have cupcakes!"

"Cupcakes?" Colt walks toward me.

"Yeah, I have these ones if you won and these ones if you lost." I point to them as he looks over the two sets of cupcakes. "See? Fuck bitches. Get money. Because Erickson is a bitch and you make twice as much as him, get it? Anyway sorry the icing looks terrible. I had to do it myself because the woman at the bakery told me she wouldn't make obscene cupcakes. I also didn't have a contingency plan for a tie. But it's the thought that counts right?"

Colt's face contorts and his lips quiver before a loud laugh rumbles through him, and he pulls me to him and kisses me. He smells like soap still from his last shower and the stubble on his jaw scratches against my skin as I kiss him back.

"You're the best." He grins at me when he finally pulls back to look at me and the cupcakes again.

"Are you going to introduce me?" I raise an eyebrow and look back at his brother.

"Joss, this is Cody, my younger brother. Cody, this is Joss."

"Joss?" Cody's eyes light with recognition.

"Joss," I confirm, holding my hand out, and he shakes it giving me a bright smile as he looks me over again with what looks like a new understanding. Apparently, Colt talks about me to his brother. Interesting. My heart flutters a little and I try to regain my composure. "Like I said, I didn't know your brother was coming back with you. I'm sorry."

"I didn't either. He surprised me by getting a flight back.

He left the game a little early and told me to pick him up at the airport. Luckily, we landed at similar times."

"I just wanted to surprise you."

"That's going around today." Colt flashes a smile at me.

I grin at his brother wanting to support him in the same way. Glad that whatever his strain might be with his parents, he at least has one family member in his corner. And from the way Cody looks at him, I'd guess Colt is his own personal superhero.

"Do you want a cupcake?" I ask Cody.

"That sounds fucking amazing." He sits down at the counter, and I pass one to him along with a napkin. "What do you want to drink?"

"A coke?" he asks.

"Coming right up." I go to the cabinets to get a glass.

"Now suddenly he gets waited on?" Colt feigns hurt.

"What would you like to drink?"

"Just some ice water." He grins.

"All right." I grin back at him and work to fix their drinks like I'm some sort of domestic goddess that gets up in the middle of the night to wait on company. I don't know what this guy is doing to me, but it's definitely a new experience.

I hear them whisper something behind me, and I know it has to be about me, so when I set the glasses down in front of them, I give them both a surly look. Cody grins at me in response, and it's unbelievable how similar his smile is to Colt's, just younger and more boyish. As I glance between them, I really see how much Colt has changed.

"How old are you?" I ask Cody just as he takes a bite of the cupcake.

He chews and swallows, wiping some of the frosting off his lip with the napkin before he responds. "Twenty-one."

"A baby. Jesus. Is this really what you looked like when we

met? Was I this much of a cougar?" They both laugh in response. "I'm serious, it's eerie. You should let your future wife know there's a built-in younger model to trade in for. Just in case," I tease Colt, and Cody whistles low and then bursts into laughter.

"I don't play football like a god though."

"That's to your advantage for those of us who don't care about the sport."

"You don't like football?"

"Well, I don't dislike it—anymore. Your brother cured me of that because he looks so fucking sexy playing it. And I like watching him light up when he talks about it. Like a little kid on Christmas. But it's definitely an acquired taste."

"Fuck. I love football. I wish I'd been half as good as him. Instead, I get to go back to the farm when I'm done with college later this year."

"I bet the girls love that though. Working with your hands, riding your tractor... I bet it's bucolic bliss." I lean over, staring at him as I flutter my eyelashes, and he laughs.

"I'm gonna need you to not sound like you're hitting on my brother." Colt's arm wraps around my waist and he hauls me back toward him. I turn around to tease him when the robe I have on starts to fall open, and I remember that I'm still half naked.

"I should probably put clothes on, huh?"

"I'm not one to encourage it normally but..." Colt's eyes slide to his brother. "All this trade-in talk with a cougar in the house has me nervous."

"All right. Be back in a minute." I laugh and give Colt another chaste kiss on the cheek as I leave the room.

THIRTY-EIGHT

Colt

"THAT'S JOSS?" Cody looks at me wild-eyed once she's out of earshot.

"Yes."

"You didn't accurately describe how hot she is. That's a lot of tattoos, and are her nipples fucking pierced?"

"Don't look at her nipples." I glare at him.

"I mean, kind of hard not to when she's all..." He gestures, and I slap him upside the head.

"For my eyes. Not yours. Do. Not. Fucking. Look," I repeat, and he tries to look remorseful and fails miserably.

"Mom and Dad would die if they saw her." He takes another bite of the cupcake she gave him. He's not wrong. They'd hate a lot of things about her.

"She's none of Mom and Dad's business."

"Mom still thinks you might come home and sweep Mary off her feet."

"Mom has a lot of crazy ideas about what my future looks like."

"Is Joss your future?"

"Joss is my friend."

"Cagey as fuck."

"You'll learn when you get older."

"I fucking know what a situationship is bro. I've had a few. Fuck I have one right now. Mom and Dad would hate her too, but you should see what she can do with fruit snacks."

"She... what? Never mind. I don't think I want to know."

"Oh, you *want* to know."

"Who the hell are you hanging out with at college anyway?"

"Well, I'm not Mr. All-American Quarterback, brother. So I'm sure they wouldn't be up to your standards."

"I'm just saying you should be careful."

"Trust me. I learned my lesson a while ago when one girl gave me head and then wanted to know when she could meet you. If you'd be at the next family dinner."

I try to stifle the laugh.

"It's not fucking funny. Living in your shadow. Looking like you. Like Joss said... sometimes it feels like I'm a substitute."

"Not to Mom and Dad. He's training you to run the farm in the summers, right? Wants you to take over?"

"I know you're not fucking jealous over the farm. You wanna run the farm, and I'll play ball for hundreds of millions of dollars while hot chicks wait for me half naked on my kitchen counter when I get home? We can trade bro. Anytime you want." He's half kidding but I don't miss the hint of bitterness in his tone.

"I wouldn't mind seeing you on a farm. Wearing those cute little overalls and a flannel shirt. Hands dirty." Joss grins, her eyes flashing between us as she senses the tension mounting in the room when she returns. "Ooh or better yet, Levi's and no shirt, all tan and sweaty while you toss bales of hay around. Tell me there's hay bale tossing off a truck involved. Please." She grins wide and Cody laughs while I shake my head.

She grabs a cupcake and sits next to him at the counter then, asking him a million questions about college, his major, his girlfriend, and his hobbies. He's thrilled to have that amount of attention focused on him, and my chest aches a little at how easily she makes friends with him.

AN HOUR or so later I've got Cody set up in the guest room, and I've pulled Joss back into my bedroom after she offered to go home and give me some real rest. Swearing up and down I got sleep on the plane, because I want her here with me tonight.

"I'm sorry the game ended in a tie," she laments as she starts to get undressed for bed. "I really wanted to see him get what he deserves."

"Better than a loss."

"But still. He stole your girl. Was she there? Did you see her?"

"Can't steal someone who wants to be to be taken. And no. Thankfully. I guess she wasn't on reporter duty since he was playing. Conflict of interest and all that. And I didn't stick around after to chat. Just got on the bus to get to the airport."

"Well, she's clearly insane to choose the lesser option and marry it. Ugh." Joss shakes her head in disgust. "Although I guess she gets what she deserves. Because she definitely doesn't deserve you."

"I don't care about her."

"No? Don't want a little revenge for old times' sake?"

"No. Barely crosses my mind. The woman who gets me

obscene cupcakes and waits for me in my kitchen after the game though... I can't ever stop thinking about her. And now, thanks to her sheer robe neither will my brother."

She grabs a pillow off the bed and launches it at me. "I had no idea your brother was coming home with you."

I laugh and kneel across the bed to grab her and pull her down onto it with me. She falls under me, a pile of giggles and limbs, and I grin at her.

"I mean, I think that's what you get for pulling a stalker move."

"See, I thought it was cute until I was sitting there in the dark. But then it was already too late." She looks up at me, her fingers wrapping around the back of my neck, delicately tracing lines over my spine.

"I mean it was hot as fuck. We might have to reenact it when he's gone. Take the icing from one of those cupcakes and paint you with it." I kiss her, and she parts for me, letting me taste her and her legs wrap around me.

"I think I did it partially out of jealousy though," she whispers the confession.

"Jealousy?"

"I don't know. I have a wild imagination. I imagined her realizing how much she fucked up and chasing after you to tell you, *you're* the one she really wants."

I sigh because I really don't want to talk about Kate right now when it's late, and all I want to do is be buried inside of Joss. But I don't want her to think I'm keeping anything from her.

"Oh my god." Her legs drop away from me, and she starts to sit up. "Did she? Because she better stay away from you, or I will kick her ass. But if she's trying to cheat on him with you, I mean I guess good for you."

I shake my head, running my tongue along the inside of my cheek.

"No, she didn't chase after me. But she's a sports reporter, and she's interviewed me a few times. A couple of them when it was just one-on-one with the videographer."

"And?" Joss's brow raises.

"She's implied she'd be open to it. Nothing blatant but obvious enough all the same."

"Well..." Joss lets out a little sigh. "I guess I can't blame her. Do you want her back?"

"Fuck no."

"Are you sure? Because I remember what you were like when she got with him. You really loved her a lot. It broke my heart to see you like that. I know even with all the stuff Ben had going on with Violet he was worried about you."

"That was years ago, and I was young and stupid. I didn't even know what love was then." I realize what I've said as soon as it comes out but before I can backtrack, she smirks.

"I mean, I did try to tell you that."

"I don't mean with you. I mean with her. With you—"

She puts her fingers to my lips. "You don't have to explain, Colt. Jesus, real love or not you were still heartbroken over the fucked up shit they did to you, and finally getting head for the first time in your life. So I didn't blame you for the confusion." She laughs a little to try and disrupt the tension between us but my chest tightens all the same.

My heart thuds in my chest as I remember confessing I was in love with her and her looking at me like I'd lost my fucking mind. Scrambling out from under me a second later and putting her clothes back on while she made excuses about forgetting she needed to meet someone and running out of my place a second later. Another memory of trying to go to her at her apartment and explain the next day, and her telling me she thought I should probably just go to a party and fuck someone my own age comes just after... And I'm surprised when the wound still reopens just that little bit all these years later. I open my eyes, and her hand slips over my jaw as she studies me.

"I'm sorry I was such a heinous bitch to you back then. You scared the fuck out of me. You were so sweet. So raw and honest, and just everything I had no idea what to do with. I didn't deserve you, and you deserved better than me."

"You were exactly what I needed, Joss. I just wasn't what you needed. That's the problem for us in this universe—we're never the right people and it's never the right time."

"But I like pretending it is," she whispers, her green eyes so intense that I get lost in them for a long minute as I look at her and run my fingers over the long line of her neck and over her chin and lips.

I hook my fingers in the waistband and pull her panties down her legs, kissing her stomach and her thighs as I go. Then I stand to finish stripping down, and I move to the nightstand when her hand goes around my wrist.

"I'm on birth control if you want to take me bare."

"Is that what you want?"

"I want you to fuck me like I belong to you."

I climb back on the bed, dragging her body underneath me and sliding my cock through her wetness. Because I'm not wasting a fucking moment I have with her or any opportunity she gives me to have something of her I haven't before. It makes me think about what it could be like if she was here for me all the time. If she belonged to me for real.

"If you belonged to me on a night like tonight, I'd just come home tired from the game and want you naked in my bed. So I could slide inside you and fuck this sweet pussy awake. My fingers bringing your clit to the edge by the time your eyes flutter open because I know exactly how to touch you."

"Fuck, Colt..." she moans as I drag the head of my cock over her clit, back and forth slowly as her hips roll up seeking more friction. "I want that so much."

"You'd wait in this bed naked for me every time?"

"Yes. Every single time."

"Maybe a few when you're in the kitchen too." I tease her with the tip, barely dipping in before I pull out again.

"Anything you want. Just as long as you fuck me. Please," she begs, and her eyes open, giving me a pleading look.

I take her then without another word, grabbing her and sliding deep inside. The feeling of nothing in between us, like she's actually mine, and I fuck her like this all the time. It has me barely able to last for her. It takes all my focus not to lose my control, and when she starts whimpering for more a few moments later, telling me how close she is and how big my cock feels, I lose it.

But luckily, I'm not alone and I feel her clench down on me as she rides out her own wave with me, the first time we manage to come together like this. At the same time like we're meant to fuck in the middle of the night after we both confess our fantasies about being a couple.

Because I need this woman like I need air. She's mine now and always. I just have to make her see it before she leaves.

THIRTY-NINE

Joss

LATER THAT WEEK I'm in Violet's office, pulling some documents for the nonprofit she's kindly letting me keep in her safe when I see a folder with my name on it that I haven't seen before. I pull it out and open it. Inside there are dozens of pages but as I flip past the cover documents I come to a deed for a building, one that's listed as a live-work building, and I frown. I page through to the signature and see Colton St. George.

"Did you find the incorporation documents?" Violet asks, and I jump a little.

"More than that." I look at her, frowning, holding up the folder and deed that I've found buried in the safe.

"Shit," she curses sitting her morning coffee down.

"Yeah, shit," I echo her.

"I can explain."

"Why there's a folder with my name on it here and the deed to a building that belongs to Colt?"

"Yes." She frowns and the guilty look doesn't fade.

"Explain." The two of us don't fight. It's insanely rare. I can think of maybe twice ever and it was when we lived together because if you live with someone long enough, you're bound to fight with them no matter how much you love each other.

"Colt bought a studio space for you. It has offices downstairs too that he thought you and Harper could use to run the nonprofit out of."

"That's... incredibly sweet of him." I bite my cheek because I am not about to cry.

"But there's an apartment upstairs. One he thought you could use while you are in town. But he was worried you'd be freaked out that he bought you a place, and he didn't want to upset you. So he raised the idea of Ben and I giving it to you. Except I said you deserved to know it came from him. That you would love it. And that if he explained it the way he explained it to me, you wouldn't panic. You'd know he did it out of the goodness of his heart to help you." The tone she's using is telling me how I'm going to react, rather than an actual prediction of how she thought I would react. Because my heart rate is definitely speeding up and skipping beats as I stare at the deed.

"He bought a fucking building. When?"

"A couple of weeks ago. I think it was just an impulse purchase when you were upset about everything with the donors. He just wanted to do something to help, and this is what he came up with."

I run my fingers over my lips as I stare at it, trying to process it along with all the other emotions I'm having lately when it comes to him.

"He shouldn't have done that."

"But he did. Because he cares about you—a lot, Joss. You need to take this in the spirit he meant it, and you need to not freak out on him about it. I love you lots, and I have your back all of the time, but on this one, you will break his heart if you don't listen to me. And I love him too." Violet gives me a meaningful look.

I start crying then because I don't know why exactly. I can't process emotions like this. The kind of tender thoughtfulness he shows all the time isn't something I'm used to. People don't treat me with kid gloves. People besides Ben and Violet don't buy me thoughtful gifts to try and help soothe my anxiety—and they sure as fuck do not buy me entire fucking studios to make my life easier. The only gifts I've ever gotten from men were because they wanted something in return. But he was going to keep it a secret and let me think it came from our friends rather than tell me. Just to protect my feelings and keep things good between us before I leave.

The soft stream of tears coming out of my eyes turns into an all-out ugly cry, and I buckle over at my waist. Violet runs over to me.

"Joss! Oh my god. What's wrong? Joss, he meant well. I promise you."

"No. No. I know he did it's just, Violet, I've fucked up so horribly." I crouch down to the floor because I feel like I might topple over if I don't.

"Fucked up how?" She leans down and wraps her arms around me.

"Because I love him. Like an idiot. We're supposed to be fixing our friendship and instead, I love him." I sob into her shoulder. I've cried more in the last few weeks here than I've cried in years.

"Joss, it's okay. You're allowed to love him. We all love him."

"No, Vi. I'm *in love* with him. And I—" I try to get air in my lungs. "I don't know what to do with that. Or how to tell him. If I *should* tell him. I don't know what to do with being in love with someone. It doesn't feel good. It doesn't feel safe. It feels like everything that matters to me is just out there, exposed for anyone to fuck up and trash at any given moment."

"I promise it's not that bad."

"It is that bad. I told you when I came here, Violet. He's not Ben. Ben's in love with you above everything else. Colt is in love with football. Just like I'm in love with my work. It's the one thing we get about each other."

"I don't think that's true. I think Colt has plenty of room to love you as much as football. More even."

"It's true. He told me so himself. He said it's the reason he's single. That any woman is second place. That it's football before all else for him. All he cares about; all he gets up and does every day is try to get the team to the finish line. And I get it. He has a lot of people he wants to prove wrong. Just like I did when I was his age. His parents. His hometown. His ex. Her asshole of a husband. All these fucking sports reporters who I have to listen to all the fucking time say that he's anything but amazing. Saying that there are guys better than him. It's bullshit, honestly. I should send them all glitter bombs in the mail for being morons. Celebrate their stupidity in style."

"I think we're getting off track..."

"I just... fuck all of those people. I want to see him prove them wrong. I get why he says he doesn't have room for anything else."

"He made room for you these last few weeks. I haven't seen him this happy and vibrant in a long time. I mean, Colt's never unhappy, you know? He's always stoic and smiling. Making little jokes when he can. But since you've been here... he's been a different person. The guys have all noticed and commented on it. I just didn't want to tell you because again... I didn't want it to upset you."

"Jesus, you all act like I'm a fragile little thing who's going to break at any moment," I grump.

"Not break. Pretty sure you're unbreakable. But run? You're good at the running." Violet eyes me carefully.

"I'm good at getting out of the way and staying out of places I don't belong. Making sure that I don't fuck up people's lives, and I ran because I wasn't good for him, Violet. He deserved so much better than me. A person who couldn't even return simple affection when he was already so heartbroken over his ex. All I could think back then was how suffocating the idea of a relationship was. I felt like a monster."

"Well, you're not a monster now. You just said yourself, you're in love with him."

"And what am I supposed to do with that?"

"Be the badass bitch you are and fucking own up to it. Tell him."

I press my lips together and glare at her. "Yes, Violet. I will just tell the most eligible bachelor in the country who also just happens to be the most famous quarterback, that no big deal, I'm in love with him. And when I run away because my biological clock strikes midnight, and I'm about to turn into a fucking pumpkin, he'll find out and decide yes, that's what he wants all along—being married to a runaway pumpkin."

"Joss, what the fuck are you talking about?"

"I don't know Violet!" I yell, setting the deed papers down on her desk. "I'm going to be sick."

"Okay. I think you just need to take some deep breaths right now."

"Don't try to yoga me out of this, Violet. Let me have my meltdown."

"Fine. You do that. Then pull yourself together. Because I'm going to text Ben to tell Colt to take you out tonight and give you the deed. And to tell you it's from him. And you are going to act insanely surprised and thankful and very cool about the entire thing. Because I'm not keeping these secrets anymore."

"Fine."

"And then after, you're going to tell him, you love him."

"Not fine."

"Joss."

"Violet."

"I don't ask you for much. But I'm asking you to please do this."

"Maybe." I take a deep breath, despite the fact I don't want to. I know she's right. That I have to tell him. I need to be honest and let him know the truth. Give him the chance to react to it how he wants. Even if that means ending our arrangement early.

FORTY

Colt

THAT NIGHT AFTER I SHOWER, shave, and get dressed, I drive to Ben's to pick Joss up and take her to dinner. Violet's going to distract Joss for a few minutes so Ben can hand me back the deed to the building, and I'm going to take her to dinner and tell her I bought it for her. Or at least I think I am. Right now I feel like I'm going to throw up as I climb out of the car.

I know Violet's right. The right thing to do is tell Joss the truth about the building, even if it means I blow things up in the process. And in all honesty, I'm glad that she forced my hand because I hate the idea of lying to Joss. Even if it's just a lie of omission. I can't stand the idea of anything like that between us. Not after everything we've worked through so far.

Which means I also have to make sure she knows about the tabloid photos. The ones my publicist has been hounding me about. Because when we were at the restaurant with the donors and Harper and Alex, we'd been spotted leaving the restaurant. Partly because Harper and Alex are the new it couple in the city. I hadn't thought about it when I'd grabbed her hand on the way out. I'd just been thinking she had a rough time dealing with their bullshit, and I desperately wanted to get her home.

But now the tabloids are speculating who we are to each other, and the posts I've made on social media that link back to their foundation have people online starting to ask the same questions. And I've been avoiding my publicist because I honestly don't know how to answer this. I don't want to say anything that's going to jeopardize my situation with Joss, no matter how little time I have left with her.

THE RESTAURANT I've picked is a romantic one with an art nouveau interior I'm hoping she'll appreciate and dark secluded corners that I hope are going to still give us the privacy we need away from prying eyes and ears. Especially when I bomb her with the reveal that I bought her a studio, and her reaction might be to walk out on me.

We order our drinks and salads, and she smiles at me, dragging her shoe along the inside of my calf as she smiles at me.

"You seem stressed tonight. Something wrong at work, or just one of those days?"

"One of those days." I smile at her, taking in the sweet way she's looking at me right now.

"Well, we can call it early and go fuck in your car if we need to." She smirks at me as I nearly choke on the sip of ice water I was taking.

"You love doing that, don't you?"

"Yes. It's one of the greatest pleasures of my life." She grins, and I wipe the water off my lips and set the napkin down.

"I have to tell you something, and you might freak out a little. Or a lot. Frankly, I'm terrified to tell you, and I just need you to believe me when I say my heart was in the right place when I did this. I wasn't thinking at the time of how it might make you feel, so I'm sorry for that."

When I finally work up the courage to look at her, her smile has faded and her brow is furrowed but she still seems to be calm, waiting for whatever I'm about to say next.

"Okay..."

I pull the deed out of my suit jacket and slide it across the table. She opens it, and her eyes drift over the page.

"You bought a building?"

"A studio, for you." I take a breath as my heart starts to race. "It has some offices downstairs too that I thought you and Harper could use while you get things figured out with the nonprofit. You could hold meetings and do your shoots there without always having to worry about booking other spaces."

"Downstairs?" she asks.

"Yeah. The main floor. Upstairs is an apartment. It's not huge or fancy or anything, but I thought if you wanted your own space away from Ben and Violet... I'm not expecting you to move there permanently or anything. You could rent it out too for some extra cash or whatever you feel like. I just thought in case you wanted a place to crash when you have to come back to town to work on foundation business, it'd be useful." I swallow against the lump in my throat as I wait for her reaction.

"Oh... Yeah. That makes sense I suppose." She lifts her eyes to meet mine, and a small smile forms on her lips. "Also an easy place to take my hookups after I photograph them too. Better than just riding them on the couch in the studio."

The server chooses that moment to bring our drinks and salads, and I raise my eyebrow at her as we wait. She takes a sip of her wine and watches me with an amused expression.

"Yeah, that's a condition of the building," I say when the server is finally out of earshot.

"What's that?"

"The only person you fuck anywhere in that place is the one whose name's on the building."

"Well, that's too bad. What if I want to fuck myself while he watches?"

The server chooses that moment to return with our bread, and I hear him nearly choke on his own breath as he hurries off again. She laughs at his retreat and her eyes sparkle as they meet mine again.

"You're gonna kill someone with that mouth of yours one of these days."

"Well, I have every intention of making it you." She grins and my heart tightens in my chest.

"Gonna be a rough murder trial for you. Killing the golden boy."

"Yeah, but I'll probably get a fantastic nickname like Black Widow or something. And in the trial, I can brag on the record about how good you were in bed."

"Well, at least that will be on the headstone."

"Of course."

"So you're not pissed at me?" I look her over carefully, worried at how calm she's being about all of this. That she's making jokes instead of lecturing me about the entanglements and bolting for the door.

"No, I'm not pissed. It's insanely sweet of you, Colt. I'm grateful, honestly. The studio space will be huge, and I know Harper will be thrilled to have proper offices instead of her working out of Alex's place and me trying to carve out a corner at Ben and Violet's." Her eyes drift over me, and she smiles. "Thank you. I don't deserve you; you know."

"I'm just relieved you like it. I wasn't sure how you'd take it."

"Well, I'm glad I can surprise you sometimes."

"Sometimes..." I echo, even though I'm pretty sure it's a nonstop revelation to have her in my life. She is definitely not for the faint of heart, but she is everything I've ever wanted.

FORTY-ONE

Joss

WHEN WE GET BACK in the car after the valet brings it
around, I'm cursing myself for not having discussed the elephant
in my head at dinner. Now in the car it's going to be a million times
more awkward. When Colt walks around to get in, he smiles at me
as he slides onto his seat, and I feel like I'm about to ruin a perfectly
good evening with my emotions. But before I can open my mouth,
his phone connects to the speakers and it's glaringly loud.

"Holy fuck!" he yells, and I start laughing as he struggles to
press the buttons to turn it off. "Jesus. I don't drive this car very
often. That's what I get for trying to be hot shit tonight. I'm
sorry. Hang on."

But he presses something else and suddenly his voicemail
starts playing.

"Two messages. First message. From Mom. Hi Colton. It's
your mother. I wish you'd pick up. I'd rather have this discus-

sion on the phone, but I guess I'll have to have it with your answering machine. Cody set it up, so I have an alert on my phone that sends me any news about you. So I can know about your games and things. And it sent me photos of you and some woman out together holding hands."

My stomach bottoms out. But technology doesn't give a fucking damn about my feelings, so it rolls on.

"And I am just very worried about you and what that city is doing to you. That woman looks like a prostitute. With those heels and those tattoos and that nose ring. Ugh. Disgusting. Her dress isn't fooling anyone. I hope you're not dating prostitutes, Colton. Your father nearly died when I showed him the photos. He's as worried about you as I am. We both think you need to take some time off and come back home. You need to find a good woman to marry, Colton, to keep you out of that sort of trouble. That woman is the kind men keep as a mistress. Not a wife."

"Jesus. Fucking. Christ." I hear Colt growl as he tries to find the right combination of buttons.

"You know Mary, Gene's daughter. She still asks about you every time I see her at the grocery store. Wants to know how you are. Tells me how handsome you are. She's still single you know. She's the kind of girl who would make you a good wife. I know boys like to sow their oats but, Colton, you've got to think long term, and I know you don't want—"

The recording cuts off abruptly as Colt manages to finally sever the Bluetooth connection.

"Fuck," he curses again.

"I think they're waiting for you to move the car out of the way," I say softly as I see the valet bouncing back and forth trying to decide whether or not to chastise his favorite quarterback for blocking the valet stand.

"Fuck." He kicks the car into gear and pulls out of the spot, making his way back to the main road.

We sit in silence for a minute, and I try to keep the tears from burning through but fail. So I turn my head toward the window hoping that he doesn't see them. His mother's words play on a loop in my head. I know once he finds his words, he's going to tell me she's wrong. That they barely speak, and she doesn't speak for him, ever. But the problem is that I don't know if she is wrong.

Colton is husband material. He has a whole house he built with a wife and a family in mind, one he built three years ago when he was even younger than he is now. He has a good guy image and if the tabloids caught pictures of us out looking like we're a couple, I can only imagine that his publicist is hyper-ventilating into a brown paper bag somewhere. Probably wondering how the hell she thought she took the easy gig and got stuck with a problem like this.

And it hits me then. What Ben and Violet said about Alex. How quick he was to come get Harper and her things out of the house once they handled Drew. That Colt has all the space for a partner but instead, he bought me an apartment and studio in the city. Because he knew what I would like. Where I belong. Because I'm not wife material, but I could be mistress material. Just like his mom said.

I hear Violet's voice in my head, shouting at me that I'm wrong. But a lifetime of experiences to the contrary has me questioning it. The fact that all I've ever been to him is good sex. That he thought he loved me when he was a boy but hasn't said a word about love now that he's grown up. That's what boys do—fall in love with the girl they like to fuck, not neces-sarily the woman they want to marry. The person they can see having a home with, raising a family—that's the woman they marry. And God knows if I'm not wife material, I'm definitely not mother material.

I swipe at the tears on my cheek. I need to pull it together because I'm spiraling out with my train of thought right now and it's not helpful.

"I'm so sorry, Joss. I'm so embarrassed, I don't even have words right now. I had no idea she left that message and even for her it's fucking low as hell."

"It's fine, Colt. She didn't mean for me to hear it. She's just a mother being protective of her son. She cares about you."

"She doesn't care about me. She cares about what gossip the neighbors will drum up if they see pictures. She worries that they'll whisper about her at the salon or at the back of the church. That's all she's ever cared about."

"Well, she lives in a small town. That's the kind of stuff that can get you ostracized. When are the pictures from? Do you know? Did you know about the tabloid?"

"Yes. I was planning on telling you at dinner, but then everything was going so well that I kept putting it off. Then I was going to tell you in the car on the ride back. Except my mom decided to tell you first. The pictures are from when we were out at the donor dinner with Alex and Harper. The paparazzi have been following them a lot, and I just didn't think, you know. I was caught up in getting you home that night."

"So you could rail me over a desk. Guess your mom was half right." I try to make a joke, but it doesn't land.

"It's not funny."

"I'm sorry, I was just trying to lighten the mood."

"Don't. The things she said were unforgivable."

"Colt she's just—"

"She's not *just* anything. She wants me to marry some nice girl from back home because she thinks they'll convince me to leave Seattle. Raise a couple of kids and help Cody with the farm. She sees all this as temporary, and my dad isn't much better. He at least loves football enough to understand why I left, but deep down he'll still never forgive me for leaving the farm. Going to college to play instead of just being the local high school star. I hope you know it's not about you—the things she said, they're about me."

"I know. She wants to protect you. It's what moms do. Mine was the same. Before she died, she's the one who told me not to trust guys. That they were fun times, but they never lasted. Wouldn't be there when you needed them. She taught from her own trauma. Wanted to be sure I didn't repeat her mistakes."

"I'm sorry. About your mom, that she never had anyone she could trust." He reaches over and puts a hand on my thigh, and I place mine on top of his, brushing over the backs of his knuckles with my fingers.

"Me too. I wish she'd lived longer. I keep thinking maybe if she'd met someone, had some love before things got so hard for her... Oh god. Okay. I'm going to start blubbering, and we don't need that. Anyway, what I'm saying is, it's fine. She means well."

"I don't care what she means, Joss. No one fucking talks about you like that. Not her, not you, not anyone. You are the love of my fucking life and you're just a mind-blowingly amazing person. You just came in here and pretty much single-handedly helped Harper figure out how to save her museum and help a bunch of other museums and organizations in the process. You managed to get Ben and Violet to finally see eye to eye all those years ago, and I don't know what any of us would do without them, let alone without you. I don't want to hear a single bad fucking word about you. Not even from you."

My heart constricts in my chest, tightening as I try to

process what he's said with his mother's voice still in my head. All my reasons for why I don't feel worthy of someone like him resurfacing, drowning me and stealing my words. Afraid anything I say will be the wrong thing, so I just stay silent.

He pulls into a random parking lot and puts the car in park. I glance around and raise an eyebrow.

"Fuck..." He scrubs a hand over his face. "I rented a suite at a hotel down here. I made that joke about the house and the hotel. You showing me what was better. I thought it would be fun to get room service dessert, and I had some other plans. Plus if we stayed down here, we could stay in bed an extra hour because it's so much closer to the stadium than my house. And I know I won't see you for long after since you have to catch your flight early in the morning."

My heart twists even tighter at how much he has thought it through.

"But thanks to what she just called you, I don't want to take you there now. So now I'm just trying to come up with a new plan."

"We can still go to the hotel."

"No. I'm too fucking pissed off."

"Okay... then you can just take me back to Ben and Violet's. I've got some packing up to do anyways so that I can enjoy the game tomorrow without worrying. I'll still see you after and we can celebrate your win."

I make up a stupid excuse that's only halfway based on truth because it's obvious neither of us is in the mood anymore. It's all become way too awkward and complicated. There's no way I can confess my feelings to him now. And now he's so focused on being pissed off at his family, there's no way either of us can get out of our head's enough to enjoy anything.

"Oh... Okay. If you're sure. We could go to my place." He offers, his brow furrows as he looks up at me.

He looks tired and frustrated and I feel guilty that I'm the source of it, even if it wasn't my doing this time.

"No. You should get rest anyway. You have the game tomorrow, and it's an important one. Gotta stay focused on the end game." I grin at him, trying to be reassuring.

WHEN HE DROPS ME OFF, he parks the car and walks me to the door like the gentleman he is.

"I'm sorry about tonight. About the call and losing my shit there for a minute. I meant everything I said though."

"It's okay. It was a good night up until the little voicemail mishap. We can just pretend that part didn't happen." I smile at him, and there's still the faintest bit of the light that returns to me in his eyes despite how emotionally exhausted he looks.

"You'll be at the game tomorrow? We can get dinner after and spend the night together before you have to leave."

"Absolutely. Wouldn't miss it for the world." I kiss him then, because I'm not cut out for anymore discussion tonight. I just want a shower, bed, and time alone to process and recover. He kisses me back, and something flickers over his face as he looks at me when he pulls away.

"Okay. I'll see you then. Goodnight, Joss." He kisses me one last time before I walk in the door and he heads back for his car.

When I get inside, Violet's just heading up the stairs to bed, and she stops to look at me.

"I didn't tell him." I hurry past her on the steps.

"Then you tell him tomorrow. But you're telling him."

"Tomorrow," I repeat the word but whether or not I can follow through with it is a problem for another day. One when my heart doesn't feel like fragile cracked glass that's about to shatter.

FORTY-TWO

Colt

AS WE STRETCH on the field before the game, I run over the scenario for the fiftieth time in my head. I should be thinking about the game, running over my plays in my head. And I am, but I'm also trading off thinking about how to win her over. What I might be able to say before she gets on the plane tomorrow that will make her come back after her next project is done.

She's at least agreed that she'll use the apartment over the studio. That there'll be opportunities for her to travel back and forth from wherever she is in the world back to us—back home to me. I've settled for that promise. The chance to see her again.

I'm furious with myself for not asking for more. For not telling her right then that I want her for good, however we have to make that look so that she can still pursue her career. Then my mother's voicemail fucked things up in a way that I don't know if I can repair. Joss is resilient and she gives very few shits about what people outside her inner circle think of her or her life choices. But she's vulnerable when it comes to the people she loves, and that my mother might have been able to pierce through because of me makes me never want to speak to her again.

I hadn't returned any of her calls before or since and have no intention of doing so. Anything I could say to her or my dad right now would likely sever our relationship for good. It's already on thin ice. While I'm absolutely going to make it clear that they'll never ever fucking talk about Joss that way again or it will be the last time they speak to me at all, I still have a small stupid hope that they'd see her for who she really is. How much she means to me. How I can't see a future without her in it.

"You all right there?" Ben asks as we move to start doing some warmup passes.

"No."

"I figured that might be the case."

"Word travels fast."

"Violet said she was wrecked last night, and she didn't say much this morning before I left. She was smiling and looked like everything was fine, but I know when she's that quiet it's not good."

"She overheard a voicemail she shouldn't have."

Ben stops abruptly and looks at me like he might murder me. "Not another woman."

"Hell no. Are you insane? Even if I wasn't gone for her, she's more than I can take on a good day."

"Then what?"

"My mother, spitting vitriol about her and me finding a *real* wife and not a prostitute."

"The fuck?"

"You know how she is. Everything that isn't what she grew up with is wrong in her eyes."

"That's fucked."

"Yup, and I think it might mean I've lost my chance where Joss is concerned. She just had me take her back to your place when dinner was over."

"You have tonight to talk to her. When we go to dinner, or after—tell her."

"I know. I will. I just hope she'll still listen."

FORTY-THREE

Joss

I'M SITTING in the box with Harper, Violet, and Mackenzie for today's game—this time on a ticket Colt provided and wearing his jersey as promised. I'm trying to be lighthearted and pretend like everything's fine. I still haven't told Violet the details of what happened, and I definitely don't intend to tell Harper or Mackenzie. I'm not even sure I can muster the courage to tell Violet at the moment.

Everything about the situation hurts. That there are tabloid photos he has to explain, that his mother not only thought I looked like a prostitute but was pressed enough to call him and leave a voicemail over it, and that I awkwardly had to listen to it. I'd been so stupidly hopeful before. I was all ready to confess everything to him. Pour my heart out and just let him decide. I hadn't even thought about what the consequences of having me as a girlfriend would be for him. I'd just been thinking about how much I wanted him. How much I loved him. That maybe we could finally be something.

Now, I barely want to be at this game. If it wasn't for the fact that I know some future version of me will appreciate the memories—being with Violet and the rest of these badass women, watching him play the game he loves the most—I wouldn't be here at all.

I stare down at the field, watching as they line up for another play. They're doing well today for as much as I understand about the plays. They're up fourteen points, and it's not even halftime yet. Every shot the camera gets of him, he's smiling and patting his guys on the back for a job well done. And now they're about to score again, closing in on the end zone while the crowd roars to life after every play and quiets again as he gets ready to throw.

But this time when he steps back, he falters a bit, struggling to find someone open to throw to and his eyes are glued to the far side of the field when the worst thing I've ever seen in my life happens. A guy from the opposing team has an open line to him, and he's running like he's a cannonball fired directly at him. He slams into him, and the ball goes flying at the same moment Colt slams into the turf.

The hit is brutal, and I have to look away for a minute. I don't normally shy away from violence but it's a different story when it's your loved one out there getting smashed into the ground. When I look back, I expect to see Colt slowly but surely rising to his feet again. Just like he always does when he gets hit. But he doesn't move.

The rest of the team has taken off down to the other side of the field, chasing after the ball the other team recovered. But Colt just lays there.

"Violet?" I ask, reaching out for her arm, my voice high-pitched.

I watch as I see Ben approaching Colt, going down on one knee to look at him and then quickly signaling for the Phantom staff to come off the sideline.

"Violet!" I start to feel the tears coming and her arms wrap around me.

"It's okay. It's okay. He might just have the wind knocked out of him."

"He's not fucking moving, Vi."

Ben takes his helmet off and kneels next to him while the trainers rush onto the field, and I look to Violet for answers. I can feel the anxiety zipping up my spine, the tears clawing at my throat, and I grip her arm tighter. Everyone in the box has gone quiet, and several people have moved forward to stare at what's happening on the field. As the rest of the stadium catches on to what's happening it goes quieter too, a rumble of whispers rattling through it, and more of Colt's teammates come back to kneel in a circle around him.

The trainers start moving in, making it impossible to see what's going on, and the cameras that were trained on him for a moment on the big screens switch to other views. One pops up a cartoon of a mascot running across the field, and I glare at it.

"Tell me it's not what I think, Violet."

"I'm sure he's fine. Sometimes it looks a lot worse than it is. That's why the medical staff is down there though. He's in good hands whatever it is. It's probably something simple like the wind being knocked out of him. Or he tweaked something and doesn't want to move until they assess it. That's happened a few times with Ben." Her voice stays calm and level as she talks, and that gives me a little bit of reassurance. Like maybe I'm overreacting to what I'm seeing. She's here week after week watching them play and has witnessed scenes like this a million times. If she's calm, I'm calm.

Then I make the mistake of looking at Ben. He runs a hand

through his hair, and I watch as Waylon, Mackenzie's husband, and another good friend of his, walks over to talk to him. He shakes his head, scrubbing a hand over his face again as Waylon pats him on the back and kneels beside him. Ben looks worried. Ben doesn't look calm, and I look to Violet again as she exchanges looks with Mackenzie.

I swallow against the lump in my throat. "Just tell me, Violet."

"I don't know, Joss." Her grip around me tightens and we hug each other as we stand there.

THE NEXT FEW minutes drag on and fly by at the same time. It's a blur of staff, announcements that there is a delay due to a medical issue, and then I watch as they bring a stretcher onto the field. My heart takes off at a million miles an hour like it's running a race all by itself, and it feels like it's going to tear straight out of my chest. They slide the board down, and I take a step forward, like somehow, I'll be able to see around all the staff and see his face from up here.

"Oh my god," I mutter, the tears starting to sting my cheeks. "He has to be all right, Violet."

"Joss, don't worry too much yet okay?" Mackenzie gives me a sympathetic look because right now Violet is as shell-shocked as I am.

"She's right Joss. Even if it's just a concussion they'll do due diligence to make sure until they've checked him out. He might be fine, but they just want to be cautious." Harper puts her hand on my shoulder, trying to reassure me.

Time stretches on, and I shift on my feet, wishing I could just be down on the field talking to him. See him. Hold his hand. This is torture, standing up here, hopelessly watching and knowing I can't get close to him. The crowd is restless now.

Chanting his name out in intervals between hushed discussions. I'm sure they're all wondering the same things I am.

The staff start to move then, and I can see glimpses of them getting him on the board. They're working to strap him down and get him up on a medical gurney they've wheeled out, and I hold my breath as I see glimpses of him again. Whispers break out around the room, and it makes the uneasiness slide over my skin again. I feel hot and cold at the same time, my hands are clammy as I grip Violet, and we lean our heads together.

A second later and they start to wheel him across the field. It's impossible from this distance to even see if he's conscious or not. But then he does a thing I could kiss him for, he holds up one hand and gives a thumbs-up sign. The whole crowd erupts. Standing on their feet and clapping. Cheering so loud that the stadium practically shakes with it.

I take a deep breath and the tears come a little harder, happy tears now because at least I know he's conscious and able to move.

"Oh thank fucking god," Violet whispers as she tightens her hug around me.

"Holy fuck..." I curse, squeezing her back. "Okay. At least it's not the worst. But what do we think it could be?"

"I don't know. Concussion maybe? We'll have to wait to find out."

"Can we go see him?"

"No. They won't let us back there. They usually won't even let family back at first. Until he's assessed."

My heart thuds hard against my chest, dropping to my stomach. Because as much as I feel like I'm Colt's family—that Ben and Violet are his family—I'm reminded in moments like this, that we're not.

"WE SHOULD GO to the hospital. I feel useless just waiting around here," I say as I pace around the box for the hundredth time in the last hour. I'm ready to leave the game and rush over, but the women in the box, the experienced veterans of this sort of thing, explain that there's no use. That he'll be evaluated for a concussion and a battery of other tests. That they won't let me see him. That I'll be waiting just like any other stranger for news, and I'm better off being here. Because here we might actually get an update from the staff or one of the coaches.

Harper gives me another hug, trying in vain to comfort me to the best of her ability.

"I know you want to go to the hospital, but they won't let us see him. We're not family." Violet reminds me of why I need to pull it together, but even though I know all the logical reasons, I can't make myself believe them. I'm also incredibly tired of being told I'm not family when Violet, Ben, and I are as much his family as anyone who's blood.

"Which is stupid because he has no family here. We *are* his family," I argue the point with Violet, uselessly.

"Yes, but they don't care about that."

"Are they going to let Ben in?" I look up at her as the thought hits me we might eventually get an inside source.

"I don't know. He's going to go with one of the coaches. Either the head coach or the offensive coach when the game is over. He said at half time."

"Well, I hope they at least let him back. Insane that he's in the hospital, and they won't let anyone who cares about him in." I pace the floor back and forth.

"Everything I've heard is that he's fine, and it was just a mild concussion at most."

"Mild concussion my ass. Did you see the way he fell?"

"Ben will keep us posted with any information he gets. You know he will."

She's right. He will. But right now I can't help the sick feeling in my stomach that I can't go and check on him myself. That I can't talk to him and find out how he's doing. I've already sent him a dozen text messages, but I have no idea if he has his phone or when he'll see them. I just want him to know I'm here for him if he needs me, and I can't even do that much.

FORTY-FOUR

Colt

THAT NIGHT as I get home, I'm exhausted. It's late, and it's been a long day. It had been one test after another while they poked, prodded, evaluated, and re-evaluated every single thing they could think of and eventually decided I had a mild concussion. They'd finally let me go home, and my quarterback coach had insisted on driving me back himself. Ben followed in his car, after spending most of the afternoon and night with me in the hospital when I told them that he's my emergency contact. I'd barely been able to talk to Joss since my phone was at the stadium until Ben brought it when he came over, and even then with all the tests they'd been running, I'd only been able to send a quick "I'm okay" text.

Violet and Joss are waiting in the house when I get there, both of them hurrying over to hug me as soon as I shrug out of my coat and shoes.

"I was so fucking worried about you," Joss hugs me tighter as Violet steps away, and I wrap my arms around her.

"I'm okay. Just a little bump on the head."

"Well, that's not what it looked like."

"I know. I saw the video. I'm sorry I scared you."

"It's not your fault. That stupid giant fucking ogre of a bastard on the other hand better hope I never find him."

"He was just doing his job," I say softly.

"And I'll just be doing mine when I kill him."

I can't help but laugh at that.

"All right. So what's the protocol then?" Violet looks between me and Ben.

"Should have someone here to check on him but no need to wake him up. At least one of us should stay."

"I'm staying," Joss says immediately.

"You have an early flight."

"I can stay with him," Ben offers.

"No. I'm staying. I'll figure out the rest of it, but I'm staying here." She steps closer to me like she's ready to fight if someone argues with her about it.

"All right, well maybe we'll stay too, so we can all get some sleep." Violet looks meaningfully between Ben and me, glancing at the back of Joss's head as she buries her face into my shirt.

"Whatever you guys want to do is fine with me. There's plenty of room."

"We'll stay. That way Joss has backup if she needs it."

"All right. I just really need a shower right now. Haven't gotten one yet."

"I'm going with you," Joss announces. "You could get dizzy or something and you shouldn't be alone."

"I'm fine."

"She's right, and I really don't want to have to be your

shower buddy. So let her go?" Ben gives me a look, and I realize it's probably half because Joss has been worried all day. While I hate that she spent the day so worried, it feels good to know that she cares that damn much.

"Fine. I'll submit to being treated like this for a few more hours. But by tomorrow can we please all just realize this was a mild concussion, and I'm fine?" I grumble.

No sooner I say it, I realize it won't matter. At least not where Joss is concerned because she'll be on a flight back to Europe. So far away it won't matter what I'm doing here. I've lost most of my last night with her, and I was given strict instructions that I rest and not participate in any strenuous activities. A lecture the doctor felt he needed to punctuate with the clarity of, "That includes sex." So my last night with her will be spent like most of the rest of this trip—barely being able to touch her.

"Agreed. Let's get you cleaned up and in bed for some rest," she says as she finally releases the tight hug she's been holding me in.

"Do you know where everything you need is?"

"We'll figure it out. Don't worry." Violet smiles at me.

I'm incredibly grateful right now that I have the friends that I do, and these three especially to be here for me when I'd otherwise be alone. I don't know what I'd do without them.

AFTER I TAKE MY SHOWER, during which Joss patiently sits in a corner with her back turned to me for my "privacy" while she reads up on her phone how to care for concussion patients, she helps me into bed.

"Do you care if I sleep in here? I promise no touching, doctors' orders will be obeyed. I can even sleep on the chair if you want. I just want to be close in case you need something."

"Of course you can sleep in here. Jesus. If it's my last night, you're definitely sleeping with me. Just make sure you wake me up in the morning before you go."

"I'm not going. I'll be here in the morning."

I pause pulling back the sheets to look up and stare at her. "What do you mean?"

"I don't know yet. I'll reschedule or get a different flight. But I'm not leaving. I'll be here in the morning somehow. So don't worry."

"Are you sure?"

"Yes, Colt. I don't want to be anywhere else right now. Not after I saw you on that field. I need to know you're okay.

"All right."

"I'm gonna talk to Violet and Ben, working out a schedule for checking on you in the night. Hopefully, I can do it, but just in case I sleep through an alarm or something, I want to be sure."

"Let them take turns with you. That's what they're here for. I feel stupid that they have to be here at all, so let them at least be here for a reason. And you look like hell Joss. Let one of them sit with me while you take a shower and relax a bit, okay?"

"Okay." She nods and starts to leave the room before she stops. "Colt?"

"Yeah," I say as I lay back against the pillows.

"I'm glad you're okay. I just... can't imagine life without you in it, you know?"

My heart squeezes in my chest, and I give her a small, cracked smile. I want to confess everything to her, but I know I don't have the energy right now. I need to take it easy and trying to convince her to do a thing like risk it all on me and my love for her is going to take everything I've got. So instead I just nod.

"I know, Dollface. Same."

She smiles back and then hurries off to find Violet.

WHEN I WAKE up the next morning the smell of breakfast is wafting toward me and as I open my eyes, I see Joss standing there with a tray. She smiles at me when she sees my eyes open, and the sight of her makes my stomach twist and my heart squeeze tight. Because she's still here. Which means she didn't take the flight she was supposed to. She didn't leave, and she meant it when she said she was going to stay.

But my heart aches all the same because she doesn't want to be here. She's just worried because I don't have someone to look after me besides hired help, and she knows my family won't want to come out, and my brother can't.

"I sent Ben and Violet home to do their thing, but they want to come back and check on you later. Your brother called and I told him you were good, and I promised to tell you so you could call him back when you were awake. But I want you to eat first. I made you eggs, toast, and some bacon. The bacon's a little burnt but not bad. And there's a little fruit bowl because your trainer said to take it easy but not to let you have too many treats. I also made the protein shake to his directions, but it's still in the kitchen. I'll go get it," she explains as she sits the tray down on my nightstand and then evaluates my position in bed.

"Thanks," I mumble, she looks back at me and my position and frowns, turning and walking back toward the bed.

"Here let me get you some pillows, help you sit up in bed."

"I can move the pillows."

"But that's what I'm here for. To fluff pillows and bring you food and not let you overtax yourself. Give your brain time to heal."

"Grabbing a pillow is not going to overtax me."

She reaches over the bed despite my protests to grab more pillows and motions for me to sit forward.

"I know you're used to being super independent with everything. But right now, you're going to have to let me be in charge. You need to get better, and the more you rest the more likely that is. Everyone's worried about you. They're lost without you. So the sooner you're back on your feet—the better."

"And I need to hurry up, so you can get back on the road," I say bluntly because we both know that has to be a consideration. Her awkwardly staying here looking after me doesn't make sense.

"I'm here as long as you need me."

"I appreciate that, but you should get back to work. I don't want you wasting your time here when you have clients waiting on you."

"I'm not wasting my time being here for you. You would do the same for me—look at what you did with the studio. I can't buy you a studio Colt, but I can be here for a week while you recover from a brain injury."

"Brain injury," I snort, shaking my head. "I just bumped my head."

"A concussion is a brain injury. The doctors are treating it like one, so I'm going to treat it like one too."

"Being treated like a child is going to make me grumpy."

"I think you might already be a little grumpy." Her brow raises at me but she smiles. "But that's allowed given everything going on. I'll do my best not to treat you like a child. I just... want to be here for you." Her eyes go soft as she looks at me, and it makes my chest go tight in response. I look out the window, trying to distract myself.

"I appreciate it." I nod, because deep down in a more selfish part of myself I'm glad she's here. I'm glad that she canceled her flight and presumably her shoot and is at my side. Because I want her with me like this always. But her job is her lifeline. Being on the road is what she loves. Every moment she's taking care of me is a moment she's not doing the thing she loves and I don't want her to have to make choices like this.

FORTY-FIVE

Joss

"COLT," I say softly, curled up on the couch next to him as we watch television. I set my phone aside because it's been nearly a week of our nurse and patient routine, and he's been allowed to return to practice. The team might not have him for this weekend's game, but it won't be long before things are back to normal. He's mentioned it several times already, and I know the unspoken question is about when I rebook my flight.

I've been putting it off, and then just now, looking at flight prices like a coward. Instead of doing the thing I know I need to. That Violet told me to do way before now.

"Yeah?" he asks absently.

"I love you," I blurt out.

I've lain awake at night coming up with ways to tell him. Speeches. Elaborate workarounds and build-ups that would put this whole thing into context. But I forget all of them and just let the words fly out on their own.

"What?" He puts his phone down and looks up abruptly.

"I love you. I'm in love with you, I think."

"You think *what*?"

"Well, I've never had it happen before so... I was going to tell you. The night we went out to dinner. And then after the game. But then things kept happening and it never seemed like the right time. Now it's just... I'm trying to find a flight to get back on the road, and I don't want to leave without saying it."

He stares at me blankly then, and my heart constricts in my chest and my lungs feel like they're tightening so much I might lose my ability to breathe. I'm just left hanging here, suspended in space. The kind where you've stupidly told your friend—frenemy with benefits? Fuck buddy? That you've fallen for them, and they do nothing but stare.

"Oh... so this is what it feels like then. Well fuck, I guess I get why you were upset then."

He blinks and then scowls a little, puzzling like he doesn't understand again.

"What are you talking about?"

"When you told me you had feelings for me last time and I freaked out on you. No wonder you were so hurt. I get it. The chest pain alone..." I rub my sternum. "I'm sorry. I shouldn't have said anything. I thought... I thought you'd want to know. Maybe. I mean I guess like you said before... We're never the right people for each other at the right time. I bet we're happy in that parallel universe though, right?" The tears are starting to form and holy fucking hell is that embarrassing. I'm just the queen of waterworks lately, showing up here and having all my pent up emotions pour out like I can't control them.

I'm really feeling very sympathetic for a younger Colt right now. And I wasn't nearly as kind as he's being. He's just sitting here silently while I make a fool of myself. I had said unkind things and then fled. Although I have to say the silence is a little cutting too.

"Could you say something please?" I ask at last when it stretches on too long.

"Sorry. I'm just thrown off right now. I swear to God, you just told me that... that you're in love with me, and now I'm trying to decide if I call the team doctor, or we just go to the emergency room. Did they say what to do if I start hallucinating, do you remember?"

"Colt... don't make jokes right now." I cough a little.

"I'm not joking. It's fucking freaking me out."

"Jesus, Colt. You're not hallucinating. I said I'm in love with you, and you're acting so weird. I know I probably deserve it, but I thought I might have earned a little grace after everything."

"You're serious?"

"Yes, I'm serious."

"You're in love with me?"

"Trust me. I'm already questioning it now." I glare at him and swipe at my tears.

"Marry me then."

"What?"

"Marry me."

"Jesus Christ, Colton. Maybe we do need to call the doctor."

"We can do it this weekend. It's an away game in Vegas." His face lights with amusement. "We can have Elvis do it. Tell me it wouldn't be perfect for you."

"Okay. You're scaring me now. Did I break you? Is this from the swelling? I'm going to call Ben and ask him what to do." I reach for my phone.

"I'm fine. But yes, call Ben and Violet. Tell them they have to be our witnesses for our wedding this weekend." He jumps up. "I'll call my assistant. They can help you find somewhere to get a dress. Do you want Harper there? I can call Alex."

"You do not seem fine. I tell you, 'I love you,' and you stare blankly into the void for several minutes and then say you want Elvis to marry us."

"And?"

"And you are not a get married by Elvis in Vegas person, Colton. You're a house already built for the wife, picket fence owning, elaborate wedding with four hundred people that takes two years to plan—having person."

"Yeah well, fuck that. Elvis it is."

"Oh my god. Stop this. You haven't even said if you love me back yet!"

"Do you have a brain injury? Because I thought it was just me."

"Colton!"

"What?" He looks at me with a giddy smile.

"I am not kidding when I say you are freaking me out. Can you please just be sensible right now?"

"Okay. I'm being sensible."

I give him the side-eye and then motion for him to sit down. "Do you love me? I mean, seriously. Don't joke about Elvis. I'm trying to have a serious conversation about this."

"I'm not joking about Elvis. I'm just trying to get you tied down before you run off again because you get scared in the middle of the night when you overthink it. If there's a paper trail and legal grounds, I can at least try to run after you this time."

"This time?"

"You were in love with me last time too. That's why you ran."

"I was not in love with you. I was terrified that you were serious about being in love with me."

"Yeah. I don't buy that. The way you look at me? The way you fuck me? That's from a long-term obsession. Years of missing someone you wish you could have back."

"*Please.*" I try to feign my way out of this.

"Trust me. I know."

"You want me to believe that you were in love with me this whole time?"

"No. I want you to believe we've been in love with each other this whole time, and stupidly fucking denying it. But yes. I've been in love with you."

I scoff because I have a very hard time believing that.

"You don't believe me?"

"Not really. When I got here... that was not someone in love. The way you acted. You weren't even happy to see me."

"Joss, I was scared to see you. All the feelings I knew it was going to dredge up. I never really stopped being in love with you. I just accepted it would never be returned. Seeing you, thinking about you—it hurt like hell. You were still in my head all the time."

"I'm sure."

"Your birthday is still the password on my phone. That's why I wouldn't tell you. That and the fact I still have pictures of us on it..."

"What?"

"You heard me. I compare every fucking woman I date to you and none of them measure up. You ruined me for anyone else, honestly. There's no one who comes close. So I'll take you in this universe or any other that you'll have me."

He kisses me, and I'm lost in it for several minutes. Imaging this world where Colton St. George has been in love with me. All the while, I stared at him on TV and on magazine covers. Heard from our friends how well he was doing in the pros. How he was taking the whole league by storm with Ben and

Tobias's help. But somehow was secretly missing me. That doesn't seem like it should be possible.

"Wait... but you built a whole house for a future with a wife and kids and all the things. You skipped straight over the bachelor's pad to this... This monument to everything you should want."

"I told you. I accepted you weren't going to love me back, and I tried to figure out what I wanted if I couldn't have you."

"And?"

"I thought I wanted the perky future PTA mom. I tried. Fuck, *I really tried.* Would have made my mom so happy. Could have at least made one of them proud of me for doing what they wanted. But it just didn't work."

"Why not? Seems like you would have had plenty of options to choose from."

"I did. But you haunted a house you'd never even lived in. You were there in the shower, naked and telling me to fuck you. You were in the kitchen replating food you ordered and pretending you made it for me while I played along. On the couch explaining to me why The Crow should never be remade and ranting about the inferiority of most remakes. And Christ, all your rants live rent-free in my head. How the hell am I supposed to fall for anyone else when you're always there? It's impossible."

FORTY-SIX

Colt

"I CAN COOK A FEW THINGS!" She's deflecting again, talking about something else because she doesn't want to face facts.

"Yeah. I'm sure you can. So you're in love with me?"

"Yes, I'm in love with you." She looks so wide-eyed and vulnerable right now like she could just shatter into a million pieces.

"But you're still looking for flights?"

"I mean... I was."

"Do you need to get back on the road?"

"I don't exactly have to. I should. But I don't need to leave immediately. If you want me to stay until you're back to playing again, I can do that."

"That is not what I'm asking, and you know it. I asked you if you'd marry me."

"I thought we established that wasn't serious."

"I'm dead-fucking-serious." I shouldn't take this approach with her. I'm cornering her—hard and there's a high likelihood she'll bolt from the pressure.

"Where's the ring?"

"What?"

"I mean, if you're asking there should be a ring, right?"

"You need a ring?"

"No, but I need what the ring stands for."

I hesitate to tell her the whole truth. Because once I do there's no going back. All my cards will be on the table. She'll know the extent of how gone I am for her. But she's come far enough to tell me she's in love with me. I owe her the same vulnerability in return.

"I bought you a house."

"What?" She stares at me like I've just told her time travel is real.

"When I bought the studio. I was telling the realtor about you, in hopes she could help me find something you'd like. And we found the studio, but she also showed me this cottage. It's not a cottage really. It's actually a decent-size house, but it looks like something out of a fairy tale. It's painted all pastel right now. So it needs work. I'm sure you'll want it all painted black. But otherwise—the space, the details, the gardens... all of it looks like you belong there."

"Why didn't you tell me when you told me about the studio?"

"I was scared enough to tell you about the studio. Afraid of how you'd react. And when you didn't freak out on me, I didn't want to push my luck."

She winces.

"What?"

"I did freak out. I found the deed in Violet's office."

"But you acted like you didn't know."

"I lied. Violet told me to pull my shit together and be thankful that I have such an amazing person in my life."

"So you hated it..." My heart sinks in my chest.

"No. I didn't hate it. I bawled my eyes out when I found it. That you wanted Ben and Violet to give it to me instead. I loved it, and it broke my heart at the same time. That you felt like you had to lie to me to do something nice. I get it though. I can be a very difficult person to love, and I never gave you very much reason to trust me or my reactions. But when I saw it... I couldn't hide from it anymore—that I love you, I mean."

"Why not tell me sooner?"

"Your mom. My own stupid brain telling me things that aren't true. This house. What I thought I should do."

"Were you just going to leave again?"

"Were you just going to let me walk away again?"

She had a point. I'd been so set on letting her live her life the way she wanted, I never thought about trying to show her she might want a different one.

"I think we belong together. I think we're meant to be together, even in this universe. I just think we ended up in a version that's a little harder than the rest. But I'm willing to do it anyway if you are."

"I think you're right. It's going to be an uphill battle. With your career and mine. With how independent we both are... You sure you're up for that?"

"As long as at the end of the day I get you—always."

"Then yes."

"Yes?" My heart thuds hard against my lungs, the pounding echoing in my ears.

"Yes. But not Elvis in Vegas this weekend. I mean, I like it..." She grins. "But Violet will die when she finds out and will want to put me through all the torture of wedding planning like I did her. And I want to do cake tasting with you. Plan a honeymoon. See you take pictures with your groomsmen. And... I want you to have time to figure things out with your parents. How you want to handle it. Plus I don't want a quick Vegas wedding. Nothing is impulsive about this. I'm not running. You don't have to nail me down. I want this. I want you."

I stare at her for a long minute, trying to process this version of Joss. I'd spent so much time focused on showing her I'd changed and grown up; I hadn't noticed how much she had.

"What's wrong?" She frowns.

"I just... I'm not dreaming, right? Or dead?"

"Not unless we both are."

"I love you."

"I love you too."

I wrap my arms around her and kiss the top of her forehead. The woman is an enigma—somehow a hurricane and the calm waters I need all wrapped up in one perfect person that I'm finally going to get to call my own.

FORTY-SEVEN

Joss

> You're family member free tonight, right?

COLT:

Yes... why?

> Figured you could use an opportunity to get out some post-game aggression given how much those refs suck.

The refs, eh? Not the interception I threw?

> Interception wouldn't have mattered if the refs weren't playing for the other team.

You've been spending too much time around Violet.

> Well, she's a smart woman.

At any rate, I'm in your bed, naked, and waiting for you.

Our bed, and fuck yes you are.

Language.

Sorry, learned it from another smart woman.

HE SENDS ME A SMILEY EMOJI, and I grin and toss my phone aside, laying back and staring at the ceiling. My thoughts drift when I think about all the things I need to figure out right now. What I'm doing about the rest of the shoots I have lined up for the year overseas, and what I can use the studio for locally. I've been toying with the idea of doing boudoir shoots again like I used to in grad school.

When Mackenzie and I realized I'd been the one to photograph her and her friends before, she asked if I'd be willing to do a follow-up shoot for them when they're all back in town for a reunion in the summer. I agreed and it gave me nostalgia for how much fun I'd had taking gorgeous photos of everyday people rather than always having to be subject to editorial guidelines or corporate deadlines for the brands and celebrities I worked with.

I'll just have to work it around the onslaught of work Harper and I have now that things are really starting to get underway with the nonprofit. Not to mention finishing the book, having it published and printed, and then scheduling a release-date party where people can get signed copies.

Then there's all the work for the new house. The one Colt bought for me and gave to me as an engagement gift. We've got to line up a general contractor, decide on paint colors, and then pick out furniture. We're planning to live in the current house until it's all finished, but we're both eager to be in a place that feels more like a home than this one. One that's closer to our jobs and our friends.

I'm making a list on my phone, and so entrenched with my to-do list that I don't even hear him come in until he drops his bag at the door to the room.

"Holy fuck. I thought you were exaggerating about waiting for me naked."

"Nope." I turn my phone off and toss it on the nightstand, a little embarrassed to be caught working when I'm supposed to be seducing my fiancé. But if anyone understood what a workaholic I was, it was him.

When I look up at him, he's wearing gray sweats and a tight tee that hugs his shoulders and my jaw drops a little. In the soft glow of the room he looks insanely hot, and it's moments like these where I have to remind myself this is real life. I'm actually this fucking lucky.

"I see what you did there, with your little slut pants and tee. Very unfair."

He laughs and pulls his shirt off, tossing it onto the chair. "The woman I'm seeing is a lot to keep up with. Have to keep it interesting for her."

"Oh yeah?"

"Yeah," he says, leaning over the bed and kissing me. His hand brushes over the soft band I have on my thigh, and he looks closer in the low light, his fingers running over it. "What's this?"

"Soft restraints. Just Velcro, but if I put my wrist here, and wrap it..." I demonstrate for him, and now it's his turn to stare at me agape.

"Oh fuck me..."

"Or in this case... fuck *me*." I grin at him. "I thought it'd be fun to try. If you feel like it. If not, I can take them off. They also come off the thigh part and link together with this little clip. They're magnetized though so if I pull hard enough..." I show him how I can undo them with force. I'm not sure how much he is ever into these things, so I try to make sure it's something he wants to play with.

A smile tugs at his lips though, and he reaches to put the one I'd started to undo in place around my wrist after he pulls it off the thigh strap. "What's your safe word?"

"I see you read the stuff I sent you."

"I did." He grins. "So... safe word?"

"Dragon."

"Dragon?" He gives me a bemused smile.

"I was talking to Harper about her grad school work when we were putting the website together the other day. And do you know what St. George was famous for?"

"Being tortured? At least I could relate to it."

"Slaying a dragon."

His boyish grin flits across his face as he laughs, and he leans forward to kiss me. "You kill me. You know that?"

"You kill me, apparently."

He raises a brow and shakes his head as he stifles another laugh, taking the other restraint cuff off my thigh and wrapping it around my wrist. Just watching him doing it is making me wet already, and I chew on my lip as I watch him finish the job. His eyes darken, and he looks me over.

"Kneel for me."

I climb up on my knees on the bed and look at him.

"Holy fuck you look gorgeous like this. We're gonna have to take more photos, you know?" he promises as his hand courses up the inside of my thigh, sliding between my legs and gently dipping the tips of his fingers inside to test me.

"I only trade."

"We can arrange that." His eyes drift over me, landing hard between my thighs.

"How do you want me?"

"Every way possible... but right now? Ass up, face down on this bed, begging for me to take you as hard as I can."

"Holy shit," I whisper under my breath. I don't know if I will ever adapt to how hot bossy Colt is, but I start to move into position. Watching him out of the corner of my eye as he stands and pulls his sweats and underwear off.

His hand slides over the curve of my ass when he comes back to me.

"Can never decide which way I like taking you better, so we might have to do a few tonight."

"As long as it's rough."

A stuttered breath leaves his chest, and he grips my thigh. He lines up with me, just barely testing me first, making sure I'm wet even though he has to know by now it's a state I'm always in for him when he's like this. Then he fucks me, fast and deep on the first take. I gasp and bury my face into the sheets.

"This how you want it?"

"Yes. Deep and hard. Like you own it."

He takes instruction well, even though he's the one in control. He fucks me rough, his breathing ragged, like he's been untethered from whatever held him back in the past. Finally having the permission to do what he wants with me in the dark after a long day of being frustrated. He edges me closer to my orgasm, and I cry out to warn him when he grabs me and pulls me up, flipping me over and tossing me back onto the bed.

"Not fucking yet. You're gonna watch me fuck you like this first."

His eyes rake over my body, and he takes me to the side of the bed where he hooks my hands over the post, angling me toward him and propping pillows under me before grabbing my thighs again. He looks sexy as hell like this, sweaty and mussed as he works his frustrations out on me.

"I can't take much more before I come," I whisper.

He smirks. "You come if you have to, Dollface. I'll just work more out of you."

"Fuck..." I mutter and close my eyes because I created this monster, and now I have to live with it every day for the rest of my life. I smirk.

"Eyes open and on my cock," he barks before I open my eyes again.

I watch as he slides inside me, slower this time, trying to drag it out, and I writhe for more friction. I'm so close to coming, and I can't stand waiting anymore. He leans over and slides his tongue over my nipple, making my hips rise with the sensation. His wide hand presses back down on my stomach and pushes me into the pillows behind me as he starts to fuck me again.

The combination of his tongue, the way I'm pinned against the bed, and how good he feels inside me is too much, and I come loudly a few moments later, moaning and gasping as he pulls me up off the mattress. He fucks me harder then, his rhythm matching the waves of the last of my orgasm as he comes inside me, groaning into my chest as the sweat drips down his face and slides over my stomach. It tickles as it rolls down my body, and I twist underneath him as he takes another stuttered breath and looks me over in confusion. When he sees the source of my discomfort, he dips his tongue out and licks it up, flattening and sliding it up my abdomen and over the underside of my breast as he pulls out of me.

I can feel the warmth of him against my thigh as he reaches up over me to unhook the cuffs, making my hands fall. His eyes drift down to meet mine and the determination and lust there has melted into reverence.

"I love you," he whispers before his lips brush over mine in a soft kiss.

"I love you too."

He stands, lifting me up and cradling me in his arms as he carries me to the bathroom.

"Gonna get us cleaned up in the shower and then we can sleep like the dead for a while. At least until I have the energy to fuck you again."

"Sounds like a plan," I grin at him, pressing a kiss to his shoulder before he puts me down on the edge of the shower bench.

He cranks on the shower and then turns to me as we wait for the water to warm up. His hand slides under my chin, lifting it so my eyes meet his again.

"You make me feel so fucking lucky."

"Like four leaf clovers?"

"Exactly like that." He smiles at me.

"Me too," I agree, and another stupid smile comes to my face because around this man I can't stop smiling.

FORTY-EIGHT

Colt

VIOLET AND BEN are hosting an engagement party for us. One that's a little bit rushed because Halloween is coming up, and Violet knows Joss will loves the idea of doing it with a theme. Since it's so soon, it's just friends from the team and a few others here in Seattle attending.

But my mother, by some miracle—likely influenced by my brother, has offered to host another one if we want in my hometown. Which I'll only consider agreeing to if they both come out here to meet Joss first, where she can feel safe and I can send them packing if I need to.

But it's a worry for another day because today I have everything I want as Joss, dressed like the Wicked Witch, stumbles back into the room linked arm and arm with Violet who's dressed like Dorothy.

"We need to make the boys do the bobbing-for-poisoned-apples thing. I need my nightly amusement," Joss jokes to Violet and Harper.

"Just don't let Waylon go first. He's freakishly good at it, and it'll ruin the game for everyone else," Mackenzie adds.

"Here are your graveyard cupcakes," Ben calls from the kitchen, sliding them onto the counter as he finishes them with the last of the candy pumpkins, summoning half the intoxicated adults into the room.

Which reminds me... "Has anyone seen Tobias yet?" I ask.

"No. He said he was coming. I thought he'd be here by now." Alex shrugs.

"Yes, he told me I'd appreciate his costume," Joss says, walking up and leaning her head on my shoulder.

"I bet he did," I grumble.

"Oh, stop. You have exactly zero to be worried about, and you know it."

"You guys haven't seen the news?" Scarlett asks quietly.

"What news?" Harper turns to her.

"Uh... If you don't know, I don't think I want to be the one to say. I just accidentally found out when I was scrolling earlier because it's trending now."

"What's trending? I've been too busy helping Violet prep," Joss asks.

"Same," Harper answers.

All eyes in the room turn to Scarlett and she flicks a nervous look around, her cheeks going pink.

"Uh... here. I'll forward it to you, Harper," Scarlett mumbles as she pulls her phone out.

Harper raises an eyebrow at her but pulls out her phone from her purse and looks at the message. She clicks and scrolls and then her brow furrows. Her eyes widen, and she gasps.

"Oh. Oh fuck. Um. Alex. Here, you can... yeah, you can look at this." Harper tosses him the phone like it's burning her.

"What is it?" He looks at her with confusion and then down at the phone. "Oh... yeah. Fuck..."

"Is someone going to fill us in?" Joss asks at my side.

Alex turns the phone around and right under the headline "Westfield Makes a Sex Tape" is a blurry-looking screenshot that's got black bars across it.

"God fucking damn it!" I curse, closing my eyes. "I've told him so many fucking times."

"I mean, he looks hot though," Joss muses at the image.

"He's not gonna look hot when they call him up for breaking fucking morality clauses in his contract."

"Morality clauses? This another stupid thing like making you all sleep in a hotel together the night before an away game?" Joss rolls her eyes.

"Yes. And it can get him benched. Which we can't fucking afford right now. We have one of the hardest second-half schedules in the league."

"Well, I mean, it doesn't even look like he necessarily knew this was being taken." Joss takes the phone from Alex and scrolls down. "Is there a video?" Her eyes flick up to Scarlett, and Scarlett looks like a deer in headlights and then shrugs, making some sort of inaudible sound.

"Try not to scandalize your new friends with your eagerness to watch my friend's sex tape at our engagement party," I tease her while I look over her shoulder. I'm not eager to see my friend fucking someone, but I am curious how it got leaked. If the article has any information or if we just have to wait to hear Tobias's side of the story.

"I'm just saying. Talk to him first before you assume he did it," Joss says defensively as she hands the phone back to Harper.

"We'll see when he gets here," I say.

"If he gets here. Maybe that's why he didn't come. Didn't want to be the gossip of the party," Harper suggests.

"Tobias has never given a fuck about it before. Trust me." Alex grunts.

"I mean, I know, but still..." She looks worried.

"All right. Until he's here and can tell us himself, let's just move on and not gossip about him," I say. "We doing apple bobbing or the Ouija board?" I ask Joss.

"Not light as a feather, stiff as a board?" Violet asks, smirking at her.

"Nah. That's for the slumber party Colt and I are having after this one," Joss jokes, and everyone has a laugh and relaxes a little.

I roll my eyes and kiss the top of her head. "Let's go try the apple bobbing. I don't need to be summoning any more demons than the one I already have."

A COUPLE OF HOURS LATER, I pull Joss aside, kissing her softly before I pull the box out of my pocket and slip it into her hand while she's distracted.

"What's this?" She glances down at it and smirks. "Another vibrator?"

I laugh. "No. Something else. Better."

"Better? I don't know. We've had a lot of fun with that..."

"Just open it?" I raise a brow at her.

Her fingers slip along the edge of it, and when she opens it her jaw drops.

"Oh my god, Colt. It's gorgeous. Huge but gorgeous." She pulls the ring out and slips it on her left ring finger.

"Figure it's not a true engagement party if you don't have the engagement ring yet. I know we were looking, but I saw this one, and I knew. It was like the house, you know?" I'm hoping she likes it because it was incredibly hard to get.

"I love it. What is it? An emerald?"

Harper, Violet, Scarlett, and Mackenzie all flock over to look at it, oohing and ahhing over it once they realize what's happening.

"Demantoid garnet."

"Oh shit," Harper gasps.

"What? Is that good or bad? Demented what?" Joss looks up.

Harper laughs and tilts Joss's hand, so she can see the reflection of the light in the gem. She looks back at me and raises her brows. "I can't tell. Horsetail?" she asks.

I nod.

"Damn. Your guy really loves you."

"I mean yes, but why do you say that?"

"Because this is incredibly rare. It's a rare gem, period, and this kind here is usually only mined in a very specific part of the Ural Mountains, mostly in the nineteenth century. They were popular among the aristocracy because of how hard they are to get. One this size... had to have been up on an auction block," Harper's eyes drift back to me and I nod again. "This is like an impossible get. I don't even know how he found one so quickly. Jewelry like this comes up so rarely. They're usually heirlooms that only go up if there's an estate being divided."

Joss tilts it and then looks over at me, suspicion in her eyes. "Because he didn't just get it. Did you?"

I shrug. I'm not prepared to admit all this in front of a room full of people.

"You said you didn't have a ring."

"No, I said I didn't have *the* ring. I had a ring—one that needed to be reset into a band and setting that was right for its owner."

"Colton St. George!" She starts to cry then, tears falling down her cheeks.

I close the distance the women have put between us while they were admiring the ring. I wrap my arms around her, smiling and kissing her before she buries her face in my shirt, little sobs choking her as she tightens her grip on me. Everyone takes a few steps back, letting us have a moment.

"Don't cry. It's not that serious."

"It is that serious. How long have you had it?"

"For a while, Dollface. You know—this universe or another one I was going to have you, and I needed the rare one that matched your eyes when I got the chance."

AS THE PARTY winds down and people are starting to leave, Joss is curled up on my lap on the couch half asleep. Ben and Violet are ushering out the last of the guests, and Harper and Scarlett are busy chatting in the opposite corner of the room.

"You ready to start heading home?" I whisper, brushing her hair out of her face and sweeping some of the green glitter from her costume off her cheek.

She yawns softly. "Yeah, we can. Just let me summon the energy to get to the car. You sure you're awake enough to drive? I'm sure Violet won't care if we stay here."

"I'm sure." I kiss her again and she leans into me.

I want her at home in our bed tonight. As much as I've loved sharing tonight with everyone, I want to end it with her curled up next to me in our bed at our place. Because this is the happiest I've been in a long time.

"Jesus Christ," Alex bursts in through the door to the deck, where he'd just been taking a phone call.

"What?" I ask, my heart stopping when I see his face, and everyone in the room looks up.

"That was the hospital. Tobias didn't make it here tonight because he was in a motorcycle accident. They didn't have details, but it sounds bad. I've got to get down there. I'm his emergency person and fuck...They need someone down there to make decisions, call his family... " Alex runs a hand through his hair as his face twists with anxiety.

"I'll drive," I say and somehow, I manage to stand, despite the fact it feels like a bomb has just exploded in the room.

"I'll call East on the way," Ben volunteers.

"And I'll drive the rest of us." Violet looks solemnly at the rest of the shell-shocked faces in the room.

Tobias has to be fine. Somehow. Someway.

EPILOGUE

Joss

"SO MIKE, tonight the Seattle Phantom are fighting for their postseason lives. We really thought after the way they started the season that they were going to march straight to the playoffs. But now they're just trying to eek out a spot for themselves in Wild Card Weekend," annoying sports reporter number one says to the screen and then turns to his asshole colleague.

"Yeah Jim. They seemed unstoppable at the beginning of the season. There were people that had them picked to go all the way after week two. That now infamous pick and kiss play by Xavier sent everyone into Phantom Fever. Unfortunately the team has been riddled with injuries in the second half of the season. St. George suffered that concussion and missed a couple games. And then no sooner he was back on the field, their star wide receiving duo was broken up when they lost Westfield to that horrific motorcycle accident. They've just struggled to find their rhythm, Jim, and St.

George has struggled with more than his fair share of interceptions as well."

I turn from the screen that's playing in the box and hurry up to the window, spying the guys talking on the TV down on the field and give their miniature sized selves a giant double middle finger salute.

"Joss. You know they can't see you from up here," Violet admonishes me.

"It's the fucking thought that counts."

"All right. Continue thinking then."

"They're winning this and they can take all their opinions on St. George and shove them—"

"He's coming in now." Violet interrupts, motioning to the field.

Even if she hadn't said anything I'd still know because the crowd erupts the second their guy—and mine—steps on the field. I grin through the glass at him.

"He will never stop looking hot in that uniform, will he?"

"Hasn't gotten old for me yet." Violet grins.

"Agreed." Harper and Mackenzie chime in.

They introduce Colt by name and the crowd gets even louder.

"You hear that assholes? Why don't you report on that?" I shout down at them.

Harper laughs and wraps an arm around me. "I'm so glad Violet brought you here and Colt has convinced you to stay at least part time."

"Most of the time. I mean, I'm still going on the road occasionally and hopefully dragging him with me in that narrow window of off time they get. But I like it here."

"Well we like you here." Violet leans her head on my shoulder. "Especially when I get to put you through grueling hours of wedding planning."

"You know, I was mostly focused on your honeymoon and what you were wearing for that."

"We can do both." She grins brightly.

My phone dings and I look down. A message from the assistant Harper and I hired for the foundation pops up, letting me know that the auction is going incredibly well for the limited edition signed photo books we posted today. I hold it up for Harper to see.

"Oh shit! That's awesome."

"One of them is up to five figures already?" Violet gives me a shocked look.

"Right? Thanks to these guys being good at football and hot with their clothes off. Maybe this is the secret to funding arts and culture programs across the country."

They both laugh and then we get settled in to watch the game.

SEVERAL HOURS later and I'm two beers, one pretzel, a funnel cake and half an order of nachos that I shared with Waylon Jr. deep and the game is deep into overtime. The clock is running down and everyone in stadium is getting restless—including me.

The guys set up for the next play and I watch as Colt hands off the ball to the guy that normally runs with it, but he turns around and quickly tosses it back to Colt. I blink and raise a brow, confused as to what's happening. Colt takes a step back and then launches the ball downfield. I must not be the only one confused because Ben is wide open, catches it steps away from the end zone, and walks it in without a defensive player anywhere remotely close enough to stop him.

The stadium erupts again—cheering, music, and lights—all

going wild at the score on the board. Violet screams and grabs me, jumping up and down and turning us both around in a circle. I grin at her.

"Was that supposed to happen? I'm so confused."

"Yes. It's called a flea flicker," she answers breathlessly before she moves on to hug Mac and Harper who are also screaming at the top of their lungs.

"A flea what?" I say.

"Flicker!" Harper answers instead, wrapping her arms around me. "We're going to playoffs!"

"Yay!" I scream and hug her back.

"The guys are gonna be so fucking happy." Mac grins down at the field where the guys are losing their minds on the sidelines.

"I can't wait to see them in the playoffs," I say, and I'm shocked when I realize I mean it. This game has never been my thing, but watching Colt doing something he's so passionate about makes me love it too.

"Are you excited Way?" I look down at the little boy who's pressed up against the glass staring out at all the excitement.

"Yeah!" He grins up at me and I pick him up so he can get a better view of the field while Violet and Mackenzie chat excitedly about who we're playing next.

"Do you see him down there?" I point out the burly lineman who currently has his helmet off and is smacking Ben on the ass in congratulations.

"Yeah. Daddy is the best!"

"He is. And it looks like we get to share more funnel cake together. I got a big question for you though."

Way turns to me, his eyes wide.

"Me and your daddy's friend Colt are gonna get married. And someone special has to carry the rings up. I was thinking since we've become funnel cake buddies, that you might be the right guy for the job. Do you think you could do that for me?"

"Well... I'd have to ask my mommy." There's an intent look on his face.

"I asked your mommy earlier and she said it's up to you."

His lips twist to the side like he's considering the offer.

"Will there be funnel cake?"

I laugh. "Maybe not funnel cake. But cake for sure. I can get you a big piece of cake as payment."

He frowns for a minute like he's thinking hard. "Yeah. Okay. I think I can do that."

"Yay!" I give him a hug and he wraps his arms around me in return.

"All right. I gotta tell Mommy I'm getting cake for helping."

I set him back down on his feet and he takes off in a hurry, launching himself at Mackenzie and spilling the news to her. She grins at him and picks him up, nodding at me and exchanging smiles.

Violet looks over her shoulder as Way tells Violet about his new job and she grins at me.

"A ring bearer!" Harper gives a mock gasp. "That's a very special task. You are so lucky Way!"

I grin so hard my cheeks hurt, because I'm so thankful for this group of women that have adopted me so easily. Taking me in like I've always been here and made me feel at home just like Violet always has.

I CAN BARELY CONTAIN myself when I see Colt coming out from his presser and I run full force and launch myself at him. He catches me and braces us against the wall when we nearly topple over, laughing.

"You are amazing and I love you!"

"I love you too." He squeezes me tight and sets me back on my feet, leaning down to kiss me.

"How excited are you? The playoffs. That's like a big deal right?"

"It's kind of a big deal, yeah." He smiles, and his eyes light up.

"That flea flicker thing was pretty badass."

"How do you even know what that's called?" He threads his fingers with mine as we walk toward the car, grinning at the idea of me knowing something about his work.

"I know things. I study football."

He shoots me a skeptical look but his smile never fades.

"Okay, maybe I just know women who know football and they explain it to me. But that should count."

"We'll let it count."

"I think I kind of love them too."

"The girls?"

"Yeah. They've all been so kind to me. Oh and Mackenzie's son, Waylon? He agreed to be our ring bearer."

"That's great Joss. I'm glad. I didn't know if you'd want to be up there every weekend. I know this isn't your thing, but—"

"It's my thing now. You're my thing." I stop and kiss him again.

"You're my thing too." His eyes drift over my face.

"I've been thinking about venues. How it'll be hard to get privacy here because everyone wants to gawk at you getting married... What if we rent a chateau in France during the off season and get married there?"

He pauses for a moment, thinking and then a smile tugs one side of his mouth and he nods. "Yeah. I think I love that. Will make sense for it to be smaller and my parents won't want to travel that far so it'll be an easy out for all of us."

"Your brother though?"

"Oh my brother will be dying to go. He'll claim he's gonna meet some French woman and move there."

"Good. Well I mean that he'll come not the other part. Although in my experience time on the road does make for a clearer head and better decisions."

"Yeah, well... I'm thankful for that when it comes to you but I think my brother would just get into trouble."

"Maybe. So French chateau in the off season. Next year or the year after?"

"Fuck that. This year."

"This year?" I stop at the car and turn to stare at him because he has to be kidding.

"This year."

"But I mean... off season is soon. I mean hopefully not until after the—you know—I don't want to say and jinx it, but still... Really soon."

"I can put someone on it. I'm sure someone knows someone."

"I thought you'd want a long engagement. Time to plan and all the things." It's my turn for skepticism.

"No. I was serious about marrying you in Vegas. As long as Ben, Violet and my brother are there and you're marrying me? That's all I need to plan for. The sooner the ring is on your finger and we're moved into our new house, the better. I hope more of the guys can make it and if you want to have it at a chateau, great. But I just want you, Joss—the sooner, the better."

"I mean... All I want is you. If you're sure..."

"I'm positive." He kisses me one more time and then opens the door for me. "Now let's go celebrate getting into the play-offs with everyone, and we can tell them to start planning for France this spring."

ALSO BY MAGGIE RAWDON

Plays & Penalties Series

Pregame - Prequel Short Story

Play Fake - Waylon & Mackenzie

Delay of Game - Liam & Olivia

Personal Foul - Easton & Wren

Reverse Pass - Ben & Violet

Seattle Phantom Football Series

Defensive End - Prequel Short Story

Pick Six - Alexander & Harper

ACKNOWLEDGMENTS

To you, the reader, thank you so much for taking a chance on this book and on me! Your support means the world.

To Kat, thank you for your constant help, support, and patience. There's no way I'd ever get a book out without you and your team and I'm so incredibly grateful for you!

To Autumn, for all of your support, feedback, and handling the many rambling messages about whatever book thing is in my head at the moment. I have no idea how I got things done without you!

To Emma and Shannon, thank you for your humor, encouragement and constant support. I'm so lucky to call you friends and can't imagine this writing journey without you!

To Thorunn, thank you for the reminders to consume caffeine and cookies when things get a little rough. I'm so grateful for your friendship and support.

To Lindsey, for always holding my hand through beta reads and believing in me and my characters. Your friendship means the world!

To my Promo Team, thank you so much for the recommendations you pass to friends and the support you give my characters and books. All the hours you spend creating videos and posts are truly appreciated. I wouldn't be able to do this without you and I'm so incredibly grateful!

ABOUT THE AUTHOR

Maggie loves books, travel and wandering through museums. She lives in the Midwest where you can find her writing on her laptop with her two pups at her side, in between binge watching epic historical and fantasy dramas and cheering for her favorite football teams on the weekends. She has a weakness for writing characters who banter instead of flirt.

Join the newsletter here for sneak peeks and bonus content:
https://geni.us/MRBNews
Join the reader's group on FB here:
https://www.facebook.com/groups/rawdonsromanticrebels

instagram.com/maggierawdonbooks

tiktok.com/@maggierawdon

facebook.com/maggierawdon

38011745R00166